RAvaGE

STEPH MACCA

Contents

Triggers and Warnings

- ANAL

- ASSAULT

- BETRAYAL

- BLACKMAIL

- BLOOD & GORE

- BODILY FLUIDS (INCLUDING TORTURE)

- CHASING PLAY

- CHEATING (NOT BETWEEN MAIN CHARACTERS)

- CHILD ABUSE/NEGLECT (OFF-PAGE BACK STORY)

- CHOKING/HAND NECKLACES

- DRUGS/DRUGGING

- FIRE

- GROUP SPICE

- GUNS/SHOOTING

- INHUMANE EXPERIMENTS

- KIDNAPPING

- KNIVES

- LOSS OF A PARENT

- MASKS

- MENTAL ILLNESS (INCLUDING BUT NOT LIMITED TO CPTSD, PTSD, BORDERLINE PERSONALITY DISORDER, SCHIZOPHRENIA, ANGER MANAGEMENT, OCD, DEPRESSION, ANXIETY, SUICIDAL TENDENCIES AND IDEATION, BIPOLAR DISORDER, NARCISSISTIC PERSONALITY DISORDER, INTERMITTENT EXPLOSIVE DISORDER)

- MIND GAMES

- MORGUES

- MURDER/THREATS OF MURDER

- PERMANENT SCARRING AND MARKING

- PRIMAL PLAY

- REMOVAL OF BODY PARTS

- SCARS DUE TO TRAUMA

- SEXUAL ASSAULT (OFF-PAGE/BACK STORY)

- SPANKING

- SPITTING INTO MOUTHS

- STABBING

- SUICIDE

- SWEARING (INCLUDING THE WORD 'CUNT')

- TORTURE

- UNETHICAL BEHAVIOR FROM PROFESSIONALS

- VIOLENCE

- WEAPONS

Oh, you're back again...

It's the morgue scenes, isn't it?

Don't worry... they are loud enough to wake the dead in this book too.

Recap from Echoes

"Ring around the rosie. A pocket full of posies. Ashes... Ashes... We all fall down..."

I give him a brief nod, meeting the guard in the hallway as we head down to Dr. Elsher's room. I'm not keen on seeing that quack again, but I have little choice.

His doorway is open when we arrive, his stern face looking up from his desk, uninterested, as I walk in.

"Ms. White," he sighs. "Are we going to make any progress today?"

"You tell me," I mumble, flinging myself into the chair across from his desk.

Dr. Elsher shakes his head, making a note in my file. "Un-cooperative, as usual."

"Maybe you could try being less of an asshole," I suggest. "I don't really vibe well with that."

He ignores me, raising an eyebrow as he makes another note.

We sit in silence, my arms folded as I wait for him to speak. Finally, he looks up, putting his pen down.

"Frankly, Ms. White, I don't believe you have the capabil-ities for successful therapy."

"So, you're saying I'm incurable."

"I'm saying," he says a little louder. "That until you *want* to be helped, you're going to remain as you are."

My eyes narrow on him. "What's wrong with who I am?"

"Tell me—do you have any remorse for your father's death?" he asks, blindsiding me.

"Of course I do," I sputter. "I think that was made clear in my notes with Dr. Smith and from the court documents."

Dr. Elsher leans back in his chair. "Dr. Smith didn't make excessive notes about your sessions. Most of your initial sessions very little was discussed. It appears he only really targeted your mental health, not the actions that led you here."

I raise an eyebrow, annoyed. "*Obviously* I'm here because I accidentally killed my father while attempting to take my own life. The whole event is the reason for my mental health."

"Is it?" he snorts. "I'm going to assume because of your childhood you already had these mental illnesses. I'd say they very much contributed to your father's death."

I clench my teeth, trying my best to remain composed. "That's a very clever observation, Doctor. Of course it was linked—did you not just hear me? I was trying to kill myself."

"With a fire though?" he questions, scoffing at me. "What made you decide on that? Because surely a reasonable person would expect that a fire would have the possibility of inflicting harm upon others. Most people who commit suicide opt for different methods such as asphyxiation, exsanguination, or unloading a bullet into a main organ. Most of these methods would be far quicker, less painful, and without the risk of harming others."

I stare at him, angry at his audacity. He's known me for a short amount of time, and already he thinks he knows me better than I know myself.

He's trying to insinuate that I intentionally killed my father.

Nothing to do with the fact that my house—the same one I found my dead mother in, the same one I received all my abuse and torture—was the catalyst. I wanted to escape, I wanted to leave.

And most of all, I wanted to burn those memories to ash. If the house was gone, then no one would ever have to suffer abuse inside those walls again.

Once I was dead, my father would just find someone else to torment and hurt. He'd lure someone in, repeating the cycle like he did with my mother and I.

My father had no job, very little money. His biggest asset was that house, and I wanted to take that away from him so he couldn't use it as a weapon.

Those walls were painted with my screams, embedded into the gyprock like muscle memory. I deserved to have the final say in what happened with that house.

I knew I was going to suffer. I knew that the fire would burn me alive. But at the time, I didn't care. Whatever pain I suffer at the end, I was ready to accept, because it was no match for the mental torture I was living with. It would end eventually, returning me to the earth from which I came.

"Some people kill others before they kill themselves," I point out. "I didn't plan to do that."

Dr. Elsher lifts an eyebrow. "Why didn't you seek help? According to the court documents, there is no reference to you seeking help from any professionals."

"What professionals?" I argue. "I wasn't allowed to go to the doctor because we didn't have insurance. The few times I was taken to the emergency room, it was obvious that I was being abused. What sane person would pull shards of glass out of someone's back and assume it was there by accident? What sick and twisted person would look at my bleeding intimate parts, surmising that I'd had normal intercourse? They all had their chance to report it, but if they did, nothing was ever done. The people with authority had opportunities to pull me out of that house, but no one ever came."

"But did *you* seek help?" he asks again. "No—you left people to assume. In fact, one of the hospital reports indicated that you stated you fell and injured yourself."

I gawk at him, bewildered. "What about women in domestic violent relationships? They often lie too, terrified that their abuser will hurt them more for trying to tell the truth. Sometimes they get murdered trying to escape."

"I think the truth is you kept it to yourself because you thought you deserved it—so you accepted it."

For once, he's not completely far from the truth. I was so beaten down, my soul broken and crushed, that I did often believe I deserved the abuse. But I know now that I was wrong—no one deserves that.

"I was trained to believe that," I say quietly. "But I deserved better. I deserve to be happy and loved."

He looks at me with a bored expression. "While you might believe that now, you still don't want to heal yourself. From what I'm told, you're too focused on having others heal you. I assume that's why you are dating multiple people. Do you think you're too much for any one person to handle on their own?"

It's like a slap in the face. He might as well have gut punched me, painting a picture in my head that can't be unseen.

Is that why I want to love them both? Is that why I let Damon kiss me?

The more people that want me, the more I will believe that I'm worthy?

I didn't kiss Damon back at first, but I didn't stop him straight away either. And while the whole situation had shocked me, sending me into a moment of frozen confusion, I think I kissed him back for a split second.

Damon would be the ultimate validation. He hated me so much that I wanted him to like me. I told myself it was because of Grey—I wanted his best friend to like me. But now... I'm not so sure.

If I could make someone who hates me change their mind about me, it would start to undo all the words and damage my father did. It would prove that I was likable—loveable—after all.

I go to open my mouth to speak, trying to figure out words to respond, but my head starts to spin. I rub my temple, closing my eyes to get a grip on myself, but when I open them again, the room is still fuzzy.

There's two Dr. Elshers sitting at the desk, swaying from left to right. I can't see straight, things quickly losing focus.

Sounds start to muffle like underwater noises, and I faintly register a knock.

"Is she ready?" a voice asks.

Someone walks in front of me, kneeling down to look at me face-to-face.

"Ms. White, how are you feeling?" Mr. Whittingham asks coldly.

"It's... woozy," I slur. "What's happening?"

His blue eyes scan my face before he turns away, nodding to someone by the door.

"Take Ms. White to the lab. The doctors are waiting for her."

Chapter 1

Avery

They say when you die you see a white light.

Everything is meant to be clear and serene, with all your loved ones waiting for you with open arms.

The pain is meant to end, all anxiety swept away, as you fade into the sunset happily.

So why does it feel like I'm in hell?

Fluorescent light blinds me, a haze poking at my peripheral vision as figures move beside me. I can hear faint, muffled words—the sounds drowned out by a thudding in my ears.

I hear my name spoken a few times, snapping my senses back into place—well, as much as they can through the fog that's consuming me. I blink rapidly, willing for some control over my body that's fighting whatever is coursing through it.

Slowly, a face comes into focus, and I stare sharply, keeping my gaze on a freckle on his nose to calm the waves. He notices me watching, lowering his clipboard with interest.

"Hello, Avery. I'm Dr. West," he says nonchalantly.

His relaxed manner is off-putting, making me nervous. I try to move my body but I can't. I struggle harder, realizing that my arms are tied down by my sides.

"Where am I?" I ask groggily. "Let my arms go."

Dr. West ignores me, writing some notes down on his clipboard. "I can understand it's a little scary but rest assured, you're in good hands."

I've never been so unassured in my entire life.

I force my neck up, straining to gaze down my body. Brown faded leather straps are crossed over my body, two over my torso at either end, one across each wrist, and a large one pinning my legs down. I wiggle my ankles to see if there's any room, but they just rub together, the leather digging into my skin.

"Is she awake?" another voice asks curiously.

"Yes," Dr. West answers, giving someone a smile opposite him.

I turn my head, spotting a female doctor, her auburn hair tied up in a tight bun. She's dressed in white like Dr. West, their matching lab coats devoid of embroidery.

I don't need details though. Flashbacks start rolling back through my mind, images of Dr. Elsher and Whittingham appearing. I remember being angry before everything started to get blurry.

I was drugged.

But the question is when?

Thinking back, I retrace my steps, heart sinking at the realization. Dr. Markel gave me a tablet in his room. It looked similar to what I usually take, but then again, lots of pills are white and circular. It could have been anything.

Did he betray me too?

I shouldn't be surprised, but a small part of me is. I guess it goes to show you never know someone's true intentions.

"Hi, Avery. I'm Dr. Cromwell, but you can call me Melanie."

My eyes scan over her face, narrowing at her cerulean-colored eyes. "Where am I?" I ask again through clenched teeth.

She smiles. It looks almost genuine, not sinister like I would have expected. "You're in the Emerson Lab. There's nothing to be afraid of. We're just going to be conducting some tests."

"On me?" I spit out in disgust, tugging on the straps again.

"Yes," Dr. West interjects, leaning over me with a penlight. He lifts my eyelids, shining the light into my eyes. "She's definitely more lucid now," he says to Dr. Cromwell. "Make a note of the timeframe for our records. That's quite interesting."

Anger floods through me. They are speaking about me as if I'm not here—or a human life.

"I'm not your guinea pig," I shoot back, turning my head away from him. "You can't do this. It's inhumane."

He sighs, switching the penlight off. "Does her file state anything about irritability? Or is this an effect from the medication?"

I gape at him. "Are you fucking serious right now?"

Someone places a hand on my shoulder, pulling my attention away from him. My gaze snaps over to Dr. Cromwell, her relaxed face giving me a reassuring look. I feel like a child being placated, and it dawns on me that I'm correct. I'm not a human life at all to them, at least not one worthy of respect. I'm just a test subject.

"Try to take deep breaths," she murmurs. "Your blood pressure is starting to rise."

My eyebrows furrow as I look down at my arm, noticing the pressure cuff deflating. "You're going to regret this," I mutter angrily. "You have no idea."

Dr. West snorts, somewhat amused at my comment. "Making threats," he says to himself, writing a note on the clipboard. "Definitely interesting."

"Stop writing shit down!"

He pauses, peering at me over the top of the clipboard. "We'll trial her under group B. I think she's a good candidate."

"What would you like me to start with?" Dr. Cromwell asks.

"Immersion, please. I would probably take her now. The medication is wearing off and she's likely to become physically aggressive once she's fully mobile again."

Dr. West gestures to someone out of sight, the sound of footsteps approaching. I spot two men in their thirties, dressed in black. They move next to me as the doctors step back. They start unbuckling the straps, and when my legs are freed, I try to lift them. I manage to elevate them an inch or so before they fall back down onto the bed, the muscles straining.

What the hell did they do to me?

The men lift me from the bed despite my protests, sitting me down in a wheelchair. I hastily look over at Dr. West, his chestnut eyes watching on with interest as he twirls his pen. He's waiting for me to do something, observing me like a wild animal.

I finally notice his faded hair, the once brown strands now mixed with gray, aging lines on his face as he frowns with curiosity. He should know better, but something tells me he doesn't care.

The wheelchair is pushed away from the bed, Dr. Cromwell walking beside me as we head to a large metal door. She uses her key card to scan us through, punching in a code like the Lilydale doors.

Am I still in Lilydale? I would have to be, right?

If I was a betting woman, I'd wager we are underground like where the morgue is. Except the hallways don't look familiar as we push through. If anything, the walls look brighter, cleaner. The Lilydale staff don't care about the condition of the facility on the inside, but whatever this place is, is well maintained.

The wheels squeak quietly as we head to a large door down the corridor. Dr. Cromwell walks ahead, opening it for us as we reach it.

"What's going on?" I try to ask her, but one of the men puts a hand on my shoulder, silencing me.

"Don't speak unless you are spoken to," he scolds.

My head snaps toward him, taking in his stubble and vomit-green eyes. "Go fuck yourself."

"She's fine," Dr. Cromwell asks calmly. "Through here, please." She directs them to a side room, the light dimmer. I have to squint to look around, immediately finding a large steel tank in the center of the room. There's a lid on top with handles and a small hole, but I'm jolted away from it, abruptly stopping to face the wall.

I watch as Dr. Cromwell puts her clipboard on a counter before opening a drawer to pull out a sealed plastic bag. Behind me, I hear the sound of running water and I turn my head to spot one of the men lifting the lid off.

It's a bathtub?

"How would you like her?" the other man asks.

Dr. Cromwell looks at me, lips twitching in thought. "To her undergarments, please."

My eyes widen as he steps toward me, my voice rough as I shoot him a glare. "Don't you dare fucking touch me."

He ignores me, reaching under my arms to bring my numbed body forward. I let out a yelp when I feel his hands on my back, lifting my shirt up. Immediately, fear crashes through me, panic rising as he pulls my clothes off. I can't resist or fight back, my muscles and limbs heavy. When he goes to reach for my shorts, a soft hand touches my shoulder.

"You're safe, Avery."

Her voice does nothing to calm me, tears prickling my eyes. Rough hands pull my shorts down my legs, leaving me in my bra and underwear, slumped in the wheelchair. When he goes to reach for me again, a scream escapes my throat against my will. It doesn't deter him though, arms snaking around me as he lifts my body off the seat.

It feels like poison ivy against my skin, the burning and itch of unfamiliar touch, lifting my unwilling frame.

I'm carried toward the metal tub, eyes looking down at the water pooling inside. As I'm lowered toward it, I feel a small ounce of relief, but it's short-lived when ice-cold water engulfs me.

A sharp gasp leaves my lips as my body sinks into the water, eyes wide as I look at Dr. Cromwell. "It's freezing," I say, hoping she'll realize they forgot to turn the hot water on.

She nods slowly. "It's called ice submersion therapy. You should adjust in a few minutes."

The men lift the lid off the ground, bringing it atop the tub. As it slides toward me, I realize with sickening horror what the hole is for. The lid clicks into place, the metal surrounding my neck as my head pokes out the hole.

My body starts shivering violently, teeth clattering as I try to move my arms and legs.

"You can go now," Dr. Cromwell directs the men, grabbing a rolling stool from the counter and sliding it to the end of the tub. She sits down, facing me with her clipboard, crossing her legs gracefully. "Please return in thirty minutes."

They give her a quick nod, vanishing from the room as the door slams closed behind them. I stare at her wide-eyed and I'm almost certain my lips match the color of her irises.

"Why are you doing this?" I manage to stutter out, voice shaking.

She pauses for a moment before giving me a soft smile. "It's nothing personal, Avery. It's just part of the job. It's for a good cause though."

People make the mistake of assuming that ice will numb you. But they are wrong. I'm quickly realizing that there's a point beyond the numbness where your skin starts to burn. My muscles scream in pain, desperate for warmth, despite the burning sensation which brings no relief. I tilt my head back to hide the tears that have pooled, blinking at the ceiling.

"You torture people for a good cause?" I mutter sarcastically, tears sliding down the side of my face.

"I know it doesn't seem like it, but it's true," Dr. Cromwell answers, the sound of her pen scribbling something. "Science is always evolving, new answers breaking through."

I laugh dryly, shaking my head. "And yet, we're still in the 1800s apparently."

When she doesn't respond, I bring my head forward, noticing her watching me closely. I know she can see my tears, but thankfully she rests the clipboard on her lap instead of making more notes.

"Our methods might be old but they were proven to be helpful. This is for your benefit too," she points out with blind optimism.

"If I survive that long," I shoot back, neck banging painfully into the metal as I shiver. "What else do you have planned?"

Dr. Cromwell smiles, but this time it doesn't reach her eyes. "We'll adjust our methods and research as we progress based on our findings."

"Are we still in the Lilydale facility?" I demand quietly.

"I can't answer that, Avery. I'm sorry."

Shaking my head, I glare at her, images of Grey, Theo, and Damon appearing in my mind. "You better hope for your sake that we're not," I say. "Because if we are, I have no doubt that you've just started a war."

Chapter 2

Grey

I'm fast.

Probably faster than most people my age. Ever since I was young, speed has always been on my side. It's what came in handy whenever my father had one of his episodes. It's also the reason I learned to be able to move around without making a single sound.

But that doesn't matter right now. I couldn't give two shits who hears me.

My footsteps thunder down the hallway as we head to Elsher's office. It's echoed by Theo behind me who, impressively, manages to keep pace rather well. I have no idea if Damon is following, but I would assume he's still with Jillian.

FUCK!

We should have seen this coming. I promised myself and Avery that I would keep her safe. Did we get too complacent? We knew that cuntface was potentially on the verge of making a move, but I thought we had him blocked. Alexander should have been the tipping point, giving us an indication that they were coming after us. But I told myself that things were different this time.

Six months ago, we missed the signs. We didn't have the technology and power available to us to fully stop it until it was too late. We upped our game—but Arthur did too. He led us to believe we were one step ahead, letting us think we had absolute control.

It might not be too late.

I try to convince myself that it's fine. I just need to reach Avery before they do. Once I have her, I can tie us together. If they want her, they'll have to go through me first. Besides, she's in session. They wouldn't make a move right now. It's not their style—too many witnesses and obstacles to jump through.

Rounding the doorway, I skid to a halt in Elsher's office. My eyes scan the empty room wildly, heart thumping in my chest.

"Where is she?" Theo snaps behind me, shoving past me to look around.

I can't move. I can't breathe. For the first time in my life, I'm completely paralyzed in place as it dawns on me. Bile threatens to spill out of my body as red-hot rage builds inside.

She's gone.

They fucking have Avery.

Theo does a lap around the desk, pausing to look at me with dark eyes. "Grey!" he shouts.

It snaps me out of my trance, my body moving on its own accord. I pick up the patient chair from against the wall, flinging it across the room. It narrowly misses Theo who doesn't budge an inch, shattering the barred glass window behind him.

Immediately, an alarm starts to sound from somewhere, but it's faded in my ears by the rushing of blood.

I'm going to kill them all.

One by one, I'm going to hunt them down and rip every single organ out of their bodies with my bare hands.

"Grey," Damon's voice floats into the room from behind me. "We have to go—now."

I swing my head around to find him standing in the doorway, looking composed somehow.

How?

Does she really mean that little to him that he's not even bothered by this? Avery is missing and he just looks completely unfazed. It makes me want to put my fist through his face.

"No," I finally speak, firmly glaring at him. "I'm going to search for her."

I start to move past him but he swings his arm out, blocking my path. "Grey—"

"Get the fuck out of my way," I warn him, ready to throw hands, even if he is my best friend. "Theo?"

"I'm coming too," he answers.

Damon's gaze flicks between us. "We will find her, Grey. I promise you that. But right now, we need to be smart about this. The guards are on their way and we can't help her if we're taken to solitary confinement or arrested. You know that will be their plan."

His words stop me in my tracks, the irrational monster inside screaming that he doesn't give a fuck and he should pay. Hell, he needs to move out of the way before I bulldoze through him. He's eerily calm and it makes me angry.

That's what happened last time.

That's why she's dead.

I shake my head slowly, not voicing my thoughts. But Damon's face softens slightly, and I know he can read me easily. He steps forward, putting a hand on my shoulder.

"Let's get back to the rooms and make a plan. They will be expecting us to go in with guns blazing. All we can do at the moment is go against their plan—it's the only way."

Theo appears beside me, glaring daggers at Damon. "You better start fucking explaining or else I'll shove your plan into your chest cavity and do what I want."

"Calm the fuck down, Ashwood. This is for your benefit too. Do not threaten me," Damon says coldly, lowering his hand from my shoulder as he turns and silently orders us to follow.

I take two deep breaths before my feet move, going against the urge to run in the opposite direction to find Avery and slaughter Arthur on his expensive wooden desk.

We quickly head back to Damon's room, the three of us barreling inside and locking the door behind us. Jillian and Byrone are already here, sitting on the bed as they smash their fingers down on the keys of their laptops.

"Well?" Damon demands, leaning against his desk. "Anything?"

Jillian looks up, shaking her head slowly. "They've installed new firewall software. The encryption is hard to break through..."

"But?" I snap, sensing her hesitation.

Byrone sighs, putting his hand on Jillian's knee at my outburst. "We can see *one* file."

"What's the file?" I ask quickly.

They fall silent, the small flicker of hope in my chest starting to be smothered out. Damon breaks the silence, laughing dryly as he hisses angrily.

"Those motherfuckers."

I whip my attention over to him, watching as he rubs his hand over his face. "What?"

"It's *our* file, isn't it?" he asks Byrone in a knowing tone.

The two of them nod slowly. "It's a collection of our saved recordings from the cameras," Byrone confirms.

"They accessed our files?" I ask Damon.

He shakes his head. "They were watching us the whole time. They waited to boot us out of the system. It makes sense—Arthur fired the old IT people months ago. The new ones must have gotten through our security and been lurking until they were given the go ahead."

"Someone better start giving me some answers because my patience is wearing fucking thin," Theo growls from the corner near the doorway.

Jillian and Byrone look over, slightly alarmed at his temper. Damon gives him a curt nod, slumping slightly in his place.

"Arthur has been desperate to resume testing for quite some time. We initially overrode their IT systems so we could see who was being admitted to the facility and keep tabs on the cameras. They led us to believe they didn't have access, but clearly they did. Christopher said Avery has been on their radar for a while, which we also assumed. That's why we kept her close to the society."

"But you used her," I mutter angrily under my breath, glancing over to him. "You dangled her right in front of their faces like prey."

Damon raises an eyebrow at me. "I *used* their own tactics against them. They were trying to get information from Avery about us, so I returned the favor. It was the smart choice, even you agreed—despite your motives being different to mine."

"What the fuck does that mean?" I snap, louder.

"You fucking fell in love with her," he retorts, frustrated. "Your focus became cloudy and went off-track. You had no problem supporting me because it meant you could stay close to her. The goal was to keep everyone in the facility safe, not just her."

"Don't you *dare* talk to me about getting close to her," I warn, noticing Jillian and Byrone shift awkwardly on the bed at our rising voices. "You're one to judge, Damon. And so much for keeping her safe. Look how well that turned out!"

He raises his hand, taking a sharp breath in frustration. "Enough, Grey! This is not the time nor the place to discuss anything other than our plan. We don't have much time. Two patients are now missing. Arthur has already told everyone that Capello is dead. He's likely going to run with the same story for Avery. We all need to be focused and stay in control. You can't lose your shit right now."

I lean against the wall, falling into deep thought. "What do we do then? They've never done it during the day before. We need to go underground."

"To the closed rooms?" Theo interjects. "Is that where she will be?" There's an edge to his tone, threatening to leave this room right now to go hunting. Damon senses it too, choosing his words carefully.

"Possibly," he says slowly. "But they also know that we know the locations of those rooms. Besides being heavily guarded, I wouldn't put it past them to have relocated."

Byrone nods. "A trap."

"Precisely. They want us to go down there. They will be waiting and ready."

Sighing, I look at Theo, noticing the same pained expression behind his eyes as mine. "We'll get her back," I tell him. "We have to."

He glances over at me. "How much time do we have?"

Damon kicks off from the desk, crossing the room over to Byrone. He holds out his hand, reaching for the laptop that Byrone offers. "A few days, likely."

"I'm not leaving her down there for a few days," Theo snaps.

Putting the laptop on the desk, Damon throws him a quick look. "I'm not suggesting we do." Tapping a few keys and clicking the keyboard, a document pops up on the screen. "According to our previous calculations, they generally have a testing time of four to seven days maximum. It depends on variables."

"What do they do with the patients afterwards?" Theo asks.

"That's the variable," Damon murmurs quietly. "Sometimes they come back—particularly if Arthur announces them as merely missing. They are usually *miraculously* found. Or sometimes we are told they were in solitary confinement."

Theo narrows his eyes. "And if he announces that they are dead?"

He's a quick learner, I'll give him that.

"They don't come back," Damon answers coldly.

The room falls silent, Theo's face rapidly changing as he processes the information.

"What do they do with them afterwards?" he asks dangerously.

Damon straightens up. "We don't know," he answers honestly. "All we know is they aren't seen again."

"I'm not going to let that happen to her," Theo promises. "I'll do this with or without you."

"With us," I say quickly, making them all look toward me. "We're in this together—for Avery."

Theo nods at me. "What do you need me to do?"

This time, I look to Damon for direction. I might be mad at him, but this is still his call. This is what we planned for, what we trained for—this is our sole purpose. If we have any hope of getting her back, it's because of him. Damon isn't just *in* Cirque des Morts...

He is Cirque des Morts.

The society is everything to him and right now, he's our only chance. And that's why I'm giving him the benefit of the doubt.

"I need you all to go to classes as usual. We wait for Arthur to make his announcement so we know what timeframe to follow. In the meantime, we wait a few hours until we make our move. Let them lower their guard down and get cocky. Keep a listen out for information—see if anyone saw anything, if the staff or guards know anything. Gather anything and everything possible. Jillian and Byrone, keep working on the decryption coding. Grey, go and find Leighton and Jemison. Get them to go over the blueprints to see where a relocation could have been moved to. We meet in the library after dark—spread the word."

I nod slowly, fighting the frustration of having to wait to get my girl back. "What else do we need?"

Damon looks at me with a serious expression. "It's time to break out the gear, Grey."

Chapter 3
Avery

My teeth have barely stopped chattering when I'm thrown into a tiny, padded room. The walls are spongy and white—exactly what I'd imagine a mental asylum to look like.

The Lilydale rooms remind me of prison cells, but this? This is *actually* an asylum—go figure. All I need now is a straitjacket to restrain my limbs. Given how cold I am from the ice bath, it would be almost welcoming, if not for any reason but the extra warmth.

"We'll bring you some food shortly," Dr. Cromwell says softly as she watches me stumble to catch my footing. I swing around, glaring at the two men who disappear out of sight behind her.

"Don't bother," I snap. "I don't think I'll be staying long."

It's the only thing that got me through the torturous freezing water—knowing that the guys will notice I'm missing. Someone will sound the alarm and they will come looking for me. I can feel it in my bones. We haven't come this far for them to give up on me now. I just have to make sure I don't give up too.

I'm not sure what these sadistic creeps are planning but I have no doubt this is just the beginning.

I wish I could say I'm not scared or worried, but that would be a lie. I know the danger I'm in. It doesn't make sense, but I have to stay focused.

This place has to be connected to Lilydale—Whittingham made that clear by showing his smug, disgusting face before I blacked out. Plus, Dr. Cromwell said it was the Emerson lab. That was her name, right?

I knew Lilydale was too good to be true. In what universe would a bunch of strangers have any interest in rehabilitating unhinged youths? They treated us like scum—prisoners. I was right in thinking we were a cash-grab for them, I just didn't realize to what extent.

They don't want to save us.

They want to use us.

We're not even human beings to them. Though, if I'm being honest, they aren't human either because from what I've seen, no normal person with a shred of humanity would do this. Melanie Cromwell can pretend this is for the greater good, but we're victims too.

Traumatized by our pasts, betrayed by the people we trusted, our stories were crafted by others. And now we're here, being tortured all over again for the sake of sick fucks in expensive suits.

Why, though?

And what does this have to do with Lilydale?

"You need to eat," Dr. Cromwell sighs. "You need energy."

My gaze shoots over to her, narrowing on her relaxed frame. "And pray tell, why is that? What else do you have planned for me?"

She has the audacity to shift slightly, eyes looking away as she shakes her head. "We'll be back soon."

I watch as the door swings closed behind her, blocking out all sounds except my breathing. The light is so bright in this room—a stark contrast to the dull rooms I'm used to. It makes me feel like I'm on reality television without a break. Instinctively, I search the roof, spotting the small camera in the corner pointing down at me. The red light blinks slowly and all I can envision is some doctor sitting in a fancy office, making notes as they observe their newest experiment.

Flipping the bird toward it, I turn away, sitting on the ground with my legs folded underneath me.

I just need to wait. They will come. It will be okay.

"Are ya sure?" My father's voice echoes in my head. *"Why would anyone come for ya?"*

Tears prickle in my eyes and I shake my head. I drown him out, reminding myself that he's dead. His reign of hurt and pain is over—he can't touch me anymore.

But still...

The doubt is there.

No one ever came when I was on the outside, even when I was a walking cry for help. Teachers, friends, doctors, adults... they all overlooked me.

I can't help but wonder what my life would have looked like if just one person had seen me for what I really was—a broken specimen of fading life.

Why did they not check on me after I found my mother's dead body?

Why did no one raise the alarm when I was treated at the hospital for injuries?

How did no one realize that someone had hurt me without my consent, taking away the most womanly part of my body and soul?

Hell, even after Paige died, there was no one.

I'm not that person anymore...

I'm not invisible.

Theo and Grey see me. I mean something to them.

Fuck... even Damon. We fight all the time but he's never hurt me. He even kissed me—surely that means I'm worth something if I'm visible to even the great, ruthless Damon?

Would my life be better if someone had saved me? If I was on the outside, would I have escaped? My father was adamant I was never leaving, but what if I was able to? With more time and money, maybe I could have made a dash for it. I always wanted to go to Florida—I could have lived my life out on the beach in Miami.

But would I have been happy?

There comes a point where we adapt. You become so used to the trauma and pain that it's all you know. When it disappears, you don't know how to cope without it. Your body stays in that survival mode, constantly on edge until you start to go insane.

If I ran away, I'd be free—but at a price. I'd be alone, unsure how to survive by myself. In a foreign place, I'd be invisible, blending into the crowd of people bustling around.

I'd still be nothing.

In a twisted way Lilydale freed me from those chains. I was no longer invisible, no longer a liability to people. I was just *Avery*. And in that, I found love, acceptance, and beauty. I found self-worth, strength, and a desire to live and take back my life.

I didn't have that before.

Which is why I'm not going to let these fuckers break me. Because if I do, if I give in like they want me to, I won't just be letting myself down. If anything happens to me, it will destroy Grey and Theo.

They might not realize it, but they have come far too—making the best of a shit situation. Together, we're strong, and we'll stay that way until we find our own individual strength too. We're not the product of our upbringings, not defined by what the court system or society think about us or our past actions. We deserve to be happy too.

I deserve my happy ending.

And that isn't going to end here in this shitty, white-padded room.

The door swings open, ripping me from my thoughts. I look back over my shoulder, frowning as one of the men enters with a tray of food. He sets it down on the ground, giving me a brief look of acknowledgment.

I wait for him to leave before turning my focus to the plastic bowl on the tray, filled with red soup—tomato, I'm assuming.

There's no steam emanating from it so I can already assume that it's lukewarm at best.

Looking away, I close my eyes, picturing the reasons for my existence. I hold onto the images, gathering strength.

They're coming.

"Time to move," a voice says, pulling me out of my slumber.

My eyes flutter open, blinded by the bright lights as blurry figures reach for me. I'm too slow to react, hands grabbing my arms as I'm lifted from the ground.

"Yep. Clothes are dry. She's good to go," one of them says, snapping my bra strap.

Swinging my arm back, I hit him in the rib cage. "Don't touch me!"

Hands tighten on me, unfazed by my assault as I'm dragged from the room.

I quickly find my footing, taking back some of my weight as we head down the corridor. Entering another room, I'm not surprised to find Dr. West and Dr. Cromwell waiting, chatting quietly with each other.

"Did she eat?" Dr. Cromwell asks the men.

"Nope."

She frowns at me in disapproval, scribbling on that damn clipboard. "Alright. We'll just have to make do."

The men shove me onto a reclined chair in the center of the room, reminding me of a dentist's office. The brown, leather straps are fastened over my body, but I don't fight them. Glaring at the doctors, I wait for them to speak, knowing more is coming.

"You should be eating," Dr. West scolds.

I force myself to bite my tongue, not giving them the satisfaction of an answer. They appear surprised but continue moving around once the men step back.

Dr. West grabs what looks like a sheet of paper, peeling off stickers in the form of tiny white circles. As he steps closer, I notice little prongs on top, before he shoves a few onto the side of my head. I flinch away, bobbing my head as Dr. Cromwell clicks some leads hooked to a machine to the stickers.

"What the hell are you doing?" I ask, all strength disappearing as panic sets in.

"Just another observation," she replies simply. "I need you to stay still."

I do no such thing, flailing more as Dr. West approaches me with a needle. He sighs, pausing as he looks unimpressed.

"It would be easier if you kept still."

He grabs my wrist, turning my palm to inspect my veins. I gasp, trying to tug my arm away. "Get that away from me."

"Hold her, please," he says to one of the men, a thick hand coming into view as they press down on my forearm.

"Stop!" I plead, watching in horror as Dr. West pulls the cap off the stick, bringing the needle to my skin.

"It will only hurt for a second," he replies, piercing the skin as I let out a small yelp.

My arm erupts with burning pain as the tip slides into my vein with roughness, a cannula inserted. Dr. West grabs a piece of tape from Dr. Cromwell's outstretched hand, slapping it over my skin to hold the cannula in place.

Immediately, the pain eases, but my anxiety doesn't. Reaching into a medical dish, he lifts up a vial and second needle, drawing the fluid into the syringe.

I already know that whatever is coming can't be good, but I'm helpless to stop it. The needle enters the cannula port and the feeling of cold liquid shoots through my veins.

It doesn't take long before my body slumps into the chair, muscles relaxing as my vision blurs a little. I expect to go unconscious, but I don't.

It's a horrible realization as my mind starts to swim through the possibilities of what's happening, struggling to grasp onto a single thought.

Dr. Cromwell leans over to look at me, giving me a small smile. "Feeling okay?" she asks warmly.

"No..." I manage to croak out.

"She's fine," Dr. West replies dryly, turning the machine screen to face him. "We'll start with seventy volts at an interval of one millisecond. Have you hooked up the pulse monitor?"

"Doing that now," Dr. Cromwell answers as I feel something pressed over my fingertip.

Volts...

Through the haze, it pieces together, and in a last effort attempt to fight, I throw everything I have against the straps.

They tighten and press into my skin, digging painfully as I struggle.

"Don't do that, Avery..." Dr. Cromwell says concerned. "You'll be fine."

I snap my gaze to her angrily, perplexed that something so fucking inhumane is happening. "Let me go. Right fucking now."

She sighs quietly under her breath, stepping back as she glances over my body to her colleague.

"Alright," Dr. West says loudly, the machine beeping as he presses some buttons. "Let's begin in three, two... one."

It takes a minute to process what's happening, my body and mind blanking as the sound of loud hissing reaches my ears. But then I realize I can hear a scream through it.

It's mine.

Chapter 4

Damon

I let out a little hiss as blood bubbles through the cut on my knee, stinging as I quickly wipe away gravel. It hurts—a lot, but I don't have anyone to blame but myself. Mom warned me not to take my bicycle to this part of the yard. It's become overgrown, and the recent storm that ravaged the area has spilled debris everywhere.

But I knew better.

I always do.

"Oh, Damon," I hear Mom's soothing voice as her soft footsteps approach.

Glancing up from the ground, I smile at her, the black strands of her hair dancing around her shoulders. She leans down, inspecting the graze on my knee.

"Did you come off your bike?"

I nod. "I hit a rock, I think. It hurts."

Mom brushes her hand around the cut, flicking off bits of dirt and gravel. "Let's get you inside and cleaned up," she says, reaching under my arms to pick me up. My bicycle lays forgotten as she carries me back to the house, past the construction crew working on applying new paint to the weatherboards. Father has hired some people to renovate our new house—apparently, it's old and '*if he has to live here, it better be presentable*'.

We only just moved in a month ago. I don't really understand why, just that Mom was given the house from some family member. It's bigger than our old one, set on a huge area of land on the outskirts of town. It might be old, but I like it. Apparently, Mom grew up here when she was my age, so that's pretty cool.

The glass doors on the back patio are wide open, the summer breeze swaying the chandelier above the central kitchen counter. Mom places me on top of it, heading out of the room for a few minutes before returning with a first aid box. I swing my legs happily off the side of the counter, watching as she cleans the cut and places a Band-aid over it.

Just as she finishes, I hear loud footsteps heading into the kitchen, followed by *his* booming voice as he barks orders down the cell phone.

"I don't care if James' wife is in labor. I need that report now. Tell him to get back to the office or else he can begin looking for new employment."

Mom flinches in front of me. It's subtle—almost unrecognizable, but I always see it. I know she tries to hide it, but I always see everything.

She smiles at me, straightening up as my father rounds the corner, hanging up the cell phone. He pauses, looking between the two of us.

"Why is the child on the counter? We just had the new marble placed last week."

"I was just fixing a cut on his knee," Mom answers, hastily reaching to grab me and gently lowering me to the floor.

I stand next to her, reaching for her hand. She squeezes mine back, taking a deep breath as she gathers control of her emotions. She's the best at it, and I think I know why.

My father narrows his eyes at me with disgust, finding the Band-aid on my knee. "He's a *boy*," he spits out. "Boys don't need to be fussed over." Trudging over, he rips the Band-aid off my knee, a small hiss escaping my lips involuntarily at the sudden sting.

"Alexander!" Mom gasps, but he cuts her off, backhanding me across the face.

"Enough of that," he scolds. "You're six years old, Damon. It's a tiny laceration—man up."

Immediately, I feel those walls in my mind climbing up, numbness creeping in. I straighten up, letting go of Mom's hand.

"It doesn't hurt," I tell him firmly. "It was just bleeding."

He shakes his head, muttering '*pathetic*' under his breath before heading to the fridge to grab a drink. Mom and I stay silent, waiting until he leaves the room—ignoring us as he goes.

When we're in the clear, Mom drops to one knee, facing me. "Are you okay?" she whispers.

I nod, giving her a reassuring smile. It's forced though—my mind empty of feeling. "I'm fine, Mom. He can't hurt me."

For a split second, I notice the tears well in her eyes, but she drops her head, and when she lifts it again, they're gone.

"Okay," she answers softly. "No more playing outside until the gardeners have tidied up the grounds."

I don't answer, studying her face as sadness crosses her eyes. She quickly smiles at me, standing up as she notices someone behind me on the back patio.

"Mrs. Dale, our apprentice needs access to the electrical supply. Can you or Mr. Dale take us there?"

"I'll take you," she replies quickly, giving my shoulder a squeeze as she brushes past me. "Damon, I'll come find you soon. Stay away from your father's office. He's *really* busy."

I watch as she disappears outside, leading the tradesman to the side of the house. Turning around, I head through the house, climbing the stairs to go to my room. As I walk past the office, I can hear my father speaking on the cell phone again, anger filling me at his brutal replies to the receiver. Quickly, I shut those emotions down, knowing that if I act on them, it won't just be me that pays the price—it will be Mom.

He's going to pay one day.

I don't know when, but one day, I'll get my revenge.

**** *Present Day* ****

"Deadman, we're ready."

Grey lingers in the doorway of my room, looking worse for wear. It's only been a few short hours, but I know for him, it feels like a lifetime. I can see him ready to practically rip his skin off—or someone else's. His hair is messy, and on closer inspection, I spot little flecks of blood on his hands.

I raise an eyebrow. "What did you do?" I ask curiously.

He pauses, confused for a second, before he glances down and spots the sprayed blood on his knuckles. "Oh, this. I was just gathering information."

Standing from my bed, I shake my head. "Right," I mutter, as he walks beside me out of the room and down the hallway. It's late, the dimmed lights of the corridor being the only source of glow. As we pass other rooms, fellow members of the society follow suit, joining us until there's a line exiting the Westwood wing. Ashwood is last, stepping out of his room as Byrone scans him out. Together, we head to the library, my eyes landing on Jillian first when we enter. She's gathered the females of the society, the small group waiting patiently at the tables as we all approach.

I don't say anything as I wait for everyone to take their seats, noticing that Grey and Ashwood sit together. I don't know what to do with this information—it makes me feel somewhat uncomfortable, but at the end of the day, we're all here for the same reason.

To get Avery back.

I never thought I'd miss the day where I'd have to deal with her smart mouth or docile, naïve state of mind. Or miss her witty banter while she tries to dazzle me with *friendship*.

If I'm being honest, the past few hours have been hell for me too. I've felt sick because of the whole situation. Fuck knows what Whittingham has planned or what they are doing to Avery. Worst still, it creeps into my mind the possibility that she's not in Lilydale anymore. If that's the case, she's as good as dead. I know without a doubt that if we tried to make a break for the outside, the guards wouldn't hesitate to shoot us all dead—even me. My father couldn't give two shits if I'm alive or dead. He'd definitely prefer the latter, but I'll never give him the satisfaction or reward.

He's been trying to break me since I was a child, and the more unsuccessful he is, the angrier he gets. It's that uncontrollable emotion I'm hoping to exploit, waiting until we have the necessary power to strike not only here, but on the outside too.

I just don't know if it will be too late.

"I need updates," I start, not bothering with pleasantries. "Where are we on blueprints?"

Leighton quickly shoves rolled up paper toward me, my hand stopping it when it's in reach.

"We think there's two possible locations," Leighton says. "I'd guess they would want to go as far away as possible—more barriers and obstacles to cross."

I unroll the paper, scanning the map. I'm already familiar with the layout of Lilydale, but with Whittingham changing things so constantly, it's still a guessing game.

"North or south?" I ask him, checking the map at either end.

Both are equal distances away from here, but it's going to be the least obvious. I know they want us to think it's still near the morgue, but I'm not falling for their trap. If we make one wrong move, it's all over for Avery. We have to be quick and accurate. The moment they get any indication that we are heading there, they will prepare and retaliate.

They'll take her out of Lilydale.

Or do irreparable damage with extreme measures so that she ends up in the morgue.

"My money is on the south block," Grey interjects. "There's two more doors to get there which would make it a bit harder. I spoke to Christopher today and he confirmed that the facility have been spending money on *renovations*."

"You spoke to Christopher?" I ask, slightly amused as my eyes seek out the blood again. I really hope that it's his blood on Grey's hands. I don't give a shit what he says his intentions were—he still crossed a line by meddling in our business. He might think he was helping to save Avery, but if anything, it would have pissed my father off having to retrieve her after the arrest. And because of the unnecessary drama, it made the facility look bad in the eyes of law enforcement. She would have been better off staying in Lilydale while Arthur scrambled to keep things private. I can only assume Christopher is the one who called the police too.

Grey nods. "Around the same time that they were replacing carpet from the incidentals account. He noticed more funds had been withdrawn when he lodged the request in the system."

"Makes sense," I grunt. "We knew they were planning a move. They had us distracted by the IT issues that we didn't think to look at any other accounts."

I notice him tense up, coming to the same realization. "We need to hit both ends of the underground rooms at the same time," he murmurs. "It's the only way."

"I agree," I respond, straightening up. "Jillian, Byrone... any updates on the firewall decryption?"

Byrone nods. "We managed to get into a few files. Nothing helpful though, but it's a start. We have to go in through the backend so they aren't alerted. If we try to immediately access the cameras again, they will know."

"Keep trying. If we can get through the system in time, it will be helpful to get the cameras offline when we head underground," I direct, turning my attention to the rest of the group. "Do we have eyes on Arthur and the guards?"

"In his office," Ashwood answers, surprising me. "Leaving the facility for a dinner date with that receptionist shortly."

Grey looks taken aback—albeit pleasantly surprised—as I just nod. "Good. We make our move when he's gone. Were there any witnesses today?"

Jillian raises her hand, grabbing my attention. She waits until I'm staring at her before speaking up. "I spoke to some of the girls. One of them heard a commotion near Elsher's office as they were being escorted to Markel's room. They saw Whittingham and the guards leave with Avery. Apparently, she wasn't in good shape."

In my peripheral vision, I spot Grey's fist clench on the table, but this isn't news to me. She wouldn't have gone willingly. They did something to her—I know it.

"Alright, time to get in position," I answer to the whole room, calming the nerves building in my body. "Ladies, you'll head back to your rooms as usual. Byrone, stay with Jillian and keep working on the cameras. If you get access, shut the system down for as long as possible. Leighton, take Jemison and let us know when Arthur has left Lilydale. We'll split into two groups—Grey, you and Theo will search the south block. I'll take Leighton to the north when he's back. Jemison, I need you to be on standby with the others. Stop the guards as best as possible if they are alerted to our presence up here."

Everyone nods, a somber feeling washing over the room. I gesture to the corner of the room, spotting the black bundle of fabric waiting for us.

"New attire for the underground. Get dressed. Be smart but I don't care whose blood we have to spill. Do whatever means necessary to get Avery back. You have my permission to be as ruthless and unhinged as you like. It's go time."

Chapter 5

Avery

"She hasn't moved in two hours."

"The other patients were active by now. Are we sure that the voltage was set correctly?"

I don't even flinch at the voices behind me, my legs curled into my body. I'm back in the white room, laying sideways on the floor with a migraine. I feel sick, not just from hunger or the migraine, but the reality that I'm alone with a bunch of psychotic scientists. They are torturing me as if I'm their own little toy.

"Her CT scan results were fine."

Footsteps walk further into the room, coming into the view. I stare at glossy heels as Dr. Cromwell leans down, her face twisted with worry.

"Avery, can you describe to us what you are feeling?"

I just continue to gaze unfocused at the wall, ignoring her. They aren't going to be rewarded with the satisfaction of knowing they are hurting me. Because they are. All this bullshit about the greater good is a little white lie they tell themselves—not that I believe they have a conscience. They are too objective, not seeing me for the person I am. To this place, I am nothing more than a bag of damaged goods at their disposal to play God with.

Dr. Cromwell frowns at my silence, looking past me to her colleague. "Perhaps she's in pain. We could hit two birds with one stone."

"Drug trials?" Dr. West asks, intrigued. "That could work. I'll get it started."

I sense his presence vanish from the room, but Dr. Cromwell still doesn't move. Maybe she hopes that if it's just her, I'll open up. I can see it in her eyes, the need to succeed—the determination to prove she's beyond worthiness. Except she doesn't care about me, she only cares about her job, which is ironic since to them, we're not worthy at all.

"Avery," she tries again. "We're going to give you some medication. It might make you feel better."

"Fuck off," I finally whisper, satisfied when I notice her flinch at my words.

She quickly stands as Dr. West reappears, the two of them having a brief conversation next to me. She doesn't mention my curse words and I don't fight when one of them picks up my cannulated hand.

"Should we move her to another room?" Dr. Cromwell asks. "Perhaps she should be secured."

"I don't think she'll hurt us," he answers, the feeling of cool liquid rushing up my arm. "Will you, Avery?"

I would if I could.

If I had the energy, I'd channel my inner Theo and slam his nose back into his face.

I've never been an aggressive person. My father was the only person I ever felt the need to hurt—and that was so I could escape. But, with each passing minute, those old feelings are starting to return. I hate Dr. West with a passion. I want to escape and be back with my guys. Except the difference here is I felt so guilty about wanting to kill my father—I feel absolutely nothing for this monster.

Dr. Cromwell leans down in front of me again, trying to meet my eyes. "We need you to tell us if you start feeling anything. Dr. West has injected you with a drug similar to sufentanil, but it's a little stronger. We're working with a team of medicinal chemists to develop stronger opioid analgesic for medical distribution to war-affected areas to support soldiers."

Great. Now they are drugging me. Why do these people have to use my own war to save others? Shouldn't we all be saved?

I already feel the effects of the drug working its way into my system. It's a strange numbness, making my muscles feel weird. They tingle slightly, my head foggy as thoughts become hard to find. At least my migraine is regressing, but it's way too quickly. Whatever they have given me is too strong for my body to handle.

I hate taking painkillers at the best of times. At least Dr. Markel was always mindful of that, only giving me low-dose, slow-release painkillers so it didn't overwhelm me. Not these people... straight for a drug designed for patients with extreme pain and high tolerance levels.

"You're going to kill me," I say to her quietly in a monotone voice. "How many people have you killed before?"

She looks surprised by my question, perplexed as she stammers over her words. "We're not trying to kill you, Avery. Our survival rates are very good."

"But not perfect," I retort back, watching as she blurs before my eyes. "How many Lilydale patients have you tortured and killed?"

I have no idea if my words are coming out clearly like they are in my head. I suspect they are slurred, darkness creeping into the corners of my eyes. Little black dots float in my vision, dancing around dangerously.

I'm going to die down here. I just know it.

In my heart, I know Grey and Theo are coming... but it's finally dawning on me that I don't think they are going to make it in time. It feels like I've been down here for days, even though it's probably only hours. But they would know I'm missing. If they were going to get here, surely they would have already done so.

Maybe they can't. Maybe Lilydale is just too good this time. Maybe they are too strong for the infamous Cirque des Morts.

As little demons appear in my vision, swarming around Dr. Cromwell's feet, I manage to pull one thought out of my head.

I have to fight as well.

I can't just rely on them to rescue me. I need to try to fight my way out of here too.

Where's that girl inside of me that was willing to go down in flames to escape? The one willing to end a life to fight?

She's still in there. I need her.

Mustering all the strength I have, I surprise the doctors by suddenly flinging myself off the ground. The white room spins violently, my stomach threatening to hurl all over the floor, but I ignore the feelings.

Whipping around, I find Dr. West watching with his eyebrows raised, his stupid fucking clipboard poised in his hand. I rush forward, knocking it with my fist. It flies upwards, hitting him square in the face. Quickly, I use the opportunity to dart for the open door, thankful not to see the guards anywhere.

One step at a time...

Everything is hazy—woozy—as I try to run in a straight line. The overwhelming white and monochrome colors make it difficult to focus on anything but I do my best to stay upright, ignoring Dr. Cromwell's pleas to stop from behind me.

As I get to the large metal door, I tug on the handle, frustrated when nothing happens.

The fucking keypad and access cards.

Spinning around, I find the two doctors approaching slowly, observing me carefully.

"Get the fuck away from me!" I scream at them, looking around for something to use as a weapon. There's nothing, so I do the only thing I can think of. I smash my fist into an observation window along the wall, shards of glass falling to the floor.

Bits of red explode in my vision, eyes seeking out the color desperately. I'm so sick of white. I hate it.

White is meant to be pure. It's meant to reflect innocence... but not here.

I realize the red is coming from my hand, a large cut across my knuckles from the glass. I breathe a sigh of relief at normality—blood—that's what's keeping me alive. And as long as I have blood pumping into my heart, I'm going to keep fighting.

Kneeling down, I grab the largest shard of glass I can see, holding it toward them. "Stay the fuck back. You're going to let me out of here."

"Avery," Dr. Cromwell says calmly, raising her hands up in a surrendering gesture. "Put the glass down. You don't want to do something reckless."

"It's what you expect," I snap back. "We're not even human to you. We're just pathetic reasons for you to use. You're not God!"

More people appear behind the doctors—guards, colleagues—all staring at me bewildered. Some don't look surprised though, and it pisses me off.

Dr. West steps toward me, motioning for his colleague to stay back. I wave my hand, droplets of blood landing all over the pristine white floor that reminds me so much of my arrival at Lilydale. I remember staring at the building, wondering how they got it to shine. It's an illusion, because once you step inside, it's the polar opposite.

"If you touch me, I'll kill you," I warn. "You already know I killed before."

"You and I both know that you don't have it in you to kill anyone, Avery," he says casually. "Put the glass down and we'll escort you back to your room."

"No," I argue, shaking my head. "I'm not letting you hurt me anymore."

He raises an eyebrow, continuing to move forward. "We're not hurting you. This is us trying to help you. Once we've finished our trials, you'll be back upstairs with your friends in no time."

Upstairs...

So, we are still in Lilydale.

It's like gasoline to the small flicker of hope still inside of me, embers catching alight. I'm near Grey, Theo, and Damon—we're just blocked by guards and doorways. There's still a chance.

"I don't believe you," I reply sharply. "People don't go back to Lilydale."

Dr. West turns his head, motioning to one of the other doctors behind him. I can't make out the words, but the other man nods, darting off down the corridor. I keep my position, even though my arm is feeling fatigued.

I expect him to continue to advance on me, but Dr. West stays put, waiting for something.

Less than a minute later, I hear footsteps approaching, confusion and trepidation gripping me. What is he planning?

Two people appear behind the other doctor, my eyes widening. Am I hallucinating from the drugs?

"Vivian?" I croak out warily, still holding the glass.

Her blonde hair hangs lifelessly around her shoulders, her own eyes wide. She doesn't speak but her lips part, the two of us locking eyes.

She's still alive.

"See?" Dr. West says proudly. "All is okay. You're alright, aren't you, Vivian?"

Vivian breaks contact with me to glare at the doctor, the expression making me more angry. She's not okay—not in the slightest.

"Have they hurt you, Vivian?" I ask venomously.

Slowly, she nods without hesitation, confirming my worst fears. We're not getting out of here—they are targeting us one-by-one. Whittingham told us she was dead. How the fuck would she be able to go back to Lilydale?

People don't come back from the dead. Only their ghosts remain, haunting the people they left behind.

Oh, my God. Has Whittingham told everyone that I'm dead?

My arm suddenly drops to my side, my body tensing up as icy fear floods through me. If they think I'm dead... they won't come looking for me.

No... I tell myself quickly. Damon went looking for Vivian. He didn't believe she was dead. He knew something was up.

Taking advantage of my momentary lapse of judgment, Dr. West quickly rushes toward me. I try to quickly bring the glass back up, but his arms are already up, putting me in a vise.

I struggle against him. "No!" I scream, throwing my arm upwards towards him. He lets out a pained grunt and I realize I must have sliced him with the glass, but he's much stronger than me, my body being flung chest-first into the metal door.

The glass drops from my hand before more arms grab me, pinning me.

"Vivian!" I cry out.

"Avery!" I hear her reply, my head rushing with dizziness again.

Guards lift me up, restraining me as they carry me back towards my room. I glance around wildly for her, finding her pinned against more guards as she struggles to get to me, her own hope reflecting back at me in her eyes. They drag us in opposite directions, my voice shaking as I yell out to her.

"They're going to come!" I shout desperately, knowing that she knows who I'm talking about. "Keep fighting. We have to keep fighting."

Before she can reply, I'm shoved back into my room, my body landing heavily on the floor. The door slams shut behind me, leaving me alone in the room.

Please find us in time... I plead to myself. Because I'm fairly certain I just signed my own death warrant.

Chapter 6

Avery

It takes several hours before the drugs start to wear off. At some stage, the dizziness overwhelmed me and vomit now covers the floor around me.

My body is tired, unable to move as I lay sprawled out. Part of me wishes I was dead so I could end this suffering, while a larger part whispers to me to keep fighting.

All of us have lost too much already. I'm not prepared to be another faded memory to Theo and Grey. They would never forgive themselves for not being able to save me. I wish I could believe that they'd be fine if I was dead, but I know it's a lie.

Grey would detonate, destroying everything in his path. Truthfully, I think Theo would do the same. Their actions would cost them their place in Lilydale, and they'd be shoved into the federal prison system for the rest of their lives. In turn, Damon would lose his right-hand man—and *Cirque des Morts* would go down in a fiery death.

I was too angry to see it before, but it's becoming clear now. The society isn't the power-tripping hierarchy I thought it was. They are the protectors from the real monsters in Lilydale. Is that what Damon meant by secrets? Was he protecting us all along?

If that's the case, I can't let these people win. Even if I'm going to die down here, I have to fight, otherwise more lives will be lost. Maybe that was my purpose all this time.

Still...

It's hard to drown out that little voice inside that wants to give up. There's a war inside my head—the difference is one side is fueled by my father's words, telling me I'm worthless, and making me believe I'm unlovable. The other side is a battleground, held up by the love I've come to know and receive.

It's stronger—because I'm not my father. While he didn't care enough to fight for me, when he damn well should have, *my love* is strong. I'll make sacrifices for the people I love. I'll fight for them, just as I know they are fighting for me.

I may not have known love, but we can still learn it. We don't have to become our trauma. We don't have to become the people who made us.

I'll never be him.

The door opens to the room and I lift my head weakly, mustering a glare at Dr. West. There's a butterfly bandage on his cheek and a red mark on his nose, and I can't help but feel a little sick sense of pride. He stares back at me with a touch of frustration, but remains composed.

"We'll be transporting you to an observation room," he says coolly, my eyes drifting to the doorway as three guards enter this time.

They lift me off the ground, careful to avoid the vomit, as they drag my incapacitated body from the room. I don't struggle—instead, I take the time to look around for anything that could help my escape. It just looks like a regular hospital, an administration station halfway down the hall, surrounded by closed rooms.

The staff are wearing key cards—some around their neck on lanyards, others dangling from their belts. I could try to steal one, but it's useless without the code.

As we approach a closed door, I squint my eyes as Dr. West types in the code. His body partially blocks my view, but I definitely see the number nine get pressed.

A buzzing noise brings me out of my thoughts as one of the guards pushes open the door, the room already bright with lights. I spot the familiar chair in the center of the room with leather straps, surrounded by machines. It reminds me of the first room I was in, but there's a large white drop-down screen positioned in front of the chair.

The guards throw me onto the chair, immediately reaching for the straps so as to not give me any opportunity to move. As I'm tied down, I spot Dr. Cromwell enter, her eyes carefully avoiding mine as she heads to a machine. It's a stark change in behavior, but I don't pay her any mind. She doesn't deserve my sympathy or pity—she made her choices.

Dr. West starts attaching small metal disks to my head, making me jerk away. It's useless as always, my body secured tightly against the chair. To my right, Dr. Cromwell wraps a tourniquet around my arm, grabbing a needle and syringe from a medical dish. She promptly stabs me, drawing blood as I let out a hiss.

"What are you doing?" I finally ask, watching as she seals the vial of blood and gives it a little shake.

Are they going to electrocute me again?

"Just taking a before sample," she mutters quietly.

I glance back at her colleague, eyes narrowing. "A before sample for what?"

Dr. West flicks his gaze to me lazily. "We're conducting a study on how electrical and chemical synapses in the brain respond to various emotions but release the same hormone—endorphins."

"That's not really a secret," I grumble. "Scientists well beyond your wisdom already know how that works."

His jaw ticks slightly at my insult. "It's a subjective test."

Meaning... You're the subject.

"Well, if you want to know what my brain looks like when I'm pissed off, then you'll have your answer."

The screen powers up in front of me, my attention automatically pulled away as curiosity gets the better of me. It's blank, illuminating a bright light, and I'm interested in finding out how they intend to change my feelings of anger. It's dominating, cloudy, and overwhelming—I'll never be happy down here.

"I've made a note with the time of the drug trial in case there's lingering analgesic in her system," Dr. Cromwell says. "The electroencephalogram is ready to go."

"Great," Dr. West responds. "Start the first test now."

She presses the machine button, the sound of it whirling to life, but thankfully, I feel nothing. The room falls silent as the two doctors watch the machine screen, making notes on their clipboard.

The minutes pass torturously slow, a clock on the wall ticking. The sound starts to send me insane, the ominous *tick, tick, tick* over and over while scratches are scribbled onto paper. Finally, the machine comes to a halt.

Dr. Cromwell grabs a fresh needle, drawing another vial of blood while Dr. West moves behind me, hitting the keys on a laptop. The screen in front of me comes to life, a video ready to be played.

I frown, confused. "What is this?"

"We're going to now check your neurological activity and endorphin levels while feeling pain. Don't worry though—it's not physical."

As I turn my confused gaze to Dr. Cromwell, I notice she's still refusing to look at me. Frustrated, I shoot back a reply to Dr. West.

"I'm not scared of horror movies if that's your plan. I've been through far worse than anything depicted in a fictional scene."

"Melanie, please start the machine again," he says, ignoring me.

The familiar whirling takes off again as Dr. West presses play on the video. I roll my eyes, deciding to indulge them for a second. As the clip plays, I instantly recognize Lilydale. The gray uniforms, copious amounts of sickening roses, and some familiar faces.

There must be a speaker somewhere in the room as voices echo around us, matching the video. As I watch curiously, clinging to that hope at the sight of my *home*, my eyebrows raise when I spot Grey crossing the path of the unsuspecting camera. The scene changes, taking us to the library. Grey is there again, pacing quietly by himself.

Is this right now? Is this live footage?

He looks exactly the same, except he's deep in thought. He even digs into his pocket, pulling out two candy bars.

"What is this?" I breathe out, confusion washing over me.

My eyes are glued to the screen, desperately trying to claw at reality. Is he thinking of me? Are they planning on saving me?

Suddenly, the sound of the library door off-screen opens, and Grey looks up, his eyes lighting up at the apparent appearance of the newcomer.

"Hey," he says warmly, catching me off-guard.

Footsteps slowly grow louder, my stomach turning as I try to make sense of this. Blonde hair comes into frame, my mouth dry as a beautiful woman appears.

"Sorry, I'm late," she whispers happily. "I had to wait for Jillian to program my door so I could leave the room."

Who is this?

Grey grins at her, holding up a candy bar. "Your favorite."

What?

I don't even realize that my breathing is getting ragged, heavy with small silent gasps. I can't look away, not even for a second, as I watch my worst nightmares come to fruition.

The chocolate becomes abandoned as Grey embraces her, kissing her softly. Her green eyes close, body relaxing into his as they hold each other.

I feel sick, vomit threatening to spill again from my empty stomach. Their clothes slowly come off, and I find myself burning holes into the screen, trying to check for the distinctive marks on his body—anything to prove it's not him. But there they are—the red scar on his neck, the tattoo on his body... even his nails are painted their usual black.

It's definitely him—*My Grey.*

Something hitting my chest shocks me, and I realize it's tears. The salty taste on my lips corroborates the truth—it's not fake footage.

"What is this?" I manage to ask again, choking back tears.

"Live footage," Dr. West answers sharply, eyes never wavering from the machine screen.

I finally look away when they start having sex on the tables—No, when they start making love. It's obvious he cares for her, touching her in all the same places he touches me.

"Turn it off," I demand through a cracked voice, unable to escape the sounds of their moans. "I don't want to hear anymore."

"It's nearly done," Dr. West replies, not moving from his place. "Keep watching."

I shake my head, squeezing my eyes shut.

"Everyone will leave ya, Avery. No one will want to stick around for a pathetic excuse of a person."

Right on cue, my father makes his appearance, repeating the words over and over. My chest is tight, heart beating fast as I try to fight back more tears. It feels like I might die, torn apart from the inside out.

Everyone leaves me. I should have known better. I never should have let anyone in. Letting people in only leads to agony, betrayal, and pain.

You still have Theo...

No. He'll leave me too.

They all will.

"The test is complete," Dr. Cromwell murmurs. "I'll draw more blood."

I barely feel the sting of the needle for the third time, piercing my already bruised skin. The pain inside is far greater than everything they can do to me.

"What a remarkable difference in activity," I hear Dr. West say happily. "Have them expedite the pathology results so we can compare."

"I'll run them to the lab now."

Hands grab the straps, freeing me from the chair, but I'm limp. The guards lift me, dragging my legs along the ground as I'm taken back to the white room. At least I'm placed more gently on the ground this time. But it doesn't matter—I'm already broken.

They aren't coming. No one is.

So, this is how my story ends—a fitting epilogue to the already fucked-up series of events that led me here.

The voice in my mind telling me to fight starts to fade, replaced by defeat. It weakly mutters to not give up.

But how can I not?

I don't have anything to fight for. I'm alone—maybe I've been alone all this time.

They wouldn't leave you. They love you.

It's a desperate scream in my mind, quickly silenced by the images of Grey kissing another girl. I want to believe what my heart is telling me, but my head is at war.

Be rational. Be strong.

How? How do I be strong? I don't know what's real anymore. I don't know how long I've been down here. It feels like forever.

You have to believe in them, believe that they are coming.

I'm tired. I've tried to fight. I don't want to give up, but I'm tired.

Tired of all the pain. I'm sick of fighting a losing battle. Life is meant to be hard—but not like this.

Maybe it wasn't live footage. Maybe they were just trying to hurt you for their tests.

The last part I believe without a doubt. And in my heart, I know that little voice is probably right. Theo and Grey wouldn't do that to me—Damon either. But even with the exhausted fight left in me, the thought that I *could* be left behind, stirs up a fear of abandonment I had fought against by being distant from people long before I came to Lilydale. It's hard to fight against all you've ever known.

It's a reminder of everything I've suffered up until this point. It's the reality of my trauma, making me realize that perhaps Dr. Smith was right all along. I needed to heal those insecurities harboring inside, keeping my mind hostage.

Take a nap. Gather your energy. It will become clearer soon.

And finally, I give in to the voice, my body drifting off into slumber as I try to escape the narrative planted by the monsters in white coats. I hold onto my own version of events, gripping the tether between me and them.

Just hold on a little longer, Avery. Don't let go.

Chapter 7

Damon

"Arthur has finally left the facility."

I look up at Leighton and Jemison, giving them a brief nod of acknowledgment while my chest tightens.

It's time.

I'm not afraid for myself. I know without a doubt that everyone would be happy to see me dead. But death doesn't scare me—it's coming for all of us, it's just a matter of when.

It's these people I'm worried about. I could be leading them to their end. Whether that's a casket, prison, or into the hands of the people downstairs, I don't know. But regardless, it's a lot to have on your shoulders.

I have to give them credit though. If any of them wanted to back out, I wouldn't blame them. But they are willing to go.

Especially Grey and Ashwood.

That's the hold that Avery has on us. We'd all walk through fire and broken glass to save her. What a strange turn of events.

I glance over at Grey, perched down in the corner of my room, watching as he springs to his feet. There's no hesitation at all—he's ready to fight. Nearby, Theo kicks off from the wall, staring at me with silent questions.

"Alright," I start, giving them both a little nod. "Jemison, head back to the others. I need you to be our eyes and ears. Work with Byrone and Jillian, and keep the upstairs guards occupied. Leighton, you'll come with me."

Leighton murmurs his understanding back, reaching for a mask on my bed. I follow suit, motioning for the others to do the same.

We've had these outfits ready for months now. I had just hoped that we never needed to use them. For a while there, it seemed like we were in the clear. Months have passed since any experiments have been conducted. I thought we had scared Arthur and his team off. But it was a bittersweet short-lived victory.

We were so close last time. Just a few more minutes and we could have saved them. The downfall was finding out that they may have survived after all. It was our intrusion that escalated things. The doctors panicked, distracted by our unsuspecting attack. If we were faster, maybe we could have stopped it.

But we didn't.

And now those deaths still weigh heavily on me.

I won't let that happen again. That's why we need to be quicker this time with our approach. We can't give them the opportunity to hide and cover their tracks.

Grey covers his face with the mask, the last of his skin hidden. It's a nice change from the poor quality, gray material we are usually forced to wear—donned in black sweatpants, shirts, and hoodies. I meet Grey's eyes through the red skull mask, barely visible through the darkened sockets. I can see it in his eyes though, the fire and determination. Blood is going to be spilled. He's not my normal playful friend right now—this is the man who slaughtered his own father in cold blood.

Ashwood quickly shoves his own mask over his face, body tense. But it's easy to tell it's not from fear. Truthfully, I don't think anything rattles the guy. He's ruthless, cold—a true companion to Grey's darkness.

I guess that's what makes the three of us unique. People like Avery, they make mistakes. They end up in Lilydale because of their trauma, forced to fight for their lives. But us? Humanity doesn't exist in situations like this. It's revenge and retribution, the fuel to our souls.

They will be expecting us. The question is: what will happen once it's all over?

There's no plan B here. The only plan is A—and that stands for Avery. I don't care what happens afterwards. As long as we get Avery back safe, I'll fight Arthur and my father.

It's not a common reaction for them either. Arthur has been uncharacteristically quiet about it. Usually, he puts on a big song and dance about a disappearance. We knew immediately when others had been taken. But with Avery, he's said nothing.

Without a doubt, it's because he knows we're going after her. He tried so fucking hard to keep her from us, but there's nothing we won't do to stop him now. If he thought we were strong before, he better realize there's a category five hurricane coming.

I can only assume his silence is uncertainty. If he tells people she's dead—it will lead to too many questions if she comes back. Their public cover would be blown. The moment he makes an announcement, the facility is ready with the PR team. He's trying to keep this under wraps. But why? Why target Avery at all then?

Simple. He's trying to piss me off.

He knows that she means something to my society. It's a high-risk, high-reward situation—one which has been fueled by his ego. It was a stupid move, but he's desperate to exude power.

I'll make him regret that decision.

I lead them out of the room, down the corridor. It's eerily quiet and no one speaks a word. When we enter the main hallway near the library, Jemison disappears to find the others.

The remaining four of us head toward the stairwell, the key card poised between my fingers. I shoot a quick glance back at Grey, checking for his card as well. It's there, and when he notices me checking, he holds it up.

"They will probably know we are on the move," I say to the others, glancing through my mask to the little flashing red light in the corner. "It appears the cameras are still online. Move quickly."

"Here," Grey replies, reaching into his hoodie pocket. "I brought toys."

I smirk as he pulls out some hand-crafted knives, taking one from him. He looks down at one of them, his expression unreadable behind the mask before he grips the handle tightly in his palm.

Ashwood plucks one from his other hand, twirling it curiously. "I don't need a weapon. I am a weapon."

"Consider it a gift then," Grey murmurs, letting his hand fall to his side, the knife dangling toward the ground.

I swipe the card, punching in the code. "Leighton and I will head north. You guys head south. We're going in blind and with no way to contact each other, so just do the best you can. Once you find her, get her upstairs as soon as you can. I left my room unlocked."

Our footsteps echo down the stairwell, pace quickly gaining momentum. As soon as we reach the basement level, we immediately separate. I don't bother to glance back as Grey and Ashwood take off, my eyes focused on the corridor ahead. I listen closely for sounds, blade in my hand, as I move swiftly.

Leighton stays to my left, matching my movements as we make our way to the other side of Lilydale. It's been months since I've been this far, but I remember it well.

Little drops of water ricochet off the ground from leaking pipes, and my breathing slows when we reach the north end. I spot the familiar double doors ahead, motioning them to Leighton. He nods, repositioning his knife in his grip as we slow down.

This is it. Either there's people on the other side or it's empty.

I swallow, ignoring the uncomfortable feeling of potential failure. There's no room for failure here.

"Deadman," Leighton whispers, pointing to the ceiling. "The lights are off."

Glancing up, my heart races as I notice he's correct—the cameras are offline. Byrone and Jillian must have somehow managed to get access. We're temporarily hidden. This is our only chance. They will have been alerted to the switch, probably already frantically trying to gain control again to find us.

Gripping the key card, I quickly swipe it, hitting the code into the pad. The light on the door flashes green, and I shove my weight against the metal, pushing it forward.

Bright lights blind us as we adjust to the new setting as we leave the dark corridors behind us. It reeks of chemicals and metal, and immediately, I know we've found it.

Except...

It's quiet.

I was waiting for guards and doctors at the door. The entrance is empty, silent.

Slowly, I walk in, glancing around. My eyes instantly spot a broken window along the wall, tape plastered over it to hold it together.

Approaching a desk, I head around to check underneath, finding no signs of life.

Leighton heads to the left, cautiously strolling down the hall as we stare at locked rooms.

"There's no one here," he whispers. "Maybe it's a decoy."

Ruffling through paperwork on the desk, I search through documents until I spot something.

"Here," I murmur, paper crinkling as I yank it toward my face. "Avery's name is on this."

He turns, eyebrows raised as he rushes over. "What does it say?"

"Not much," I grumble, shaking my head. "Just EEG results that I can't fucking decipher. Start checking the rooms."

Crossing the corridor to the nearest door, I swipe my card, shoving open the door.

Empty.

I go to the next room and repeat.

Still empty.

By the fourth room, I'm getting edgy, annoyed that no one is inside. When I swing open the next door, I'm suddenly taken aback by matted hair in the corner, a body hunched up in a ball.

Except, it's not Avery.

I lift the mask slightly, revealing my face, as green eyes peer over at me—slowly at first, before recognition dawns on them.

"Capello," I growl, surprised. "Fancy finding you here."

So—I was correct. She wasn't dead, after all.

She quickly scrambles to stand, relief rushing over her face. "Damon."

"Where's Avery?" I snap in frustration. It's not her fault, but it feels like I'm so close, yet so far.

Lifting her hand, she points to the other end of the corridor. "They took her that way."

My heart starts to race at her words. It's the only confirmation I need as I slam the mask back down.

Avery is here.

Flinging the key card at Leighton, I glare at him, my tone firm. "Get Capello back upstairs now. The code is 1109."

He nods, grabbing the card from me before I rush past him. Stepping out into the corridor, I look to my right, eyes scanning the closed doors.

Leighton and Capello appear behind me, my hand flying out to stop them before they can move past.

"Which room?" I ask angrily.

The small woman pauses, looking terrified at the thought of halting her escape. "I think the middle one," she squeaks back.

"Go."

I wait for them to disappear through the exit, door closing behind them. Once they are out of sight, I grip the handle of my knife, taking large strides to the closed door.

Jamming the tip of the blade into the top of the plastic access pad, I ram it down, dislodging the covering. I'm greeted with a bunch of wires, my fist grabbing them as I steadily drag the knife through them, severing the connection. The lights quickly turn off, and my hand grabs the handle, ripping open the door.

It's even brighter in here, the entire room white. But my eyes don't focus on that. They immediately fall to the ground, stomach clenching at Avery's curled up body, her long black hair scattered around her.

She's not moving and I fear the worst, feet darting forward before I can even dwell on it.

Dropping to my knees, I brush some hair away from her face, panic flooding through me.

Suddenly, her arm swings out toward my face, my own hand jarring forward as I manage to catch her wrist before her fist collides with my cheek.

Her eyes dart open—anger and pain staring back at me. It quickly vanishes, fear shining through her eyes. For a brief second, she also looks bewildered, a wall rising behind her eyes like she's preparing to endure more horrors. My fingers tighten around her wrist and I'm not sure if I'm holding onto her tightly for her benefit or for mine. I'm worried if I let her go, even for a second, she'll disappear.

"What is your obsession with hitting me?" I say coolly, relieved for once that she's trying to knock me out.

Avery's lips part in disbelief, eyes softening as her voice cracks. "Damon?"

"Obviously," I murmur, a smile creeping onto my face behind the mask. "We need to get out of here. Can you walk?"

Tears of relief well up in her eyes as she sits up, my hand still grasping her wrist.

"Yeah..."

As we gaze at each other, a loud alarm starts blaring somewhere outside of the room. My eyes glance up to a camera on the wall and I watch as the red light comes back to life, a darkness taking over me as murderous thoughts fill my mind. They're coming.

"Well then, let's go," I say, standing up as I help lift her from the ground. "Time to get you out of here."

Chapter 8

Damon

I can't help but notice that her legs shake as we hastily head toward the exit. But, for whatever reason, she chooses to stay quiet. Part of me waits for her to comment on it but nothing comes. I can only assume that she's hurting—but the idea of freedom is giving her the second wind she needs to power through the pain.

Wasting no time, I stab my knife into the access pad, dislodging it like the one outside her room. Avery watches on in silence, hovering close by.

"I need you to move quickly," I tell her, throwing the remains of the security system down to the ground. "The guards will be on their way. As soon as we can get you back upstairs, you'll be safer."

"Where's Theo?" she asks, hesitating for a moment. "And Grey?"

Against my better judgment, I pause, looking at her curiously. There's something off about her tone, almost like a pained cry behind her words.

"They are searching the other side of the facility for you," I reply sharply. "Together—believe it or not."

She nods slowly, frustration creeping over me. I don't have time to play therapist to her right now, but I'm also trying to be mindful of the fact that she's been through hell. I don't know where her mind is right now but we don't have the advantage here. There's enough dodgy professionals upstairs to help unravel that clusterfuck, but we have to get out of here alive first.

When she doesn't answer, I squeeze her wrist. "Look, I know that whatever happened down here was fucked up. I know you're in a difficult place. But right now, you need to put all that aside and help me to get you out of here. Otherwise, all that pain... all of our efforts will be for nothing."

Avery looks up slowly, eyes watering slightly. She swallows, giving me a small nod. "I know."

It's small but it's the confirmation I need, my body dragging her behind me as I pull us out into the dark corridor. I have no idea if I'm hurting her with my grip but all I know is we are facing a losing battle with time. I have no key card which will slow us down. I'm also alone without backup, meaning whatever force Arthur has guarding the place will be solely my responsibility—all while keeping her safe.

When the stairwell door comes into view, I exhale in relief. But before I can reach it, three bodies come flying around the corner in front of us. I halt, swinging my hand out to Avery's chest, stopping her in her tracks.

The guards look almost perplexed to have caught us too, taking a few seconds to gather themselves. I watch as their hands fall to the guns on their belts, one of them stepping forward with a straightened posture.

"Remove your mask," he demands.

I shake my head. "No," I reply calmly.

He stumbles for a second, not expecting my reply. "Do it. Or I'll shoot you."

Avery's hand suddenly grips my upper arm, moving closer to me. I frown to myself as I notice her step a few inches ahead, like she's trying to protect *me*, and I hastily shove her backwards with the back of my hand.

"I wouldn't try," I warn him, slipping my hand unnoticed into my hoodie pocket to grab the knife. "Consider this your only warning. Go back to your stations and I might let you live."

The guards laughs, looking to the others for support. "Really?" he questions, drawing his gun.

Pulling the knife out, I don't bother to hide it from them, the blade resting against the top of my leg. "Really."

"You brought a knife to a gunfight?" one of the other guards taunts. "You're outnumbered in every sense."

"Not really," I say coolly, stepping forward. "But I'm a big believer in *fuck around and find out*."

The other two draw their guns as well. Behind me, I sense Avery trying to move forward again, and I quickly cut her off by side-stepping to shield her.

Slowly, I use my free hand to lift my mask, watching as recognition crosses their faces. I know the first rule of being incognito is to stay hidden, but these three won't live to spill our secrets. They deserve to see the face of the man that kills them.

I want them to see me.

Two of them at least have the decency to look uncertain and rattled, arms lowering slightly as they look to their unofficial leader for guidance. I'm not familiar with him myself, but I can tell he knows who I am. The hesitation lingers on his face, gun still pointed at my chest.

"I'll give you until the count of three to make up your mind," I start.

"And what decision are we making?" he growls.

"Whether you live or die today."

He raises an eyebrow, his brown eyes glaring into mine. I know that expression well—it's the same one my father gives me. Trepidation but determined. He's afraid of me, scared of what I can do—but with a dire need to be better than me.

But this man is not Alexander Dale. He's nothing but a pathetic guard with an ego complex.

"I think you're forgetting that I'm the one with the gun," he snarls.

"True," I shrug lazily, looking away for a split second.

My blasé attitude throws them off guard. He doesn't see it coming when I suddenly swing back, launching my knife with force and power at his head. It spins through the air, blade embedding into his throat.

Gasping, he drops the gun with a loud clunk, hands clawing at the blade lodged in his neck. I rush forward, kicking the gun backwards toward Avery as I rip my knife from his throat, wasting no time in slashing it across the front of his neck.

Blood spurts out all over my black hoodie, my hand casually pushing him to the side as he stumbles and falls to the ground. Lifting my foot, I connect it with the stomach of one of the other guards and he flies into the cement wall behind them while I bring the bloodied blade to the face of his friend.

"What's it going to be?" I ask, staring down at his gun. It's pointed into my stomach, but I don't think he even realizes, his eyes wide with fear as he stares at my mask.

"I-I..." he stutters, shaking his head.

In my peripheral vision, I spot the other guard trying to get to his feet, hastily fucking around with the hammer on his gun.

Sighing, I turn my attention to him, watching the repugnant excuse of a man stumble pathetically in the face of danger.

"She needs to go back," the young guard in front of me says, unsure, eyes poised on the blade near his face. "We have orders to make sure she stays in the lab."

Suddenly, a loud bang echoes around the corridor, shocking even me. Metal clanks on the ground as I watch the other guard fall face-first, gun scattering away from him.

Amused, I turn around to find Avery staring at him wide-eyed, gun held in her hands.

"I'm not going back," she whispers firmly, gaze finding mine.

"You heard the lady," I say, glancing back at the last guard. "She's not going with you. Consider this your termination."

His eyes widen more before I push the blade forward, impaling his neck with it. I think it's gone all the way through, but I pull it out, wiping the blood off on my sleeve.

Falling to his knees, he clutches the wound on his neck, trying to stop the bleeding. I reach down, collecting his gun, before firing a bullet into his head. It's a quick death, full of mercy—but a statement nonetheless.

The corridor goes quiet, and I turn around, walking toward Avery. She still has the gun pointed, face full of disbelief, so I promptly take it from her hands, pocketing it.

"Good job," I tell her, watching as she stares at me bewildered.

Not waiting for a reply, I step over to the door, making quick work of the security system. When the door opens, I gesture for her to come with me, but she doesn't need to be told twice.

Avery briskly moves into the stairwell, letting out a shaky breath. Together, we ascend the stairs, until we reach the landing. I'm surprised to find the door open when we arrived, a masked figure waiting.

"Leighton," I nod. "I trust Capello is safe and sound."

He gives me a thumbs up, looking over Avery as she steps next to me.

"Vivian? You got Vivian out?" she asks urgently, voice suddenly full of power.

"She's with Jillian," Leighton answers, handing me the key card back. "But I should warn you, Christopher is lurking about."

I pause, shooting him a look of annoyance through the mask. "At this hour?"

"Apparently, the alarm was raised. He came back to check on things. Jemison and the others have kept him away but he's asking questions."

"Of course he is," I grumble, reaching for Avery. "Tell them to keep him away from the rooms. I don't have the energy to deal with him right now. Make sure the others get back safely. Avery, come with me."

Her footsteps match my pace as she lingers close, face visibly more relaxed at being upstairs. "Dr. Smith is here?" she asks warily.

"Don't worry about him. He won't be coming anywhere near you."

She nods as we head into the Westwood corridor. "He didn't do this," she mutters quietly. "It was Elsher and Whittingham."

I clench my jaw. "I know, Avery. And believe me, they will all pay for it."

When we reach my room, I'm surprised to find it empty. The thought worries me a little, but I remind myself that Grey and Ashwood can handle themselves. Besides, we probably dealt with the majority of the danger. I have no doubt that there's more guards lurking around downstairs, but Grey is stealthy. He would have seen them coming long before they found him.

"Sit," I order Avery, motioning to the bed.

She sits on the edge of the mattress as I open my drawers, pulling out some snacks. When I turn around to hold it out for her, she stares at the candy, not reaching for it.

"Eat something," I near-snap. "*Please.*"

Her eyes shoot up to mine in surprise at my unusual begging. "Please?" she repeats.

I roll my eyes. "Don't make this into a big deal. Just take the food."

Slowly, she reaches for the chocolate, resting it in her lap.

Removing the mask from the top of my head, I set it down on the bed next to her, running my hand through my hair. Avery glances at the mask before looking up at me, an eerie numbed expression on her face.

"How long was I down there for?" she asks.

"Seventeen hours," I reply, trying to read her body language. "Why?"

She looks away, alarm bells ringing in my head at her sudden change of behavior. "Do you know of a woman here? Blonde hair, green eyes?"

I raise an eyebrow. "Capello?"

"No, not Vivian," she murmurs quietly. "Another woman—someone known to Grey."

Both eyebrows raise now as the pieces start to fall into place. "We know everyone here, Avery. What exactly are you trying to ask?"

Avery falls quiet, head dropping forward. "Was he with anyone while I was gone?"

"No," I answer sharply. "Unless you count Christopher."

She gazes up, eyes desperately searching for hope. "No beautiful women in the library?"

Ahh. Those motherfuckers. I'm not surprised they brought that up. I don't know how but it's obvious something was used to torture Avery.

"She's dead, Avery."

I don't bother to sugar-coat it. Not that it needs to be. I watch as her expression changes rapidly—sadness, surprise, relief... then disgust at her own solace.

"How do you know?" she asks hesitantly.

"Because I can only assume that whoever you saw was Leah. She's the only other person Grey has ever shown interest in. And she's been dead for six months."

Chapter 9

Avery

Dead.

It was all just a joke to them—exactly like the rational part of my brain had tried to argue.

Still, it had hurt. I can't be mad at something that happened before I even came to Lilydale. But the thought of Grey loving someone else instead of me was a torture Dr. West knew I couldn't fight.

It's sickening, beyond anything I thought they were capable of. I knew they were monsters, but to exploit our biggest weaknesses—feeding into our fears and traumas. What kind of sociopath does that?

"They forced me to watch them have sex," I finally manage to say.

I'm not sure if I'm telling him this for my own benefit, to get it off my chest, or because he needs to know the lengths these people will go to. They have personal footage of patients, and the irony isn't lost on me that what they did breached so many confidentiality laws. We already know that the staff in Lilydale have no morals or ethical boundaries.

"Old footage?" Damon asks.

I shrug, unable to look at him. He hates vulnerability, but I don't know how else to be right now. I promised myself that I would be strong and escape, and now that I'm back here, I feel like I'm ready to snap and break.

Seventeen hours isn't a long time. But it felt like days. Torture method after torture method, I lost a bit of myself, and now I'm trapped in this head space of knowing I am safe, but realizing they just fucked me up worse than I was to begin with.

I don't want him to see me cry. If he makes any comments about my emotions being unstable or my lack of control, I'll shatter.

"Yeah, I guess so," I mutter back. "They told me it was a live stream though."

"You thought we weren't coming."

It's a confident statement because he always knows everything. Begrudgingly, I nod, letting him know just how messed up I am.

"We were always coming, Avery," Damon says, surprising me. I glance up at his unusually soft tone, taken aback. "We just had to be smart about it. But for what it's worth, Grey was a wreck the entire time."

"A wreck?"

"Well, a wreck in the sense of Grey."

A tiny laugh slips out of my lips. "Who did he hurt?"

Damon's mouth tilts upwards into a smile. "Christopher—among other things."

"He didn't do this," I reiterate. "It was—"

"Arthur and Elsher, yes. Regardless, there's some things we need to explain to you. But not tonight."

I don't have the energy to argue or the mental capacity to take any more information in. "Alright. I don't want to go back to my room though. I don't feel safe there."

"You're staying here," he replies, before being cut off by the sound of rushing footsteps.

My eyes widen in panic, turning to Damon in alarm. He looks unfazed, and within seconds, I realize why.

Grey bolts into the room, immediately finding me on the edge of the bed. He lets out a sigh of relief and a string of curse words, lunging forward to engulf me in his arms.

All the air is squeezed out of me as he coils his arms around me like a snake, crushing me in his hold like he's afraid to let me go. And suddenly, it starts.

I break down crying, unable to stop the tears as I cling to him back. I sense another set of eyes on me and I peer over Grey's shoulder, finding Theo hovering behind him.

My bottom lip quivers as I manage to slip my arm free, holding out my hand desperately for Theo. He grasps it, squeezing my knuckles.

"You're okay," Grey whispers, pulling back to grab my face in between his hands. "You're okay."

I can tell he's saying it to himself too, running his fingers over my cheeks, like he's checking that I'm not an apparition.

"I'll give you guys a moment," Damon murmurs. "I need to go check on the others."

I watch as he leaves the room, eyes glued to his retreating frame. It doesn't go unnoticed by Grey, his eyebrows furrowing.

"So, he got you out? Was it okay?"

Finally, I manage to break my trance, turning to look at Grey.

"Yeah," I tell him. "We ran into a few guards but it was fine."

Fine.

What a weird way to describe the fact that I just killed someone—again.

Grey nods. "We did too, but they were no match for us."

Theo squeezes my hand again and I tug him toward me, forcing him to sit on the bed. Grey, realizing my intentions, slowly lets me go, shifting to make room for the three of us.

I shuffle backwards until my back hits the wall, bringing my knees to my chest. I can't bring myself to tell them what happened—any of it. All I can do is focus on the fact that I'm safe, and the validation of that little inner voice that they came for me.

"Do you want to talk about it?" Theo asks quietly.

Shaking my head, I force myself to smile at him. "Not right now."

He nods in response. "We're here when you are ready."

They each grab one of my hands, clutching them tightly. I let them, a wave of exhaustion starting to creep over me as the fight-or-flight adrenaline wears off.

"You need to get some rest," Grey mutters. "You can come to my room if you like. Theo can stay too. We'll have Jillian program the door so no one gets in. I'll stay awake all night if it makes you feel safer."

"You need sleep too," I mumble sadly. "I don't think they will come find me here. Not tonight at least."

"Or ever," Theo snaps. "Never again."

My lips twitch at his words, a smile fighting to appear despite my current state. The validation is everything I need right now. I know I need to learn to cope on my own and not rely on others, but in this second, I cling to it. I hate having to ask for help—almost as much as I hate having a need for external validation. I used to believe it was setting me up for failure, to have my heart broken. But now I know that's not true.

Dr. Smith was right—it's normal to have connections. We need them to survive. Trust will strengthen over time, but the first step is accepting that I have needs as a person... and there's nothing wrong with that.

"Tomorrow is going to be bad," I murmur. "I wonder what bullshit they will spin about it."

Grey leans his head back against the wall. "Arthur and Alexander are masters at covering their tracks."

"Vivian was down there," I tell them, watching as they both look at me.

"We thought as much," Grey answers. "That will definitely be a PR crisis for Lilydale."

"I have no sympathy for them," Theo grumbles. "Let them panic about it."

I glance at Theo curiously, realizing that there's a lot I don't know yet. But it's a conversation for later, all of us needing sleep.

We wait until Damon returns—because truthfully, I need to know that everyone is okay. Thankfully, they are, and the confirmation eases some of my guilt.

The three of us head to Grey's room, Theo dragging his own mattress in as we create a makeshift double bed on the ground. Without exchanging words, I find myself in the middle, flanked by the two of them as we lay on the hard ground.

I was worried that I wouldn't be able to sleep, reliving the horrors. But surprisingly, once I am in my cocoon, surrounded by them, I drift straight off to sleep.

I'm not sure what wakes me up.

My body still aches and screams with exhaustion as sunlight fills the room. When I roll over to my left, I notice something missing—*or someone.*

Immediately, I jolt upright in a panic, noticing the empty spot.

"He'll be back," a voice murmurs from behind me. "He's just gone to see Damon."

An arm snakes over the dip of my waist, pulling me backwards into his chest. I relax a little, shifting slightly to mold myself further into Theo's body.

"When did he leave?" I ask, eyelids feeling heavy.

"About fifteen minutes ago."

I nod slowly, hand reaching out to the vacant spot. It's still a little bit warm, the flimsy mattress flattened slightly in the shape of a body. It's a wonder we don't all have spinal problems with the quality of the beds here.

"He said to give you something when you woke up."

"Oh?" I reply, curious. "What is that?"

Turning around to face Theo, I smile as his hand brushes my cheek, our chests touching. He leans forward, giving me a soft kiss.

I kiss him back, feeling the utmost relief that I can. For a moment in time, I believed I'd never get to touch them again.

"That," he mutters, pulling back from the kiss.

Dropping my head forward, I rest my forehead against his chest, letting his arms tighten around me.

"Is it nearly breakfast?" I ask quietly. "I haven't eaten since before they took me."

"Nearly," he replies, sounding concerned. "About half an hour. Grey said he'd be back to get us soon. They just needed to take care of some things first."

"I can only imagine what," I grumble. "Today is going to be a dumpster fire."

Theo cups my head, gently prying me back to look at him. "Listen to me. I'm not going to let anyone touch you again. You're not being let out of our sights. I don't know what

Whittingham has planned, but I am damn sure that Damon will be on the warpath today."

"I know he will be," I say, agreeing. "He didn't have to come get me, but he did."

"Of course he had to. There was never any question about it."

It dawns on me at this moment that perhaps Theo doesn't know the full story between me and Damon, and what happened between us. I know I was hesitant to tell Grey initially because of his friendship with Damon and jealousy issues, but Theo has never given me a reason to be afraid of that. If anything, he's probably the one person I can confide this information to, who will look at it in a different light.

"He kissed me," I tell him. "Before I was taken."

My eyes scan over his face, but as expected, there's nothing but calm acknowledgment.

"I'm not surprised," Theo answers—but it's a surprise to me.

"What do you mean?" I ask, confused.

Theo raises an eyebrow. "It's obvious he likes you, Aves. I can see it from a mile away."

"No, he doesn't. We tolerate each other."

"At first, sure. But not recently."

I push myself up, leaning on my elbow. "What do you mean?" I ask again more urgently.

Theo smiles at me, amused at my stupidity. "You really can't see it?"

"No?"

He runs his hand over the curve of my body. "He wants you—wants this. I'm just not convinced that he's admitted it to himself yet."

"He doesn't want me. I'm fairly certain he only kissed me to shut me up," I argue.

"It's a great method to silence you, but you should have seen them when you were missing," Theo says. "Grey was ready to throw hands with him. But Damon, he pulled together a team and made a plan. He was the mastermind behind everything."

I don't know what to do with this information, falling silent. Theo walks his fingers along the side of my body.

"No one can blame him. You have that effect on all of us."

I smile. "Even you?"

"Even me."

A little squeal escapes my mouth as Theo suddenly flips me onto my back, holding himself above me. I don't even care that my back hurts from sleeping on the ground. He leans down, kissing me with every single, little bit of longing that's been haunting him.

And it dwells on me.

I nearly lost this.

I nearly lost him.

My hands grab his shirt hastily, pulling it off his body so I can get to his skin underneath. I need to touch him—need to feel him. I need to cling to reality so that my mind stops drowning in memories.

I know today is going to be tough, and before I have to face it, I want to be lost in Theo for a little while.

Kissing him back, I run my nails down his back, pulling him closer. His hands push my shirt up my torso, gliding along my rib cage. When it's bunched up on my chest, he grabs my breasts, squeezing them through my bra. My nipples harden instantly, craving his touch. I hate that there's still clothes between us. Theo senses that, sitting up so he can remove my shirt.

I grab the waistband of my shorts, pushing them down with my underwear. Dark eyes watch on as I kick them off, quickly snapping my bra off too.

Theo scans my body slowly, staring at me like I'm his favorite tattoo—a piece of art that will last forever.

He goes to reach for me, but I playfully smack his hand out of the way, finding his pants. My fingers curl under the waistband, pulling them down just enough to see my name appear on his hip. I pause for a moment, enchanted by the sight.

"You're making it hard to go slow," he complains.

Smirking, I shove his pants down. "I hope it is hard."

He lets out an uncharacteristically loud laugh, helping me pull them off the rest of the way. I return the favor with his pants, running my eyes over his naked frame, cheeks flustered and pink by his toned physique.

I'll never get sick of looking at him. Never not be affected by his gorgeous body.

Theo hooks his arm under my knee, flipping me onto my side. He nuzzles in behind me, pressing his chest against my back as he holds my leg up.

Letting me go for a moment, he grabs his cock, guiding it to my body. In one swift swoop, he's inside me—giving me what I need.

His hand grabs my breast, using it to hold me against him as he rolls his hips back and forth. My head drops back onto him, and I turn to look at him. Our lips meet as he buries himself inside of me, slow and deep.

Our pace quickens as the urgency between us increases, both too impatient after being separated for what felt like an eternity. Theo drops his hand from my chest, sliding it along my stomach until his fingers reach my hips. When they graze over my clit, I moan into his mouth, his tongue quickly pushing into mine.

The tip of his finger circles lazily around my clit, teasing me, as his cock plunges into my pussy. It's a deadly combination—and I'm too far gone.

My orgasm rolls through me, my body tightening around him as I cry out into his mouth. He swallows my moans of pleasure, only moving his hand to my thigh when I've finished riding out my high.

Gripping my leg, he thrusts into me harder, sending my body ricocheting up the flimsy mattress. I grab his hand, holding onto him with all my strength, rocking my hips back against him as I help him chase his climax.

I'm surprised when he suddenly stops, pulling himself out of me. Before I can turn to look at him and ask why, he pushes me onto my back, crawling up my body.

"Part those pretty lips," he commands, pulling my bottom lip down with his thumb.

Pushing myself to my elbows, I open my mouth, watching as he guides the tip of his cock past my lips. Theo grips the base of his cock with his fist, stroking hard, until he pauses with an almost inaudible growl. He releases his high onto my tongue, and I'm ready to be drunk on him.

Holding his gaze, I swallow. His eyebrow twitches slightly before he leans down fast, smashing his mouth into mine.

"You're fucking perfect," he growls into my mouth. "So fucking perfect. And mine."

"Ours," comes a voice from behind him. "She's perfect and ours."

Chapter 10

Theo

Avery and I pull apart as I watch her glance over my shoulder, finding Grey leaning against the doorway casually. I turn my head to look as well, noticing that he's smiling at Avery.

His relaxed posture is a sign of huge improvement, and it's obvious that a large part of that stems from the fact that we thought we had lost her. It's amazing how your perception changes when you realize you have something to lose.

I had an inkling this could be the case after seeing Grey in the tunnels underneath. His demeanor to most is questionable—never allowing people to see what's coming next. It's as if he plays the role of a coin, and it's a guessing game as to which side you'll get.

We've all seen both sides—his notorious anger and odd fascination with blood and violence, contrasted by a carefree, happy nature. But downstairs, I saw a third side, one that I think is deeply hidden.

It's a cavernous mystery that I can assume is the reason he's in Lilydale to begin with.

Most people would make the mistake of assuming he would lose his temper if Damon clapped twice with an order. But I think the danger is far greater than that.

He's calculated. Savage.

I saw first-hand that his anger is not based on emotional dysregulation. If I had to guess, he *allows* himself to feel anger only when it's most convenient to him. And he wields it in a way so that he stays in control.

The anger he feels is more than a human emotion. It's a choice—one that he happily engages in.

He's not much different to me.

People say I have anger management problems too. They can believe whatever they want if it appeases their fragile, tiny minds. I just have little tolerance for ignorance, stupidity, and manipulation. Besides, if people see you as unapproachable, they leave you alone. They fear you, and with that comes a strange sense of respect.

It's how I've stayed *mostly* under the radar here. A few knuckle sandwiches and amputations here and there, but people quickly learn. If there's one thing patients are good at, it's recognizing their own mortality—except for dickheads like Hallman. I had contemplated chopping off his dick instead of his finger since he barely measured up to any sense of a man, but removing the part of his body that touched Avery seemed like a better idea.

"You're back," Avery breathes out happily.

I notice she doesn't try to cover up her naked body, nor does she appear embarrassed at us being caught by Grey. Whether or not she realizes, this is a huge step for her too.

Before, she'd worry about other people, scared of not being able to please everyone. She'd put her own needs aside to entertain someone else's insecurities. It nearly tore her apart. She's not designed to keep secrets and live in the dark. She's done that her whole life while stuck in survival mode. It was an unhealthy coping mechanism that got worse as time went on. But it's time for her to break free and be herself, reach the potential that she's been held back from by the people in her life that let her down.

The night in the library was the first step to acceptance of this weird dynamic for all of us. And together, it appears Avery and Grey are growing and healing whatever issues they brought into this forsaken asylum. I guess I'm growing too. In a strange twist, it's almost like I'm honoring my sister's memory—allowing peace where she found violence and a brutal end.

"I wanted to be here when you woke up but I needed to attend to something," Grey says, stepping forward. He drops to his knees in front of her, pulling her in for a hug.

She hugs him back and when he leans down to kiss her, I finally see her hesitation slip through. Grey notices too, raising an eyebrow.

"Uh—" Avery stammers, looking over at me, unable to find the words.

"I came in her mouth," I answer for her bluntly. I have no desire to drag out her uncomfortableness.

Grey pauses for a brief second, before closing the gap and kissing her anyway. She lets out a little squeak of surprise before kissing him back.

I leave them to have their moment, fetching my clothes and pulling them on. By the time I've finished dressing, they have broken apart, and Grey is helping her with her own clothes.

When we finish getting dressed, Grey shoves his hands into his pockets, giving us both a warm smile.

"We're going to escort you to breakfast. Damon and I have already made sure it's safe. So far, Arthur hasn't bothered to show his ugly head. The guards are keeping to themselves as well."

"And Vivian?" Avery asks quietly. "Has someone checked on her?"

Grey nods. "We had a few guys stand guard to make sure she wasn't disturbed. I believe she's being seen by Markel this morning."

"I don't trust him," she replies with hurt in her voice.

"We are going to look into what happened."

"How?" she asks warily.

Grey shifts in place slightly, eyes darting over to me. "You're going to be called in for an appointment with him."

"But—"

He holds up his hand, interjecting. "We're going with you. You're not being let out of our sight, and it will give us the chance to interrogate him."

Avery crosses her arms, shaking her head. "It was *his* pill that caused me to lose consciousness."

"What do you remember?" Grey asks.

She shrugs slightly. "He told me it was my usual medication. It was in a little bag with my name on it."

"Loose pill?" I question.

"Yeah," she confirms. "But that's how it usually is."

Grey nods, deep in thought. "It could have easily been switched though. Markel leaves the key in the cabinet. Someone could have made the change when he wasn't looking."

"Or he's as fucked up as the rest of the staff," Avery snaps quietly. "I wouldn't be surprised."

"We'll figure it out," I say, stroking her arm. "An interrogation sounds fun."

Avery's face cracks into a smile. "Only you pair would think so."

I share a look with Grey, the two of us smirking at each other. It would be *fun*.

As much as I hate to admit it, we work well together as a team. I normally prefer to work alone but beggars can't be choosers. When we were searching for Avery downstairs, we ended up being ambushed in the tunnels. Grey and I had agreed to go down further, to avoid being seen for as long as possible. But the guards had anticipated it—finding us in the darkness below.

Most people would freeze when confronted by guns and tasers. But not us. It was a challenge—their weapons, our hands. And I got to witness what type of predator Grey is.

He lured them in at first—acting like he was surrendering. And as they got closer, their confidence grew, and that was the fatal mistake they made. Grey lashed out quickly, slitting the throat of the first, before stabbing the next through the chest. They barely had time to see it coming. I'd almost call it a mercy kill, because I know, like me, he wanted to make them all suffer slowly.

They scrambled, of course—trying to regain control once they realized we wouldn't be going willingly. But by that time, I already had my hands on them, outshining them in strength easily.

We took them down quickly, leaving them in the tunnels. I hope Whittingham found them, seeing the massacre with his own eyes. But he doesn't seem the type to get his hands dirty. If anyone is going to suffer later for this, it will be him.

That's the difference between a coward and a true fighter. A coward will hide behind an army, while a fighter will be front and center.

In a way, that's why I respect Damon now too. He's a raging bastard, but I have to give credit where it's due. I would have pegged him as the type to hide behind his minions, but he was there—and he was the one who rescued Avery.

It will be interesting to see how today plays out. Whether the Lilydale staff like it or not, they will have to issue some type of statement and make an announcement. Avery going missing was one thing, but the other girl... she was declared dead. And now their plans have come back to bite them in the ass. While it's definitely a problem, I have no doubt that the rich fucks have a contingency plan—money can buy almost anything.

"Come on, let's get you some breakfast," Grey says, reaching for Avery's hand. "You must be starving."

"I doubt there will be anything overly filling," she complains, looking back to make sure I'm following them. "Stale toast and rotten fruit doesn't sound very appealing."

I can tell she wants me to grab her hand too, but right now, I think she needs time with Grey. She needs to reconnect and lean on him as much as she does with me. And truthfully, he needs it too. He needs his moment with her since he missed seeing her this morning because he was trying to keep her safe. As much as I want to pull her into my arms and super glue her body to mine, a dick waving contest isn't going to help anyone. Besides, jealousy doesn't exist for me. Only the unwavering desire to make Avery happy.

And he does.

But so do I.

I hope that over time Grey comes to realize that. It's not about having a maximum amount of love to allocate—love is endless.

My sister once described it perfectly to me. Meatballs can be your favorite meal, and then you eat lasagne one day. Almost the same ingredients, right? Yet... they taste vastly different. But you can still love meatballs as much as you love lasagne. It doesn't change how much you love the other meal, just the fact that you can enjoy both. Life would be boring with no variety, especially when each meal can bring you a connection and fulfil your *needs*.

So, sometimes we want meatballs, and other times we need lasagne. It doesn't take away from the other delicious food at all.

As we trudge down the corridor, we're joined by other patients escorted by guards. The guards don't bother to look at us, but the patients watch on with perplexity—blissful ignorance.

I hope they sleep well at night believing the lie that this place feeds us. They think they have a future, that they are going to be saved by the rich.

Haven't they learned the most obvious fact by now? The rich get richer and only look out for themselves. The only way to secure your future is to fight for it, but these bastards have thrown it away. The best we can do is ignore them in the hope they get sick of us. Eventually, they will realize they are wasting their money, forcing us out on the street to make room for another victim to try to manipulate.

I knew it from the second I arrived here. It was obvious—their overly confident behavior and well-crafted spiel. It's why I refused to cooperate with them from day one. I don't need saving and I don't need lectures. I'm just doing my time until whatever happens, happens. Maybe they'll let me go, or maybe they will torture me to see if I'm breakable now that I know what happens beneath the surface. Either way, the only goal I have now is to ensure Avery is safe and gets away from this hellhole. I'll happily die fighting for it.

We step into the large hall and behind them, I notice Avery's back tense up with nervousness. Grey must sense it as well because he squeezes her hand, not pausing in his movements as he leads us to the table where Damon is already sitting. He looks up as we approach, eyes lingering on Avery's frame for a few seconds before he forcefully rips them away, replacing his gaze with a nonchalant expression. It doesn't matter how well you master your emotions, you'll never be able to hide them completely.

I'm surprised that Grey hasn't picked up on it yet—then again, I think he has. He's just choosing to ignore the obvious. Sometimes ignorance is bliss. He's too focused on being *okay* with me, that he's not ready to face the reality that someone else may come into the picture. There's no rush though. It's clear that Damon is feigning ignorance too. The guy probably wouldn't recognize his feelings for a good girl even if she was sitting on his face.

"Hey," Avery greets him meekly, sliding into her seat.

His eyebrow twitches ever-so-slightly as he gives her a brief nod of acknowledgment without glancing up from his plate. *Yeah... real smooth, asshole.*

I could slice the tension with a knife if I wanted. It's a mixture of chemistry, pathetic incomprehension, fear, and the unsettling expectation of today.

"Arthur's going to make an announcement," Damon replies casually, glancing up. "Probably shortly. After breakfast, we'll escort you to Markel's room. Then, it's normal schedule."

"So, that's it?" Avery asks in disbelief. "They are just going to pretend everything is okay?"

Grey lets out a sarcastic laugh. "It's what they do best, babe. They don't want to alarm anyone and cause a riot."

She stills, contemplating his words. Then, her face flushes with a pained expression, followed by anger—like to them whatever she has gone through is nothing more than an inconvenience and insignificant.

I hate to say it, but it's true. I'm not sure what they did to her, but in their eyes, it was meaningless, only important to their own needs.

I'm calm now, but when she opens up about it, I have no doubt I'll want to avenge her. The real question is who will get there first.

On her other side, Grey gives her leg a squeeze, smiling before his eyes dart toward the door. Instantly, his face hardens, eyes glancing over as Whittingham struts into the hall with an entourage of guards by his sides.

When Avery spots him as well, she tenses up, eyes widening briefly with a mixture of apprehension and fear before she squashes it back down. She's trying to be strong, hiding her vulnerability. But it doesn't stop the tiny tremble of her frame as she acts like she isn't bothered. That alone sends a thunderous wave of anger down my spine, but I remain calm, directing those emotions with my gaze at the prick in his expensive suit.

As the guards set up the wooden podium, Whittingham glares around coolly at the room, stopping when he finds our table. His lips purse together with disapproval and dissatisfaction before he steps onto the podium, speaking into a small microphone.

"Good Morning *students*," he grunts out, choking on the word like he'll choke on my fist soon. "We have some wonderful news to share."

Avery scoffs under her breath, Damon's lips twitching to fight a smile when he notices. I shake my head myself, turning my attention back to the podium.

"We were wrongly informed of another student's passing. It turns out she was in a critical, emergent condition—thus the misinformation. I'm pleased to say she's made a full recovery and is back with us at Lilydale."

When Avery looks away, I follow her line of vision, spotting Vivian huddled in a corner with the mean looking redhead and a petite girl with blonde hair. Her friends don't seem to catch on to the bullshit, but judging by Vivian's glare at Whittingham, she won't soon forgive or forget.

Avery frowns when Vivian seeks her out too, something passing between them. My fists curl under the table, unmistakable anger ready to pop out and splatter blood all over the walls.

Whittingham flashes his pearly white teeth into a creepy smile, plastering on a relieved look as he pretends to give a shit. "And another student who was also *unwell* has re-joined us. This is a gentle reminder that if you need help with *anything*, our professional staff are more than happy to assist. You're not alone in Lilydale."

You could hear a pin drop around the room at his words, patients shifting uncomfortably at his bullshit statement and offer. But it's Avery's change in body language that has my attention, her breathing intensifying like she's fighting back a panic attack or something.

Everyone stays silent until Whittingham and the guards have vanished back through the doors, the chatter slowly returning as people go back to their food.

Avery's eyes are on the metal table, dissociating as her hands grip the edge, turning her knuckles a shade of off-white.

"Did he... did he just insinuate to the entire room that I was suicidal?" she whispers angrily to herself.

Grey shoots a glance at me over her hunched shoulders. "Don't worry about him," he says, rubbing the small of her back. "He's just trying to save face."

"At my expense?" she mumbles in disbelief, finally snapping out of her trance to look at him. "By telling everyone that I'm mentally *unwell?*"

My gaze flickers over to Damon, watching as the wheels turn in his mind. He's probably thinking the same as me—this isn't the end. They aren't going to stop. It's the perfect alibi to cover their tracks, as well as protecting their own asses if she were to go *missing* again.

"This is just what he does," Grey murmurs. "You're safe though. They won't touch you again."

"Gather everyone tonight," Damon interjects a little too roughly. "And you three meet me in the library after Markel's visit."

Chapter 11
Grey

"We're going ahead with the *ASS*," Damon says as soon as we step inside the library, his waiting frame leaning lazily against a table.

My lips curl up in silent laughter as Avery pauses in her steps, looking bewildered.

"Whose ass?"

"Your ass," I grin, giving hers a little pat as I stop next to her.

Theo glances between us, raising an eyebrow in perplexity. I had intended to fill him in before breakfast, but I was too distracted seeing Avery awake to relay the information properly. I can't help it—she has that effect on me. Plus, she's lost some weight in the past few days, enough to be noticeable. I was determined to get some food into her as soon as possible, even if it was just one pancake. She had complained that she wasn't hungry. A blatant lie, but after Arthur's little announcement, I'm fairly certain it killed all our appetites.

Just like I'm going to kill him.

"It's a new schedule we're implementing," Damon answers. "The *Avery Sleep Schedule*."

She blinks once, eyes locked on him. "So, literally *my* ass. What does this entail then?"

His lips twitch at her words, eyes lighting up slightly. I know he's missed her playful banter, and once again, that knot appears in my stomach. It twists violently like a knife, ripping uncomfortable feelings to the surface against my will.

Now that I know what I do, it's all becoming ridiculously obvious. Maybe I was being deliberately blind, turning away from what was in front of me. But ever since Avery told me about their kiss, it's put me on high alert. Every single interaction between them, I can't help but watch—their body language, the words exchanged, the tension. It's a science experiment, a chemical reaction under way. And the more I observe, the clearer it becomes.

Damon likes her.

Not tolerate, not *like* as a friend.

He LIKES her.

I've barely gotten comfortable with Theo, proud of myself for stepping outside of my cage of demons to put Avery first. To his credit, he made it somewhat easier. Theo's lack of jealousy and equal need to protect her made me respect him. I was able to fight back the hatred I felt initially because we shared the same goals. But Damon? I don't know how to feel about this.

Besides Avery, he is the person I respect most in the world. My brother and best friend, the one person who took me under his wing when I arrived. The trust between us is greater than most—there's nothing I wouldn't do for him. Well, *almost* nothing.

You'd think that would make things easier. I'd give my life for Damon without a doubt. But my girl? That's another question.

It's not because I don't trust him. And it's not because I feel the need to compete with him.

It's because I know him better than anyone here. And even then, I still don't know him completely.

Damon only lets people see what he wants them to see. I've seen multiple sides of him—the bad, the good, and the worst. And from that, I've seen the way he treated Avery when she first arrived, heard the words he spoke about her.

I've always accepted Damon as he is because I can't judge. I'm the worst anti-hero here—maybe even more horrible than him. But from the moment I met Avery, I knew I wanted her. Damon would have killed her and not thought twice about it.

With all that in mind, it drives me insane thinking that we are now here. Is he even capable of love? Would he love her like I do?

Or will he break her into a thousand pieces and make me choose?

Because I know without a doubt, I'll choose her.

Avery has this ridiculous ability to see the good in everyone. I think she lives in a world where she does so to protect herself—which is stupid and ironic because everyone has let her down.

Even me.

I don't know how she can live with the constant disappointment. Maybe she wants to be *saved* so badly that she waits and hopes that one day, her suspicions will be right, and it will validate everything in her mind.

Part of me loves that. Another part hates it.

The thought of her being hurt and let down makes me want to slaughter anyone who makes her cry.

I love that she sees flaws in people and thinks they are beautiful. I was never enough for my family growing up—I was either too much to handle or, in comparison to my father, not enough. I was forgotten and tossed aside, treated like an insane criminal. But Avery accepts me for who I am, allowing me to be the devil in her dreams *and* her nightmares.

And now I have a hard-on thinking about it.

I shake my head to clear my thoughts, focusing on the two of them again.

"Are you even paying attention?" Damon snaps at me with a raised eyebrow.

Grinning, I shrug. "I was thinking about Avery's ass."

Her face flushes with embarrassment and a hint of need. I laugh, winking at her.

"I was saying that while you were at the appointment with Markel, I spoke to the guards. Apparently, Arthur is going to start conducting '*welfare checks*' in the evenings."

"Meaning what exactly?"

Damon's eyes flicker over to Avery. "They are going to be checking the rooms to ensure people are *safe*."

"To make sure we haven't killed ourselves?" Avery asks with disgust.

"That's the general story they are running with," Damon agrees. "But I don't believe them for a second. It's just another way to access patients without witnesses."

Her face twists with anguish. "And if they notice I'm not there, it's going to raise alarm bells."

"You're not staying there alone," I interject angrily.

Theo crosses his arms, eyes narrowing on Damon. "What is the plan then?"

Damon nods. "We're creating a schedule so that one of us is always in the Eastwood Wing keeping track. We'll monitor the guards to determine their checking times and make sure no one is taken from their rooms."

"Still unsure what this has to do with my ass," Avery mutters.

"We'll be there to make sure your ass stays glued to the bed," Damon says coolly. "But in rotation so that we aren't caught out of the rooms either and get rest just in case. Byrone is working on it at the moment. It appears we have gained enough access so that we can manipulate the systems to receive notifications of which doors are being unlocked to know where they are at all times. One of us three will be watching your room specifically."

She relaxes slightly. "And what's the plan if they do try to take me?"

"We kill them," the three of us say in unison.

Avery smiles before shaking her head. "And if they kill you first?"

"You give them too much credit," I laugh. "The guards barely know their dicks from their toes—which I'll happily remove one by one."

"I've already removed fingers before," Theo teases. "Piece of cake."

"What if they try to take you?" Avery asks quietly.

Her expression changes, a darkness falling over her features. I can see her mentally reliving her time downstairs, my blood boiling when tears build up in her eyes. But they are quickly gone, her face hardening once she realizes what's threatening to come out.

"What did they do?"

My words cut through the silence in the room, asking the question that's been on all our minds. I don't know if she's ready to talk yet—but I do know some of what occurred downstairs. Damon filled me in this morning briefly and to say I'm murderous is an understatement.

They used Leah against her. Led Avery to believe I wasn't coming for her because I was with someone else.

The nerve of them, especially considering they are the reason she is dead in the first place.

I made a mistake once by letting my guard down. It will never happen again.

Avery sighs and starts pacing the library. We watch her in silence, waiting for her to speak. When she does, her voice is stronger than I expected.

"They tortured me. Decided to play God and treated me like an experiment."

Theo's fists curl next to his legs while Damon nods to himself quietly. We knew this already—just never the extent. People rarely come back from downstairs, but the few stories we've heard have all been the same.

We should have told Avery weeks ago when we knew things were on the rise again. I wanted to protect her, but by doing so, I let her down. In my mind, she was always going to be safe because we would protect her. I didn't want to scare her with tales of the monsters lurking below. But in doing that, she went in blind, unable to prepare and fight against the evil. And I hate myself for that.

"You knew this already."

Her voice is softer, gaze directed at Damon. It's not an angry accusation, just a general statement. She's a smart girl—putting together the dots and small clues along the way.

"It's not new," he answers gently, surprising me with his tone. "I was going to tell you but then you were taken."

She stops pacing, body sagging slightly. "It's the secrets you warned me about."

"Yes."

Avery's glance shifts to me and Theo briefly before returning to Damon. "Is that why your father visited me when I was arrested?"

At the mention of his sperm-donor, Damon stiffens. "My family are the owners of Lilydale, Avery."

If she's surprised by this revelation, she doesn't show it. If anything, a moment of sympathy passes across her face.

"That's why you're untouchable," she remarks.

"I'm untouchable because I made myself that way," he answers, emotionlessly. "I was their biggest target at the beginning."

Her brows furrow. "What changed?"

"I changed. I wasn't giving that asshole any power despite their best efforts. So, to keep money flowing, they entered into an agreement to use the facility for *medical research.* But I've done my best to cease those attempts. But it wasn't enough—I'm sorry."

The library falls silent again, this time with disbelief. I've never heard Damon apologize to anyone, despite knowing he carries this heavy burden personally.

Theo even looks a little shocked, shoving his hands into his pockets as he glances at the floor. Yet, in true Avery fashion, she doesn't seem astonished at all.

Like she always knew this side of him existed.

"It's not your fault," she says gently. "You were fighting a battle without resources. If anything, it says a lot about you that you tried to stop it. You could have just kept yourself safe and turned a blind eye—but you didn't. You did your best to protect everyone."

"I couldn't protect you though. I failed."

Avery slowly walks over to him, arms by her sides. "Damon," she starts, pausing in front of him. "You saved me." Her gaze flutters over to us, smiling sadly. "You all did. If it wasn't for your efforts, I'd still be down there."

Damon tilts his chin up. "We should have gotten to you faster."

It's a different knot in my stomach now—one full of pity. He knows as well as I do that we had to time it right. The reason I'm still standing here is because he held me back, calming me down from the brink of madness when I was ready to rush in without thinking. On the other side of things now that it's over, we can all agree that timing was every-thing. It was his level-headedness that got her out of there.

"No," Avery answers, shaking her head. "None of that matters. What's important is that I'm here now, and that they know we know the truth."

"They will keep trying. If not us, then another patient."

"We'll protect them," she murmurs, stepping closer to him.

Next to me, Theo shifts his attention to me, sensing the change of atmosphere. His feet turn toward me slightly, but for the first time, I don't want to punch Damon in the face for being near her.

It feels...

Almost wrong to stay here and witness this moment between them.

There's this strange sensation in my gut, making me feel like I'm intruding on an important moment. As if they both need this second to connect, to relate.

When no one says anything, it starts to dawn on Avery that she's having a moment with Damon. She straightens up, taking a small step back as her hands clasp together. She wiggles her fingers together, looking over at me with unease.

I don't know what I'm feeling or thinking, but I give her a bright grin, running my hand through my hair. "I need to go locate someone. Theo can come with me in case the guards try anything."

"Who? Where?" she asks, but I wave my hand at her.

"Don't worry about it. Stay here with Damon and work out the details of your *ass*. We'll be back shortly."

She tilts her head in confusion at my chilled response, chewing the inside of her bottom lip. But slowly, she nods.

I gesture for Theo to follow me, the two of us stepping outside the library. When the door closes behind us, he looks at me expectantly.

My eyes close for a second, taking a moment to gather myself from the strange emotions bubbling up.

"Where are we going?" he asks indifferently, just going with the flow.

Opening my eyes, I nod in the direction of the staff rooms. "We're going to find Christopher."

Chapter 12

Avery

The door swings shut behind Grey and Theo, leaving me alone with Damon.

He looks away, staring at a spot on the wall. His face is completely void of emotion, and if it wasn't for his breathing, I'd almost think he was dead with how still he is.

I remember how insane it felt to find out that his father was walking around the facility, sticking his nose into things. So, I'm surprised that I don't feel anything knowing the truth about Lilydale. Maybe they did manage to break me downstairs.

Or maybe my heart is broken for him.

For the longest time, I convinced myself that I knew who Damon was—he was the demon boy who treated everyone like his servants, forcing me to do things against my will. I hated him, despised the way he looked at me. But the truth is finally out.

He was never my enemy.

It's clear that there's more to the story, but I can't get over the fact that *he's here.* If his family owns Lilydale, then they are the reason he is locked up. Otherwise, he'd be somewhere else, right?

I always wore my trauma subconsciously on my sleeve—everyone who ever met me could tell I was fucked up. Even when I tried to hide it, I could never stop the feelings and hurt from crashing and pouring out of my soul. They just pretended I didn't exist, too preoccupied to pay me any mind. But the signs were there in every little thing I did.

I never stopped to think that someone like Damon could be hurting too. He seems so put-together, always making me wonder why it felt like he didn't belong here. There were no signs of trauma or abuse, no obvious tragic backstory. Yet, here he was.

"Damon," I say, breaking the silence.

He doesn't respond, but his eyes quickly move to mine. They are still so empty—so *controlled.*

"You're not your father," I blurt out, unsure what to say or do with this new information. But part of me wants to comfort him. If his relationship with his father is anything like mine was, then he needs to hear it. Too often we are seen as clones of our parental figures, painted as villains if they are bad people. And in here, it's easy to do so because, to society, we are the savages that need to be locked away.

If my time in Lilydale has taught me anything, it's that we're victims. We all have alibis and excuses for what we did to end up here.

His demeanor breaks slightly, eyes narrowing as he looks at me like he's just seeing me for the first time.

"I'm a monster like my father," he answers tonelessly. "Just a different breed."

"I would bet everything that I own that he made you that way."

A dark smile crosses his face, seemingly amused that I'm not denying that he's bad. "Is that so?"

I nod slowly with uncertainty, scared to push him too far. "Not all monsters are born. Some are created—like me."

Damon laughs dryly. "If monsters were the equivalent of animals, you'd be a sheep."

I feel the muscle in my jaw twitch, remembering how he called me a docile sheep when I first arrived. There's a sparkle in his eye that tells me he recalls it too.

"You'd be a donkey because you're an ass."

Standing up, he towers over me, gazing down with a crooked smile. "Careful, Avery," he warns, but there's a playful edge to his tone.

I'm not afraid, putting my hand on my hip as I hold our close proximity.

"You don't scare me anymore," I admit to him. "I've met the real monsters and survived. But also..." I pause, choosing my next words carefully. "I don't think you're a monster at all."

"That's a dangerous mistake to make."

Is it?

My heart beats a little faster. I don't know where I'm going with this conversation or why. Warning alarms ring in my head, telling me to run. It feels wrong.

But right at the same time.

Ultimately, I take a tiny step back, thinking of Grey. He was so angry when I told him about the kiss. Right now, we need to be strong. We can't risk losing sight of things by causing rifts in the group. But despite that, a part of me is still drawn to Damon.

I swallow those feelings, relaxing my posture. "Is there anything else I should know?"

Damon leans back against the table, crossing his arms. "Unfortunately, you found out the hard way about all of this. It's been happening for a while now, but Leah's death was the last time they tried to conduct their *research*."

Leah... there's that name again. It stings just as much as before, but I'm also mad at myself for feeling anger and jealousy about a dead girl.

"Did they do the same to her?" I ask quietly.

"Yes. We tried to save her but we were too late. We weren't prepared and neither were they. She got caught up in the ambush, an experiment gone wrong—or so they say."

Leaning on the table next to him, I let out a sigh. "I can see it. I honestly believed I was going to die down there."

Damon turns his head to the side, looking over his shoulder at me. "I was wrong about you. And that worries me."

I crack a smile, eyes focusing on the bookshelves ahead. "Damon worried? Maybe I did die, and hell has frozen over."

"I'm serious, Avery," he replies sternly. "You're handling all of this *too* well."

Glancing at him, I try to joke to break the tension. "First, you told me to handle and control my emotions. Now, I'm doing it too well?"

"This is different," he answers. "Controlling yourself is one thing but to completely dismiss what you went through is another. You need to take some time to deal with what happened. Otherwise it will eat you alive."

"I'm f—"

"If you tell me you're fine, I'm going to bend you over the table and smack your ass right here."

No sooner have the words left his mouth does he shut his lips tightly, realizing what he's said out loud with an annoyed look on his face. I just laugh softly, shaking my head.

"It's just... what I do," I admit sadly. "Maybe that's why I was so bad at it, because I kept everything in. I didn't have a choice."

"You have a choice now."

"I know," I murmur. "But I'm scared to admit what happened in case I lose it completely. What if holding myself together is the only choice we have? I can't fall to pieces right now—we can't be weak when Whittingham and the guards are lurking around. It's not just my life on the line here, it's everyone's."

Damon just stares at me in silence, making me question if I've said the wrong thing. I thought for sure it would be what he wanted to hear. After all, he's the prime example of not showing emotion.

"Avery," he says finally. "You're not weak. It's okay to fall apart if you need it. Just as long as you can put the pieces back together. Grey and Ashwood will help with that."

"Will you?" I whisper, looking at him.

What a stupid thing to ask, Avery.

Awkward tension fills the space between us, and just as I start to turn my head to look away in embarrassment, a hand snaps up to grab my jaw. Damon forces me to look at him despite the tears starting to well up in my eyes as small cracks emerge beneath my exterior.

"Yes."

I blink once in disbelief, forcing a single tear to slip down my cheek from the movement. He says nothing further, making me wonder if I perhaps misheard him or imagined it. His hand doesn't move from my face, still holding me in place.

Slowly, his thumb slides up my cheek, wiping the tear away.

"What did they do to you?" he asks quietly and I'm taken aback by the small growl that accompanies his words.

I don't know if it's my so-called lack of control, or the fact that it's *Damon* asking, but my resolve finally snaps, shattering it into a million pieces.

"Everything," I whisper again with a shaky voice. "Forced me to watch videos of Grey fucking someone else while they hooked me up to machines, drugged me, trapped me in ice water, electrocuted me..." I trail off, feeling a lump in my throat grow.

Anger flashes across his face and I'm worried he's about to snap. After a few seconds, he lets go of my face, eyes moving down my body like he's inspecting my physical condition. They pause on my arms, his hand grabbing my wrist and turning it so my forearm is facing upward. Bruises have emerged on my pale skin—large, circular spots making indistinguishable patterns—from the needles.

I let him look, not bothering to shrink away. His fingers gently trace over one of the bruises, then my tattoo-covered scars.

I wish I knew what was going through his mind. I want to know more about how he thinks, how he operates on a humane level. I'm desperate to see if there's another side to him other than the emotionless, cold person he portrays. I bet there is, lurking underneath.

"We'll make them pay," he says finally, resting my arm in my lap and letting me go.

"Why are you here?" I ask suddenly, watching him closely. "In Lilydale. If your family owns it then why are you here?"

The change is sudden, his walls going back up before my eyes. The anger disappears, the tension in his face—replaced by a sly smile.

"You're a curious little lamb," he taunts. "Always asking questions."

I ignore the animal comment, hugging my torso. "You don't have to answer."

Damon reaches over, pushing a piece of fallen hair behind my ear. It doesn't do much good since my black hair is badly knotted from being in hell. "It was just another way of my father controlling me. He wanted me locked up—out of fear for himself."

"Why?" I press, shivering slightly as his fingers graze the edge of my face. "What was he afraid of?"

"He knew I was going to kill him. But more importantly, it meant he could take over control of my wealth."

"Your money?" I ask, frowning. "He seems pretty rich on his own to me."

He smirks at the comment. "The rich stay rich by stealing and conniving, Avery. I would have ruined his empire and reputation—and he couldn't have that."

"I don't understand," I mumble. "How is it legal to forcefully lock up your child?"

"Money can buy anything," he answers simply. "He paid someone to misdiagnose me, to back up his claim that I was unfit and a danger to society. Then he used the money to create Lilydale as a way to make sure I'd never get out. He controls my incarceration here—he couldn't risk that power being in the hands of a federal prison or psychiatric facility because he knew I'd eventually be released once they realized. This way, he's out of my reach, in full control of all finances while holding me hostage."

My eyebrows pull together. "And the medical research?"

"A way to sustain my sentence here. The facility is costly to run and despite his best attempts to steal from me, he has to be careful of how he disposes of my trust fund unless he wants the IRS and FBI on his doorstep. By joining forces with the government, he's protected and hidden in plain sight. It's the perfect cover up for his plan—he keeps it all above board, working with the legal system so no one suspects anything. To them, he's a selfless person, giving back to society—taking pressure off their facilities for a good cause. And best of all, he gets to control me. Well, he thinks he does anyway."

His eyes dance dangerously, confirming what we already know—No one can control Damon, even from the inside of his own personal created hell.

"And Whittingham?"

"His old buddy from college."

I slump forward, shaking my head in disbelief as I let out a shaky breath. "That's fucked up."

"Yes, it is. That's why *Cirque des Morts* exists. It's a fuck you to my father, stopping the facility from running things smoothly. If the money runs out then the board will be forced to close Lilydale down unless they choose to fund it themselves. They don't want to do that—no one wants to give away their money for nothing in return. They are greedy pigs. But besides that, the people in here shouldn't be punished for my mistakes by being subjected to their *experiments*."

"Your mistakes?" I ask warily. "How on earth could it possibly be your mistake? You didn't ask for this."

Damon smiles, sadistically. "My mistake was leaving that bastard alive after he killed my mother. And I never make the same mistake twice—I always follow through on my promises."

Grey

"Christopher," I draw out slowly, resting against the door-frame of his office. "Fancy finding you here."

He glances up from the file on his desk, clocking me and Theo watching him. A laugh rips through my body at the bruise on his cheek and swollen nose, making his light eyes look even more vibrant from the color contrast. For once, he doesn't look put together like the professional he pretends he is. My artwork is splattered all over his face, traces of my assault clear for everyone to see.

I don't pretend to be innocent. I want everyone to know who hurt him.

Better still, I want them to know *why*.

"Come to hit me some more, Grey?" he asks casually, leaning back in his chair. His gaze flicks over to Theo, raising an eyebrow. "This is an unexpected alliance."

"Amazing that individuals can be brought together for a common cause," I murmur, stepping into his office. "I guess we have you to thank for that."

Christopher smiles, unfazed. "I'll always be the villain to you, won't I? It's easier to blame someone else instead of turning the mirror around."

"Villains recognize other villains," I reply. "I'm fine with what I am. *Are you?*"

Crossing his arms, he motions with his hand for us to sit down. "I assume this is about Avery," he says, ignoring my question. "How is she?"

I don't sit down and neither does Theo, the two of us glaring down at him in the leather chair.

"How the fuck do you think she is?" I spit out. "Those cunts tortured her."

Surprisingly, a faint look of despair crosses over his face—along with regret.

"I know," Christopher answers, sounding disappointed. "But I heard she's back with the other patients. Is that right?"

"What else have you heard?" Theo asks before I can respond. He cuts to the chase, more interested in getting information rather than stabbing this fucker's hands with a letter opener like I want to do.

Christopher looks over at him, somewhat surprised. I can only assume Theo doesn't speak much to the staff here, let alone show that he cares about anyone. "Unfortunately, not much. Arthur sent a brief email this morning mentioning that two students were back and set to resume their schedules."

"Are you involved in these schedules?" Theo questions.

I raise an eyebrow at Christopher, interested in his answer.

He sighs. "I'm not assigned to Avery if that's what you are asking. As for other patients, I can't disclose that information."

"Since when have you cared about doctor-patient confidentiality?" I scoff.

"If we're going to start *this* topic again, may I remind you that it was you and Damon that attempted to steal files?" he shoots back. "And I tried to stop that from happening."

Laughing, I lean forward, resting my hands on the edge of his desk. "And a whole lot of fucking good that did," I say sarcastically. "Her file still got stolen—by Vivian Capello nonetheless. That girl can barely function with her minimal brain cells, yet she was able to break in."

At least Christopher has the nerve to look guilty.

"I'm aware of what she did," he snaps with frustration. "And I've done my best to rectify that. But things aren't always within my control. You know this."

I roll my eyes. "Sure, blame your dear uncle. I'm curious—what has he had to say on the matter?"

The mention of Alexander has Christopher sitting up straight, locking eyes with me. If looks could kill, I'd be in a puddle of blood—pretty much the way I intend to go if I can't be balls-deep in Avery post-nut when I die.

"I have no fucking idea what he has to say," he answers, breaking his professional persona. "I've been cut out of all intel between him and Arthur, thanks to my involvement in trying to *protect* Avery."

Theo looks at me briefly, piecing things together silently. I've filled him in as much as possible lately, but even as an outsider, he saw firsthand the mess the whole situation created with Avery's arrest. All he knows is what Christopher told us the day she was taken—he was the one who framed her with the access card. While he can pretend to be a good Samaritan, the truth is he drove them to Avery. Between her involvement with *Cirque des Morts* and Christopher's meddling, it made her an even bigger target.

At least we tried to protect her. He blemished her record with an arrest, forcing even more trauma on her innocent self. For someone masquerading around as a professional, he made sure to fuck her up in all the wrong ways.

What was the end game here? Because if Avery was out of the picture, Alexander and Arthur would keep coming. Was Christopher going to meddle and *protect* all one hundred patients?

Probably fucking not.

"You did more harm than good," Theo tells him, echoing my thoughts. "You sent her down into a spiral, isolating her from the only people who care about her."

I stiffen slightly at his words. I agree, but the cold reminder of how I treated her after the arrest still pains me with guilt. It's not my proudest moment—I was hurt, trying to figure out why I wasn't enough for her. Even though I was mad, I was still trying to protect her from afar. I followed her every moment, making sure she was safe. I convinced Damon not to unleash his fury on her, agreeing to keep her close for the sake of our goal. But it was obvious it was for my benefit too—having her nearby, as agonizing as it was, made me feel better.

I was always going to protect her, even if I couldn't have her. But now that she is mine, the desire and need to keep her safe is greater than anything else I've ever experienced.

It also makes me recognize that how I felt about Leah was only a fraction of what I do for Avery.

I cared about Leah. I was obsessed with her—but that's all it seemed to be.

Obsession.

But my obsession with Avery knows no bounds. I was never ready to turn my back on Damon for Leah. I never considered burning my whole life down—until I met Avery.

It took ages to realize that I wasn't just obsessed with Avery. No, it was far more intense than that. It was love.

Love was not an emotion I was familiar with. It was never given and it was never something I could earn. All I knew about love was what was portrayed in fiction. It seemed sickening—full of flowers and sweetness, the need to be a certain type of person when it came to love. So, I resigned myself to the fact I wasn't capable of love because I am none of those things.

But Avery made me realize that love is more than pink hearts and romance. It's aggressive, violent—a danger. It can be all-consuming, obsessive, making every single personality trait and emotion appear.

Good and bad.

And she never once made me feel like I wasn't worthy of love. Avery loves every side of me—never shying away from the darkness that lies within me.

Most people want to tame their darkness. Not me.

I would change for her if I had to. But I don't—because she accepts all of me.

She's watched me murder people in cold blood, laid hands on anyone who dared to wrong her. Most people would be scared, terrified of what I'm capable of.

But not Avery.

And that... is love. Or at least, our fucked-up version of it.

"Avery doesn't deserve to be here," Christopher says, for once saying something I agree with.

"No, she doesn't," I answer in a low tone. "But that doesn't give you the right to meddle in our business. We had it under control. You might think you're better than us, Christopher. But your Ivy League degree, money, and expensive suits don't mean you're ready to play with the big boys. Power is not something you can just pretend to have. It's built from the ground up. You'll never be on Damon's level and the faster you accept that, the quicker we can move on."

I wait for some snarky remark but it doesn't come. Instead, he nods slowly, deep in thought.

"What is it that you need from me?" he asks, exasperated. "Because I don't have answers for you, Grey. Despite your obvious hatred for me, I'm not in bed with Alexander. I had nothing to do with Avery's kidnapping nor do I hold any decision-making power within Lilydale."

Finally, I sit down across from him, resting my ankle over my knee. "I need you to find out what happened that day. She was drugged in Markel's office. We questioned the old bastard, but he is practically senile. Short of ripping his jugular out, I don't think he had a hand in it."

The interrogation this morning went nowhere. Markel was too focused on Avery, singing stupid songs, and acting oblivious. Either he's worthy of an Oscar, or he knows nothing. Theo and I both agree that it's unlikely he was the one who switched her drugs. Someone took advantage of his less than adequate setup to instigate this. I nearly killed him for being so trusting and stupid. It was only his genuine concern for Avery's wellbeing that saved him from an untimely death.

"I can try," Christopher grumbles. "But most of the professional staff are in Arthur's pocket. He pays them well so I doubt any of them will talk."

"Try is not good enough. Someone is going down for this and if I don't have a specific name, I'll just take them all down one-by-one."

He sighs. "And where will that get you, Grey? Locked away from Avery and Damon for the rest of your life."

I slam my hands on the desk, finally losing my shit. "Don't you dare fucking use them against me. You lost the right to any opinion when you fucked us over."

Theo grabs my shoulder, jerking me backward into the chair. "Start with Elsher," he says to Christopher. "Psychiatrists can prescribe drugs. He could easily access whatever they gave her without it raising a red flag. She was in session with him when it happened."

It's right at this very moment that I'm thankful for dragging Theo here with me. Oddly enough, he's quite a calming presence for a psychopath.

Or maybe it's because I'm a psychopath too.

"I'll do my best," Christopher answers, turning to me. "*My best*. You'll have to just accept that, Grey. If you want my help, you'll take what you're given."

"If you don't want my fist in your face again, you'll be sure to obtain answers," I send back sweetly.

Theo laughs, surprising both of us. I send him a look of betrayal for breaking character, watching him shake his head at the two of us.

"Make no mistake," he says, eyes focusing on Christopher. "If you hurt Avery again, it won't be Grey you'll be answering to. It will be me—and I promise whatever he does will look like amateur hour compared to whatever I dish out."

"Don't threaten me, Theo," Christopher sighs. "You might have this little bromance, bad cop-bad cop thing happening here, but I don't respond well to threats. I'm trying to help out of the goodness of my heart. I care about Avery's well-being, as I do with all my patients. But despite whatever you might feel about *power* and *control*," he pauses, glancing at me. "I still have more freedom than you ever will. You need me—face it."

Cracking my knuckles, I lean back casually in my chair, holding his gaze. "We don't *need* you, Christopher. But one day, we're going to burn this madhouse to the ground. The question will be whether or not we'll leave you inside when it turns to ash."

Chapter 14

Avery

After finishing the schedule with Damon, which involves the three of them taking turns standing guard of my room at night, we find Grey and Theo in the hallway.

"No blood stains? I'm a little surprised," I laugh, taking note of their clean attires.

"It's still early in the day," Grey teases. "Figured I'd wait until after lunch before I make a mess."

He seems to be in a better mood, though his gaze does linger over to Damon occasionally—as if he's checking for evidence. I'm just not sure if that evidence is swollen kissed lips or slap marks.

"Did you sort out your *ass*?" he asks, lips twitching as he sneaks an obvious look at my rear-end.

I slap his arm playfully, nodding. "Damon can fill you in. He has all the details."

The four of us start to make our way to the Westwood wing, but before we can reach the door, we're stopped by a guard stepping in front of us. Dark green eyes focus on me, narrowing as he takes in my surrounding company.

"You've been summoned," Damon says matter-of-factly to me. "Who?" he directs the last part to the guard.

The guard looks a little surprised, turning his attention away from me to stare at Damon.

"Dr. Elsher, sir."

Immediately, Theo and Grey step closer to me, practically smothering me with their frames. Our hands entwine as I give them a little squeeze of reassurance.

"I'll go," I answer, startling them, before the guard ends up as a pile of bloodied flesh.

"Absolutely not," Theo snaps.

"Over my dead body—or rather, *his* dead body," Grey interjects angrily.

Damon swings a glance over his shoulder at me, trying to read the expression on my face. Holding his gaze, I give a little nod.

"I'll be fine."

They clearly aren't convinced, shooting deadly stares at the guard as if daring him to forcefully try to take me.

"He's a piece of shit," Grey murmurs quietly to me. "We can't trust him."

"I know," I answer, surprised at how little I feel. "But I want that fucker to look me straight in the face, to own up to what he's done."

Grey doesn't look pleased, tightening his hold on my hand almost painfully.

"No."

Before I can open my mouth to reply, Damon cuts me off. "Let her go."

A look of betrayal crosses Grey's face as he snaps his neck to turn to him. "Are you fucking kidding me?"

Despite the intense stare coming his way, Damon doesn't flinch, or even look at Grey. He's still watching me, face a perfect mixture of calm and detachment.

"We'll wait in the hallway," he tells Grey. "Let her do this."

"No fucking way. Theo, back me up here."

Theo stays silent, taking all of us in. Moving his eyes to the guard, he tilts his head downwards, and I don't see what he does but the guard suddenly takes two large steps back in fear.

Finally, Theo turns to Grey, nodding. "I agree with Grey."

"Thank you! At least *someone* has their sense about them."

I don't know what possesses me to do it, but I let go of their hands, gliding toward Damon.

"I'm not weak," I whisper to him. "I won't let them break me—break us. If I run, they will know they have won and keep coming after me. If we're going to take them down, we need to fight back."

Damon doesn't move, but I notice the change in his demeanor. "I'll wait outside the door. You just need to call out to us."

"Deadman!" Grey snaps, listening in on the conversation.

"Enough. Avery is going. You can either follow or you can go make yourself useful doing something else."

The silence is deafening as they stare at each other in some kind of power struggle.

Feeling the tension rise, I spin around, facing Grey and Theo. "It's okay," I smile. "I'm okay. You'll be right there and I want to prove that motherfucker wrong." Taking a deep breath, I gather my wits and courage. "I *need* to prove him wrong."

My head is high as I stroll into Dr. Elsher's office. Without a doubt in my mind, I know he's guilty of co-conspiring with Whittingham.

From the moment he arrived in Lilydale, taking over from Dr. Smith, he's hated me. At first, I had no idea why—wondering if it was just me. Was I that unlikeable?

It felt like he was trying to use my weaknesses against me, triggering all the issues that I was trying hard to overcome. He played on my self-loathing, treating me as if I was a lost cause.

It's just now that I realize how vastly different he is to Dr. Smith. I'm still mad at Smith—especially knowing he's tied up in Lilydale as part of Damon's family—but during my sessions, he never made me feel subpar or disposable.

Whenever he spoke about my mental state, he tried to make a point that I could overcome it—that I didn't have to be this way forever. It was never my fault, despite what I had been made to believe.

He tried to give me blind hope, even when I refused to listen. If I didn't want to communicate, we would sit in silence. I was never pressed or pushed, taunted or teased.

I don't know if I'll ever forgive him for his actions in leaking my file and betraying my trust, but I do know that in comparison to this colossal asshole, he's nowhere near as evil.

"Ms. White. How lovely to see you have returned."

A sneer crosses my face, but I don't bother hiding it. Instead, I raise an eyebrow, sitting down on the patient seat. "I'm sure you're so *thrilled*."

I match his tone and energy effortlessly—if he wants to treat me like a dog, then I'll act like a bitch.

Dr. Elsher starts to open his mouth, his shiny perfect teeth near blinding me, but I cut him off, waving my hand around carelessly.

"Let me guess—*am I going to be uncooperative as usual?*" I mock, air quoting him.

He raises an eyebrow, clearly taken aback by my change in attitude. Sure, the last time we met I gave it back to him before they took me to hell. But that was standing up for myself, proving I was more than the mental illness carved into my soul. This time, I'm proving that I'm strong—fearless. That I'm not going to let people walk all over me and treat me like I'm less than human because of my shitty upbringing.

I'm not going to accept that I deserved what I got because I never had a voice or the ability to take control of my own life.

"Interesting," he murmurs, but I can't help but feel it's a remark to himself rather than me.

I laugh dryly. "Are we going to pretend that my newfound attitude is a result of a *medical breakthrough*?" I scoff, referring to the torture I endured downstairs in the so-called name of science. "Another reason to pretend people like you are better than the patients here. Because if you truly believe that, then I'd ask for a refund on your tuition."

It falls silent for a few seconds, the two of us in a heated battle with our eyes. I refuse to look away, refuse to cower.

I wait for him to deny it, to feign innocence. But apparently, I've hit him when it hurts—his pride.

"I don't expect non-professionals to understand the significance of medical research," he starts, annoyed. "Best you don't try to speak about things you don't know."

"And people who have never suffered should not be a voice for those who have," I spit back. "Your textbooks might be able to list criteria to diagnose someone, but have you ever actually been through what any of us have? Do you understand on a physical and mental level what it is like to spend your life just surviving? You might understand the symptoms on paper but guess what? Every single person here is more qualified than you to understand the *actual* symptoms. So, don't speak to me as if I don't know what I'm talking about. I've been through more in one week than you will in ten lifetimes."

There's a tension in the air lingering. An invisible cord between us, the two of us playing mental tug-of-war.

"It's because of me that people like you actually have a chance at healing," he says with superiority. "Without us, you'd be lost to your symptoms. You cannot think or behave rationally, which is why you all murdered people. Normal people don't kill others."

"Here's the thing, *William*," I reply casually, crossing my legs. "While a good psychiatrist might be able to argue that point, it's moot for you. Because you are neither good nor a doctor. The truth is the people who had their lives ended deserved it. And before you say they didn't or there were other avenues, that might be true—except for the fact that people like *you* failed us. We were forced to regress back into animals, centuries behind where we should be, just to survive. In this day and age, it shouldn't be a case of '*kill or be killed*'. But that's our reality. That's our story."

His eyes narrow on me, but I don't back down.

"I never wanted to kill my father," I state, noticing that my voice shakes slightly despite the unusual feeling of strength flowing through my veins. "I tried to take the other direction, choosing to end my own life to escape a lifetime of pain and torture. But while I never intended for him to be caught in the crossfire, I know, without a doubt, that if he didn't die that day and we had both survived, I'd be dead now. His hands would have been the reason I cease to exist. A parent should love and protect, but I didn't get that luxury. So why is it that I'm being punished for trying to escape hell? Why am I being punished for *his* abuse?"

Pausing, I stand up straight, glaring down at him behind his desk.

"You can paint me as a monster all you like. In a way, I am. But for someone that took an oath to help people, you torture victims—the very ones you swore to save. So, if I'm a monster, *Dr. Elsher*, then what are *you*?"

Without waiting for a reply, I head to the door, pulling it open. Immediately, I spot Damon, Grey, and Theo in the hallway, their eyes snapping to me as they stiffen with worry and anger. Looking back over my shoulder, I notice Dr. Elsher standing behind his desk now, glaring at me with loathing.

"Consider this my resignation from your sessions. Tell Whittingham to put me back with Dr. Smith. And if you're going to tell him we're the big, bad monsters in this place, then be sure to remind him that you all created us. It's our fucking turn now, *Doctor*. And unless you want us to ravage this fucking place to the ground, I'd remember just what we are capable of... with the right motivation."

Chapter 15

Avery

I manage to survive through the night.

As much as I hated being back in my own room alone, there was some solace in the fact that Grey was lurking somewhere in the dark outside my door.

But every little creak had me on edge, wondering if guards would swoop in at any second to take me back into the hands of Dr. West.

I was surprised that Grey didn't try to sneak into my room—almost hurt by the notion. But part of me suspects it was to make sure I got enough sleep and that no one would disturb me.

Before I know it, I'm sitting in Charmaine's class, pretending life is back to normal.

Ever since my session yesterday with Elsher, I keep waiting for it—retaliation, a punishment.

Anything, really.

But nothing has come.

Today just feels odd. To everyone else, it's a normal day. People come and go all the time in Lilydale—in life *and* death. So, no one batted an eye when Vivian and I suddenly appeared again. At least not in front of me. Maybe because

I'm constantly flanked by my own guard dogs, who glare at anyone who dares to step foot within a six-mile radius of me.

I've seen Vivian around, mostly hanging with Siobhan and Eliana. She seems to be doing okay—at least on the outside. But if she's feeling anything like I am, it's a deadly curse. I'm on edge, tiptoeing across a tightrope. One sudden gust of wind and I'll fall off into oblivion.

"Psst, little killer."

A smile creeps onto my face, a rush of heat sliding over my cheeks as I feel eyes on me. Charmaine is busy pacing at the front of the room, droning on about classical literature. She takes no notice of the fact that Grey is practically rotated ninety-degrees in his chair, facing me.

"Ssh," I scold him playfully under my breath. "Pay attention."

I twirl my pencil between my fingers, stopping to point it at Charmaine. I pretend to give a shit about the so-called academia that is offered here. I can't help but wonder how much Charmaine knows—whether she understands that it's a waste of time. She's not teaching us our future—she's distracting us from our impending deaths.

Grey raises an eyebrow, his mouth forming a smirk. I watch as his eyes dart to my pencil, excitement in them.

"I'm not stabbing you," I grumble quietly, feeling a sense of déjà vu. "But I might let *you* impale *me* if you behave."

Maybe I *have* gone insane and my brain scrambled by Dr. West's machines. Never in a million years would I say something like that out loud. I nearly cringe at myself except for the fact his lips part and his eyes flash with stunned, heated need.

Quickly turning my attention back to Charmaine, I pretend to listen, ignoring the burning gaze on me which doesn't move for the rest of the class.

As soon as the bell rings for free time, I've barely gotten to my feet when an arm swings out, grabbing my wrist and yanking me toward the door. People are shoved out of our way as Grey drags me to the library, ignoring the guards that attempt to keep some level of order as patients flock out of classrooms.

I can't resist the laugh that breaks out of my throat when I'm shoved through the library doors, stumbling slightly until I gather stability. Turning around to find Grey, he grabs hold of the end of the nearest bookshelf, pulling the wooden structure until the side snaps off with a crunch.

He shoves the broken wood between the two door handles, turning around to face me. His eyes are darkened, a look that anyone else would describe as psychotic—reminding me that I'm playing a dangerous game.

"You want me to impale you?" he asks, taking a step toward me.

Instinctively, I step back, shrugging playfully. "Did I say that? I don't think I did."

He doesn't pause his movements, slowly creeping toward me like an animal about to attack its prey. I realize I only have a matter of seconds before he'll have me cornered, and I turn, sprinting to the tables, ducking around to the other side. The sound of his loud footsteps echo behind me and I quickly dash to the other end, putting a table between us.

"Do you think you can outrun me?" Grey teases, stalking around slowly.

We circle each other, my mind and body extremely conscious of the fact that he could leap across the table if he wanted to. But something tells me he's enjoying the chase—the thrill of hunting me and letting me believe I'm getting away.

"I'll keep trying," I taunt back, picking up pace when his movements speed up.

Grey laughs, eyes dancing. "It's cute that you think you'll win. I'm almost tempted to let you."

"Don't underestimate me," I shoot back. "I could be quite fast."

He stops walking, making me halt in the process. My heart starts racing as I try to anticipate his next move.

Suddenly, he pushes himself off the ground, sliding across the table on his ass. I let out a squeal, running to gain distance, but a hand swipes out, grabbing my wrist and pulling me backwards.

My back hits his chest with a thud, arms pinned to my sides by strong hands. Grey pushes me onto the table, bending me over so my chest is squished into the laminated wood.

"One would almost think that you wanted to be caught," he murmurs, locking my hands behind my back. "I guess that's what happens when you bite off more than you can chew."

"What makes you think I can't handle it?" I breathe out, my cheek pressed into the table as I stare up at him out of the corner of my eye.

Holding my hands together with one of his, he trails the other down my back, stopping on my ass. He squeezes it before lifting my skirt up in a painfully slow manner.

"Maybe you're right," he says quietly, running a finger over my underwear. "But you're already wet for me. Does being chased turn you on, little killer?"

I bite back a moan, closing my eyes. Shaking my head as well as I can from this position, I play stubborn. "Nope."

"Liar."

Grey slides my underwear to the side, exposing me to the cool air. The sudden movement makes me gasp quietly, his finger trailing down the centre of my lips. Even with his soft touch, it sends shivers racing up my entire body.

"I'm not lying," I argue weakly.

His finger dips inside until he's buried up to his knuckle. "Is that why this pretty pussy is clenching me for dear life? Dripping down my finger?"

I try to shake my head again but he curls his finger, moving his hand in and out, forcing moans to spill from my throat.

"You know—I don't think it's fair," he murmurs, deliberately stopping to stroke my g-spot. "It's cruel to say I can only have you if I behave. We both know that I'm not capable of that."

"I think you're behaving," I breathe out, stomach tightening as waves of pleasure increase with heated intensity.

Grey laughs to himself, withdrawing his finger despite my moans of protest. "Don't move or else."

I watch as he moves over to the bookshelves, scanning the torn-up and battered books before plucking one off the shelf. He opens it up to a random page, laying it down next to my head.

"You didn't pay attention today," he says, positioning himself behind me again. "I think you should do some reading."

My brows furrow as I lift my head, staring at the title of the book written across the top of the page. I almost burst out laughing, if not for Grey's fingers gliding back inside my body. Even at his mercy, the irony isn't lost on me.

"Dr. Jekyll and Mr. Hyde?" I question, biting down on my bottom lip to stop myself from crying out.

"Hm," he replies, removing his fingers from my aching body. "It's quite fitting. Now, this is what's going to happen, little killer. You're going to read—out loud to me—while I fuck you. Every time you stop, I stop. Got it?"

He presses the head of his cock against my entrance—not quite pushing in, but enough to make me roll my hips back in need. A hand slaps my ass cheek, startling me.

"Start reading," he orders. "And you'll get what you want."

My hands shakily move from my back to the table on either side of the book, my eyes barely able to focus on the faded words. Taking a deep breath in, I start at the bottom of the page, closest to my face.

"He is once out of five hundred times affected by the dangers that he runs through his brutish, physical insensibility..."

Grey eases inside my body, my pussy clenching around him as he stretches me. My eyes flutter closed on their own accord, mouth falling open as I relish in how good he feels. As promised, he stops.

"Keep going," he growls, a warning behind his tone.

"Yet it was by these that I was punished," I groan, skipping ahead because my eyes are unable to focus on the words. He buries himself to the hilt, rocking his hips torturously slow.

My fingers dig into the table as I beg my mind to focus. The words barely make sense, practically another language. My ability to speak is fast becoming a fleeting memory.

"My devil had been long caged, he came out roaring..." I trail off as he thrusts harder, sending my chest barreling into the bottom of the book. I grip it with my hands, desperate for him to continue.

"Your devil," he muses, stroking my hips. "He was caged until he met you."

A moan lingers in my throat at his words, pushing my ass into his hips to feel him more. He squeezes my hips tightly as a warning, cautioning me of the promised punishment.

"In my case, to be tempted, however slightly, was to fall," I murmur, no longer just reading words.

I used to think the worst thing that could happen to someone would be to fall into the darkness—until I met him. He *is* the darkness, and I never realized how much I needed him until I was there in his obsidian abyss.

They say that the light will save you—but that's not always the case.

Sometimes, the darkness is where we thrive, where we are reborn after finding ourselves.

It hides all your flaws, engulfing you. And when you think you can't breathe, you become intoxicated by the freedom it offers.

"My fallen angel," Grey whispers, fucking me harder. "You fell right into the Devil's arms."

I wish I had the strength to coherently explain to him that his arms are home. After all, the Devil was a fallen angel too.

"I mauled the unresisting body, tasting delight from every blow... of my delirium... struck through the heart...," I say breathlessly, pleasure shooting through my shaking body.

Grey's hand snakes around my thighs, fingers circling my clit as he senses my nearing climax. "Keep reading, Avery," he growls softly. "Don't stop until I say we're done."

My elbows threaten to buckle underneath me as my fingers grasp the fragile paper, straining to read the final words.

"Upon his lips as he com... compounded," I moan loudly as Grey picks up speed, slamming into me forcefully from behind. "The draught, and as he drank it..."

I tense up, clenching around his cock as I feel the start of my orgasm rolling through me, sending me back into the darkness that I love and crave. Grey's breathing deepens, becomes ragged, fingers holding onto me tightly as he starts to reach his own peak.

"He drank it, pledged the dead man."

The two of us cry out together, bodies trembling as we fall like dominoes onto the table. Grey's body crashes on top of mine, his face buried into my hair as his cock jerks inside me with his release.

Dr. Jekyll and Mr. Hyde are forgotten, the book laying open next to my head while he kisses the side of my face. And as we come back to reality, the last words still linger in the air.

We've both pledged our allegiance to the Deadman.

Chapter 16

Grey

She smells and looks amazing.

It takes all of my willpower not to stop her from fixing her clothes up, to bend her back over the table and go round two.

Knowing she's all over my cock right now, it's pacifying.

Having her back in front of me is the only thing stopping me from tearing this place apart. But fuck knows I want to—even Damon does. But we know that we have to handle this delicately. Too many people could get caught in the crossfire if we don't take our time.

I don't fucking care to be honest. As long as Avery comes out of it alive, let the others burn. Except I know she wouldn't be able to live with that.

When she thinks no one is looking, I catch her seeking out Capello, checking that the other girl is still unharmed.

After what Capello did, part of me wishes she would suffer. There will never be enough punishment to repay what she did to Avery.

My girl begs to differ, constantly reminding us that it appears Capello has seen the error of her ways now that her pathetic dick-on-a-stick is out of the picture.

I guess I have a *little* sympathy for what she would have gone through downstairs. It's hard not to when Avery was down there with her, experiencing the same thing. But my heart doesn't beat for anyone except my little killer. And if anything, Capello was a part of the reason Avery was taken. She started this whole mess, whether she's repented her ways or not.

"Should we go look for the others?" Avery asks, putting Dr. Jekyll and Mr. Hyde back on the shelf.

"No," I answer casually, careful not to draw her attention to anything. "I just want to be alone with you for a bit."

She nods, giving me a smile as she heads back over. "Are you doing okay?"

I raise an eyebrow at her, secretly teasing her need to always care about others while fighting her own demons. "I'm fine. Are *you*?"

There's barely any sign of discomfort at my question, worrying me.

Just before breakfast, I met up with Damon once I knew Avery was safe. He didn't have much to say as usual, but he did, in *Damon words*, express a concern about her *lack of emotions*.

I laughed it off, telling him to cut her some slack after everything that happened. But even now, I see it. She's detaching, completely dissociated from the situation as if she wasn't just tortured. A few times I've spotted her staring off into space, a battle behind her eyes as she compartmentalizes her emotions.

She's scared.

Maybe she's worried that she'll drive us away if she loses her shit. Or that it's too much to handle.

There's a greater need to reassure her, to tell her that's not the case. But there's a part of me that's worried too, terrified that I'll push her away if I make her open up.

Which is why it pains me to think that she opened up to Damon, of all people.

I know he knows more than he's letting on. He's closing down too, focusing too much on the task at hand. But I also have seen the way he looks at her when he thinks we're not paying attention.

It's unsettling.

Despite wanting to be the one she turns to and confides in, I understand they both need this. I want to be the one to keep her safe, but what if I'm not there? She needs someone else. Three people are better than two, right?

Sometimes safety doesn't come in the form of knives and fist knuckles. It's about knowing that her vulnerability is protected, her weakness not exploited when she's drowning in her own emotions.

If I can trust Theo with that, then surely I can be open to the possibility of trusting the one person who has always had my back in here.

Even though I wanted to punch him, Theo voiced the same as well. He can see it too—the tension between Damon and Avery. But that motherfucker doesn't have an ounce of jealousy in his psychopathic body, telling me to get over myself, and let things run their course.

"It will break her if she has to fight it. She'll disappear before us—ceasing to exist—if you make her believe she's not allowed to love someone."

And I fucking hate that he's right. All she's ever wanted is to be loved. Imagine if I stop that—take that away from her. It will reinstate every fucked-up thing she's ever believed about herself that we've worked hard to erase.

"You can ask me, you know," Avery murmurs, ripping me out of my thoughts.

The library comes back into view, and I register that I've zoned out, my demons pulling me under again.

But I'm stronger than them now.

"Ask you about what?" I ask, giving her a warm smile so as to not alarm her.

Avery puts her hands on my chest, peering up at me with her big doe-eyes. She's trying to calm *me* down.

"About what happened in the labs."

It's the first time since her return that she's willingly offered to talk about it, not avoiding the conversation that we all wanted to have. My smile drops, a serious expression taking its place.

"Only if you want to talk about it," I offer.

Her fingers dig into my chest slightly, eyes shaking as she recalls the events that linger behind them. But as quickly as it comes, it vanishes again.

"I know about Leah," she starts, a stabbing pain hitting me on the other side of her hand as my chest tightens. Out of everything, that's her beginning point.

Not her own pain, what they did to her.

But my ex-girlfriend.

I nod once. "I know," I mumble, not bothering to hide the fact that Damon has briefed me on the situation. As much as I want to trust them, and I don't want to break the trust developing between *them*, it would be an insult to pretend that I don't know. Avery knows that Damon tells me things—it's who we are. It's what keeps the society running.

Avery's eyes fall to her hands, avoiding my gaze. "I'm sorry for what happened to her," she murmurs quietly.

My brows furrow as I frown, immediately grabbing her wrists and holding her firmly to me. "Whatever you are thinking—stop. Don't start comparing yourself to something that happened in the past. We're here now, and that's all that matters."

"There's cameras in here," she says monotonously. I'm confused by her statement—I know there's cameras everywhere but unsure why she's veering off the subject.

Before I can speak again, she's elaborating, her tone giving the sense that she's not present.

"They filmed you. They have personal footage. Nothing is kept private."

They have footage of me and Leah.

I suspected as much when Damon told me, but seeing her reaction only makes it more real. If someone forced me to watch a video of Avery fucking someone else, I wouldn't stop until they were all dead, mangled into tiny little pieces for the kitchen to feed to the surviving staff.

The irony isn't lost on me.

Without realizing, I squeeze her wrists tightly so that she doesn't pull away. "Avery, look at me," I demand, watching as she instantly tilts her head back to meet my gaze. I try to find *something* in her eyes, but it's empty—a closed wall. "I can't change the past. We all have a history. But Leah isn't someone you need to compete with. Even if she wasn't dead, there'd still be no competition. You're the one I love. *You're enough.*"

A flash of emotion lights up in her eyes, but I'm not sure which part of my statement awoke it. Either way, I'm happy to have her back in the moment, so that I can get through to whatever she's fighting beneath the surface.

"Do you want to know what they did?" she asks, voice quivering slightly.

I nod firmly, refusing to let go of her hands even though I'm probably hurting her.

As the words fall from her mouth, I force myself to stay quiet—to listen. But inside, rage builds up, visions of the endless, ruthless torture forming in my mind as she paints a picture.

I'm going to kill them.

No, I'll do worse than that.

I'll become their living nightmare.

If they want to play God, then I'll do them one better.

I'll be the Devil.

Except there'll be no '*for the good of the science*' nonsense. It will be cold, hard revenge. They will suffer, until they beg me to stop. Even then, I'll keep going because death would be too kind for them. Death would be a sweet welcome and they don't deserve that.

Maybe I'll make Arthur watch. I bet he'd squirm, knowing he would be next.

Or maybe, Alexander too—though I doubt I'd get the chance. Damon has his name written all over Alexander's casket.

When Avery finishes filling me in, I notice the light in her eyes is gone again. But there's also something else there. I can't place it, even though it feels familiar. Maybe it's because it's coming from her—my innocent little killer.

I'm sick and twisted because my body reacts to it, shorts becoming tight as my cock twitches under the gray fabric.

There's a glint in her eyes that says she's mad. No, not *mad*.

Certifiably enraged.

Her words from Elsher's office come back to me. They were hard to hear, but we all caught them.

"It's our fucking turn now. Remember what we're capable of..."

And then it hits me. She isn't shutting down because she's falling apart. It's deeper than that.

She's hurting, it's true. Underneath that hard exterior she's still that woman that went through abuse after abuse. The delicate person who just wanted to be loved and seen. That's still there, threatening her existence while she tries to grasp another betrayal by people who were meant to protect her.

But there's also something else brewing. She's had enough of being treated like she's weak—pushed to the breaking point time and time again as people use her for their own personal gain.

Something has snapped in her. For the first time in her life, she's no longer solely focusing on the misery—the unstable control over her emotions that she learned to hide. Now, she's angry. But she's never allowed herself to feel that way, scared of standing up for herself. It's dangerous, the potential to implode once she allows herself to give into the rage. That's the hardest part—because once she does give in, it signifies much more than anyone could imagine.

It would mean that she has self-worth. That she sees her own potential.

My own words come back to haunt me, like a prophecy being fulfilled—one that only I saw coming.

"She's a dark horse. Imagine what will happen when she finally takes hold of that pain and runs with it. Imagine what she can become."

Chapter 17

Theo

It feels almost... wrong.

Well, as wrong as I could be fucked feeling for someone who doesn't give a shit about most things.

When I offered to do this, it didn't quite occur to me that I'd have access to things that have been previously out of my reach.

And truthfully, I don't think I like it.

Life's too short not to piss off people who have a superiority complex. I'm not afraid of repercussions—I prefer to set the scene. If they are tough enough to handle dishing it out, then they are more than capable of dealing with the consequences of their actions.

Just because I agreed to help, doesn't mean I have to do it Damon's way. In fact, I would argue that my way is better.

Staring at the access pad, I decide to do what any *sane* person would—I smash it with my fist.

Chunks of plastic casing fall to the floor, scattering around my feet. Anything I can do to be a financial burden to Lilydale sounds appealing. There's peace in knowing that they continuously have to replace things because of me. Let that be a financial lesson for them—don't piss off the hands that feed you. If they're going to make money off us, their first mistake was treating us like animals.

The staff card lays forgotten in my pocket as I pull open the door to the stairwell, listening for noises. It's dead quiet—only the echo of my own sounds rumbling around the concrete walls.

I take my time descending the steps, wondering if the guards will come and investigate. Apparently their alarm systems are back up and running, so they would get an alert about what's happening. It's probably old news by now that their colleagues were ripped to shreds down here, and I'd bet my ass that none of them have the guts to try to intercept.

Given how quiet things have been the past twenty four hours, I imagine that the staff are scrambling to do damage control—probably more focused on their reputation to the outside world. It's a dangerous limbo we're in—an opportunity to cause destruction without them doing much in return.

Their retaliation will come, no doubt. It's just a matter of when. But by now, if they have even half a brain when putting their heads together, they should realize that we're not going to take their bullshit.

When I finally reach the underground hallways, I take a moment to remember Damon's instructions. I'm familiar with the tunnels, but from what we know, they moved their equipment before they took Avery. Grey and I checked out the other side of this secret facility, but now I need to locate where the actual labs are.

I wouldn't put it past them to have moved again, but from what I've heard about their setup, there likely hasn't been enough time to do so.

Part of me hopes that's true. I really want to come face-to-face with the doctors who thought it was acceptable to put their hands on my girlfriend. I want to see the fear in their eyes, have them beg for mercy like their victims have done. Maybe then, they will have an epiphany. Apologies mean nothing if you don't understand a basic level of empathy. People like that will offer empty promises and apologies, too caught up in their own beliefs to acknowledge the harm they have caused.

But if they *experience* it first hand, that can change everything.

As I move down the dark corridors, I examine the area for confirmation that I'm heading in the right direction. There's only so many hallways down here, but the monotone colors, vast darkness, and closed doors can confuse anyone.

A speck of maroon draws my attention near my feet and I pause, eyes narrowing on the ground. More spots appear as I search, each growing larger in size, until I find huge stains on the concrete, hidden in the shadows.

I'd recognize bloodstains anywhere.

Confident with my sense of direction, I continue on, eyes glued to the door that appears at the end of the hallway. Its double doors are closed but I know without a doubt in my mind that I've found it.

My ears listen for sounds when I stop in front of it, excitedly imagining the scrambling of staff as they come to terms that there's a monster outside their door. I imagine their fear gripping them tightly until they can't breathe, paralyzing them with horror. Unfortunately, I hear nothing through the thick, heavy-duty doors, so I turn my attention to the access pad.

Ignoring the staff card again, I smash it to pieces, wasting no time in jerking the doors open.

Damon gave me a little background of the layout, explaining where he found Avery and that other girl. He mentioned medical records on a desk in the main hallway, specifically requesting for me to grab what I can. When I asked him what he wants me to do if I come across anyone, that's where he got a bit hazy on the details.

"Do whatever."

Avery would kill me if she found out what I was doing. I know she would worry, which is exactly why we haven't told her. She'll get filled in later—Grey was going to keep her distracted during free time so that she wouldn't get suspicious.

My footsteps are silent as I enter, noticing immediately that it's too quiet. Even if they had heard me smashing the door open, it wouldn't give them enough time to run—hide, maybe. But I'd be able to hear them.

As I venture in further, I spot the desk that Damon mentioned, giving a quick glance down the deserted corridor. Around the other side, I stare at the clean surface, not a hint of paper or stationery in sight.

I rattle a drawer under the desk and it's unlocked, completely empty too.

They've abandoned ship.

Likely only temporary until they gather it's safe to return or find a new location, but either way, they have wiped all evidence of their revolting, money-funneling antics. It's disappointing. I was really hoping to come across their setup in full swing so I could show them what real torture is.

There's a few other drawers and cabinets so I check those before turning my attention to the rooms. The padded white walls make it easy to distinguish what they were used for so when I reach the end of the hallway and open another door, I'm surprised to find medical equipment.

I couldn't tell you the difference between them or what they are intended for specifically, but I do know they were used for whatever fucked-up games they played.

Pacing around the room, I focus my attention on looking for specific items. Eventually I find something suitable in a built-in storage space, grabbing an IV bar and dragging it across the room.

It's almost weightless when I pick it up and turn it to the side, taking a few steps before I ram the metal pole into the monitor on one of the machines. It just cracks at first, but the second blow shatters it.

Readjusting my position, I swing it like a baseball bat, smashing the equipment into multiple pieces.

There's no rushing—I take my time, making sure every single piece of needed equipment is reconfigured into some type of artwork that takes on a new form of abstract expressionism—a salutation to the rage I feel. Having to pause operations is one thing, but having their expensive equipment trashed is another. I can't imagine the government agency will be too thrilled with Lilydale after this.

When I enter the next room in search of more items to destroy, I'm pleasantly surprised to find a living, breathing body. He's just as startled as I am by my sudden appearance, hands gripping cords attached to the machine as he pauses. It's obvious he's trying to save the machine, likely aware of what was coming. It's not exactly like I was being quiet.

"Well, hello there," I greet coolly. "What brings you here?"

I have to hand it to him—if he's scared, he doesn't show it. Straightening up, his eyes narrow, and it's then I take notice of a syringe laid on the chair next to him. Well, if this asshole thinks he has a chance of getting me with that, he's sadly mistaken.

"You shouldn't be down here," he scolds, like I'm a child who's gone out of boundaries.

"Neither should you," I respond. "But alas, here we both are."

My eyes scan over his white lab coat. It's clear what he is but I'm not interested in that. The only question that I want to know is whether he put his filthy hands on Avery.

He clears his throat, carefully placing the wrapped-up cords atop the machine. "Whatever you are thinking, it's not worth it. I've already called security."

I laugh, gripping the metal pole as my fingers dance along it. "I guarantee you don't know what I'm thinking. But I'm happy for an audience *if* they bother to come."

"Why don't you tell me your name?" he asks, bored. Many doctors have tried to manipulate me, so his stalling, distracting tactics aren't going to work.

"There's no need for pleasantries," I shoot back. "We won't be crossing paths again. But on the subject of pathways—do you know Avery White?"

His face is emotionless but his refusal to answer tells me everything I need to know. He was one of them.

The slimy bastard thinks he's being slick, but I can see his hand edging toward the syringe, trying not to make it obvious. I decide the best thing to do is fight fire with fire.

"What does that machine do?" I ask curiously, distracting him.

I watch as his eyes dart to it, concern finally showing on his face. "It's an ECT machine. It's quite expensive," he grunts, delirious if he thinks that's going to deter me.

"Electroconvulsive therapy?" I mutter, mostly to myself. "Interesting. Has it been used recently?"

Once again, he gives himself away with silence and my fist clenches around the metal pole. It must suddenly dawn on him why I'm asking such specific questions about Avery and this machine, his hand snatching the syringe up.

Before he can get any further, I swing the pole toward him, catching his rib cage and back. He lets out a loud groan, legs buckling as he reaches for the chair to steady himself, syringe falling to the floor.

I take another hit at him, this time purposely aiming for the backs of his knees. The force sends him buckling to the floor, while I step closer, plucking the needle up from the floor.

"I'd ask what's in this," I murmur, looking at the swirling liquid inside the barrel. "But truthfully, I don't care."

My hand shoves the needle into his neck, pressing down on the plunger as his arms fly up in an attempt to stop me. His hand grabs the syringe, ripping it out from his neck but he's too late.

I'm quicker than him, the drug already in his body.

"You stupid, mentally deranged child," he growls, trying to push himself from the floor. Whatever was in there seems to be working fast, coupled with the hits from the metal pole. He's struggling to lift his own weight.

"Not a child, but I doubt that would stop me even if I were," I reply, dropping the pole so my hands can lift him by his lab coat.

Slamming his back onto the chair, I fasten the leather restraints around him, his body getting weaker each passing second. I think he tries to speak but the words are caught in his throat as his eyes roll for a split second.

"You'll have to be patient with me, Doc," I mumble, pressing buttons on the machine. "I'm not sure how to work this exactly. But I'm a quick learner—I'm sure I'll figure it out."

Following the wrapped-up cords, I check it's all plugged in and hit the *on* button. I smirk as the screen flashes to life, grabbing the electrodes and pressing them harshly into the sides of his head.

I lean down so our faces are less than two inches apart, smiling widely at his struggling frame. His eyes roll, regain focus, then roll again as he fights the drug, finally getting a burst of energy to speak.

"What do you want to know?" he grunts, thrashing his head side to side in an attempt to dislodge the electrodes.

Even the most confident men can fall when their own life is resting in the hands of another. It's very fitting–I bet Avery felt helpless too. Now, he has scored himself a first-class ticket to the experience.

I play innocent though, letting him believe he might get his way. "You're open to having a peaceful conversation? Good."

His eyes flash, annoyed, then relieved. "Yes. I'll tell you what you want to know then you let me go."

Grabbing a stool from against the wall, I bring it to the side of the chair, sitting down. "Okay," I say happily. "Did you experiment on patients down here?"

"Yes," he growls out.

I nod, showing I'm pleased with his honesty. "And Avery White?"

"I believe she might have been down here."

Wrong answer.

Turning to the screen, I press some keys. "Which one starts the machine?"

"Okay!" He yells, words slurring. "Yes, Avery was down here. But I don't control who they send."

Pausing, I keep my finger above the keyboard in a warning. "Who decides that?"

"The Lilydale board presents to us a list of potential candidates. They are numbered in order of interest based on their diagnoses and background. Our in-house team then gives recommendations relating to which conditions may be best suited to our research methods. After that, it's up to Lilydale who they send down."

"Lilydale makes the final decision?" I reaffirm. "And why were you interested in Avery?"

His eyes dart to my hovering hand. "Her traumatic background and experience with abuse. Earlier candidates weren't able to properly adjust to our methods. So, our in-house team decided that someone with that level of mental injury might be better equipped for longer testing to allow us adequate time to draw conclusions."

I nod, keeping my face blank despite the burning rage that grips me. "And how did she handle your *methods*?"

He scoffs, remembering back. It pisses me off because he's given himself away–he did touch her.

"She's very *strong-willed*," he says with a hint of sarcasm. "It surprised us. But certain methods were more effective than others."

"Like this one?" I ask, waving my hand over the keyboard.

"This one was more catatonic than anything–" he stops himself, pressing his lips firmly together. I watch as his body tenses, regretting his words.

I remove my hand away from the machine, giving him a false sense of security. "And what one worked best?"

The question makes me feel sick. Understanding on a descriptive level what she went through is just as bad as seeing her struggle with it. Knowing and seeing what they did makes it even more real. I could see her trauma in her face the night she returned, but looking at this machine and chair, imagining her strapped down, paints a picture I'll never get out of my nightmares.

"We studied her brain waves while showing her various forms of media."

"What kind of media?" I ask him. "How do I turn this back off?" It's a lie, my finger pressing the screen carelessly like I'm confused. But in reality, I'm hitting the right-pointed arrow—underneath the word *voltage*.

He breathes a sigh of relief, slurring together words quickly. "Lilydale mentioned that she had become attached to an individual. They provided us footage of him with another former patient."

It doesn't take a genius to put two and two together. My jaw clenches as I place my hand back on my lap.

"Thank you, Doctor–?"

"West," he mutters.

"Always a pleasure, Dr. West," I say calmly, hitting the *start* button on the screen and standing up.

His screams follow me out of the room, the sound of buzzing electricity entangling around them. But by the time I get to the end of the corridor back to the entrance, I can't help but smile.

It's gone deadly quiet.

What a shame.

Chapter 18

Avery

Even though I asked for it, I still have to admit it's a surprise. I wouldn't call it *pleasant* but it's digestible at least.

"I'm really glad you are back, Avery."

I look at Dr. Smith from across the desk, his warm smile pissing me off. It's easy to tell it's a façade.

"Back in session with you or back from being tortured by mad scientists?" I ask sarcastically.

It took many hours of convincing the guys that it was a preferred option to return to Dr. Smith. One of the guards had sprung it on me late yesterday, giving us the heads up that from today, I'd be returning as one of Dr. Smith's patients. Grey was the most vocal about it, and while Damon stayed quiet, I could see his jaw ticking.

Unfortunately, seeing a psych is a requirement of Lilydale, one that *most* people can't get out of. While the three of them seem to be session-free, I don't hold the same power or confidence. And if our options are between Dr. Smith and Dr. Elsher, it's obvious who I'd choose.

I tried to pry for information about *why* they were so worked-up about Dr. Smith but no one gave me any answers. It can't be as simple as he's Damon's cousin, because that fact was already out in the open when I was seeing him previously for sessions. Still, every time he appears in conversation, I practically drown in the masculine hostility.

Dr. Smith shifts awkwardly, smile dropping slightly. Good—I've made him uncomfortable. The last thing I need is some nauseating, happy optimist who overlooks what happened to me. As much as I hate talking about it, it would be even worse to pretend it didn't exist—acting as if my trauma is not important enough to recognize. At least here, I can talk about it freely without worrying about the personal attachments. I know the guys keep encouraging me to share what I'm comfortable with, but it's their reactions that *kill me*. They are hurting for me, angry, and out for blood.

I love how protective they are—I've never had that before. However, it dawned on me that having that kind of protection comes with a price. It's not just *my* emotions that suffer—it's all of ours. And I don't want them to feel like they are drowning because of something that happened to me.

I want to protect them too. And keeping it locked away is the only way I know how.

"Yes, well..." he starts, tapping his pen on the notepad in front of him. "That's definitely a good point."

"I almost expected you to deny it," I say, sitting criss-cross applesauce on the chair. "Probably not professional to discuss your colleagues' secret side projects."

He laughs under his breath, surprising me. Placing his pen down, he pushes the notepad away and leans back into his chair. "Despite what you must think, I don't think they are professional at all. And I certainly don't wish to have them referred to as my colleagues."

My eyebrow shoots up. "You expect me to believe that you don't agree with it?"

"Of course not. You have every right to be wary and distrusting. But I'm not going to say I agree with it, regardless of what you think of me."

"You're Damon's cousin," I point out. "That means your family owns this place too."

Surprise appears on his face. "They told you that?"

I pause for a moment, wondering if I shouldn't have disclosed what I know. But it's too late now to backtrack, so I nod confidently.

"Alexander is your uncle, I assume. Isn't he the one organizing the *research* downstairs? While also paying your salary?"

"If I supported his mission, I wouldn't have jeopardized my position here by doing what I did. And now that I have you face-to-face, I can apologize for it."

I'm not sure what he's talking about, racking my brain to figure out which incident he's talking about. "The meeting with Alexander and Whittingham?" I question. "I don't think they would have placed me in solitary confinement for long."

His eyes widen slightly, apparently taken aback at my reply. "I'm not referring to that. Though I do wish I had more input when it comes to such matters. Thankfully, Damon was able to step in."

There's a moment of confusion between both of us, and I get side-tracked by his comment.

"It's interesting that Damon has so much power and you don't."

Dr. Smith looks away, pondering my observation. "There are reasons. I'm sure Damon will fill you in if he chooses to do so."

I snort. Damon is a locked vault the majority of the time. But I already know—it's the immediate family connection. The issues about wealth.

It's still strange though that Dr. Smith is treated differently... and more so, why he allows it. If he's really against Lilydale's practices, then why work here at all?

"Regardless, you'll need to fill me in. What exactly are you trying to apologize for?" I ask, getting back to the point.

"The staff card," he says cautiously, trying to gauge how much I know.

Shaking my head, I'm still completely clueless. "What staff card?"

He sighs, rubbing his temple. "I thought you knew. I assumed they would have told you already."

"Told me what?"

Light eyes peer up at me as he hangs his head in exasperation. I can see the mental discomfort that he has to break whatever news he has. "Avery, I'm the one who framed you with the staff card. Before you react," he says sternly, noticing my face tense up in anger. "There was a reason behind it that you should know."

"Are you fucking kidding me?" I snap. "What possible reason could there be for you framing me for *murder*? I was arrested."

I'm blindsided again. All my initial feelings of betrayal from Dr. Smith come rushing back. I feel like a fool. I should have stuck to my guns and held him accountable for the file incident and giving me the fake cabinet key—too quick to dismiss it.

It's hard when your options are bad or worse.

"I had gotten wind that you were a person of interest for Alexander's project," he interjects. "I knew you wouldn't have maimed someone but figured if I could get you out of here, you'd be safe. The police would realize you were innocent and perhaps reevaluate your *situation*."

Laughter threatens to bubble out. Regardless of his position and educational background, he's fucking *stupid*.

"You're not a lawyer," I mutter through clenched teeth. "Nor do I have the money for one. What exactly did you think they were going to do once I was found innocent? Just let me go free? I'm still a convicted felon. The best-case scenario would have been federal prison. I'd be alone again in an equally terrible environment."

Dr. Smith sighs sadly. "It was a rash, split-second decision. I didn't have long to consider the long-term consequences. I just knew they were coming for you, and then once Mr. Hallman's death was discovered, it raised concerns about who would take the fall. We both know that Damon and his group wouldn't. But Arthur would still want someone to be held accountable. Unfortunately, you would have been in the firing line due to the incident earlier that day." He pauses, frowning. "I just never anticipated that Alexander would intervene. He normally doesn't."

"I'm just that special," I grumble. "But if they had their sights set on me, it would make sense that he would want to bring me back."

He falls silent and it takes me a moment to realize that it's because of what I've just said.

"What?" I ask. "What now?"

"Alexander didn't bring you back for that reason," he replies slowly. "You *are* special, Avery. But he has nearly a hundred other patients to target."

My face twists in confusion. "I'm not very good at riddles. Get to the point."

Dr. Smith leans forward, resting his forearms on the desk. "Damon cut a deal with him."

"What?" I question, my voice an octave higher.

"I don't know the particulars," he responds quickly. "I'm not privy to that information. But I do know that Damon was the instigator of your return."

I fall back into my chair, trying to deal with all the new information. My head feels like it's spinning a million miles an hour, giving me a headache.

"You shouldn't be telling me all of this." It's the only thing I can muster out loud. This whole session has been well outside the box of professionalism, and I'm not sure if I'm relieved by that or frustrated.

He nods, agreeing. "Let's move on from that. How are you doing otherwise?"

"I'm fine."

"Do you want to talk about what happened?"

I snort, raising an eyebrow at him in amusement. "What do you think?"

Dr. Smith offers me a small smile. "Fair enough. How about this? How are you coping? And remember the difference we discussed."

"I'm still fine."

"That's surprisingly a telling answer," he says. "One that I believe."

My eyes focus on the cabinet in the corner of the room, drowning the conversation out. "Good."

"The normal reaction to traumatic events is to *have a reaction*. But you do appear oddly fine. Now, I don't know the particulars of what occurs downstairs, other than its medical research on mental health disorders. My instincts would tell me that they are using specific methods to observe behavioral changes."

Against my better control, my jaw tenses as my cheek twitches. "You'd assume correct," I answer bluntly.

He nods. "I don't practice that kind of psychiatry. For them, they would make a conclusive report that the behavior you are exhibiting now is a direct reaction to their investigations."

"It is," I say, rolling my eyes.

"I'm not done," he cuts me off. "In their eyes, they would seemingly have *fixed* you—for lack of a better word. *Helped cure mental illness.*"

My eyes shift back to him, somewhat curious about where he's going with this. "I'm not cured. Or fucking fixed. It's not that simple."

"It's not," he agrees softly. "And despite only knowing you for a few short months, I also know that your coping methods are a direct reflection of what you already battle with."

"Maybe I'm just getting stronger," I argue. "Or perhaps I'm used to being a punching bag for people that I'm conditioned to it."

His lips purse together. "We both know that while both of those statements may be true, it's not acceptable to be conditioned to poor treatment."

I shrug. "It's the hand I got dealt with, I'm afraid."

Dr. Smith stands from his desk, walking over to a bookshelf along the wall. He scans the spines, sliding a book out. "Do you remember what I explained to you about borderline personality disorder?"

"Yes."

Sitting back down, he opens the book, flicking through the pages. "While extreme mood swings are common, it's also just as likely that an individual might feel *numbness*. They may split from a situation or persons, dissociating to take a step back from reality."

"Split?" I ask, confused.

"It's a defense mechanism to cope with difficult situations. It manifests in different ways, but essentially you view things in black and white, good and bad."

"That's normal," I shoot back. "The world is black and white at times. People *are* often good or bad."

He gives me an empathetic smile. "While that may be somewhat true, it's deeper than that. It takes away the complexity of things. People will often shut down, go through various phases of denial to avoid focusing on any emotions they may have about a situation. Coming back to my point, you say you are fine despite what happened. I believe you are protecting yourself, separating your mind from the Avery here in the present from the Avery that was subjected to cruel means of mistreatment."

"What's wrong with that?" I ask quietly. "I don't want to think about what they did."

"There's no easy way to put this," he replies gently. "But until you face what happened and process it, those feelings are still going to be there. They are locked away, but still present. The longer you ignore them, the more likely you are to experience extreme emotions that you may not be able to control."

I fall quiet, unsure what to say. I want to give some snarky remark or make light of the situation, tell him he's wrong. But nothing comes.

Taking advantage of my silence, he presses on. "Think of it this way—your emotions are water. You've put them into a plastic bucket and sealed it closed but there's a pipe, filling the bucket. It's manageable now while the bucket still has space, but eventually, those emotions will reach the top. And for a while, you'll still manage—but it will become harder. The bucket will be shaking, feeling pressure on the sides. You'll have moments where you start to get overwhelmed by the emotions shaking but you might be able to stop it temporarily by holding down the full bucket with your weight. But then, the water pressure will be too strong for the plastic.

It will break and flood out. By then it will be too late to stop it because the water will gush out with nowhere else to go."

There's a knock on the door before I can answer. It creaks open, a guard appearing.

"Her session time is finished," he says, relieving me from Dr. Smith's mounting information.

I stand quickly, brushing invisible dust off me. "See you next time," I say dismissively, following the guard.

As we walk down the hallway, I spot Damon waiting, his eyes locked on me while silently daring the guard to try to pull any funny business.

"I've got it from here," he says when I'm within reach, grabbing my arm and pulling me to his side. "You're excused."

The guard nods, turning to leave. We wait until he's out of earshot before I plaster on a smile, looking up at Damon. "Hope you weren't waiting long."

"Come on," he says, directing me toward the library. "I've got a present for you."

Chapter 19

Damon

"A cell?" Avery asks in disbelief, staring at the tiny black device in my palm like it has razor-sharp teeth.

"No, it's a vibrator," I scoff sarcastically. "Of course it's a cell. Take it already."

I thrust it toward her, watching as she scrambles to regain cognitive ability to grab it. Once she has it securely in her own grasp, I pull a second one out from my pocket.

"I think it's important that we are all able to communicate when separated," I tell her, flipping it open so that the screen lights up. It's not a fancy cell by any means—just a TCL Flip. But somehow, I was able to convince Christopher to purchase them on my behalf and sneak them in.

The upside of his behavior recently is he seems more inclined to help—but only when it benefits others. Not me.

He was reluctant at first, but once I mentioned that my circle, including Avery, would be issued with a cell, he was suddenly willing.

The smug fucking bastard.

"What do I do with it?" Avery questions hesitantly.

My arm drops to my side, the cell dangling carelessly in my fingertips. "It's a cell, Avery. You call and text on it."

That seems to snap her back to reality, her eyes narrowing as she glares at my offensive remark. "I know how to use a cell," she argues.

"Do you?" I act surprised. "Because you are gawking at the damn thing like it's from the future."

Her face relaxes. "I just mean what would *you* like me to do with it specifically?"

I smile, enjoying the banter that I disgustingly missed. "I've taken the liberty of pre-saving all of our numbers to your speed dial. Should you need to contact us when we are not with you, just call or message."

"So, I won't be with someone at all times."

A rush of icy discomfort goes through me. "Unfortunately, no. As much as we want to make that work long-term, it's not going to always be possible. But this way, you can reach out. We'll always have tabs on your whereabouts, but if you are in session or in your room, we'll know you need us at that moment."

She nods. "I can't pay for this," she murmurs. "Assuming there's going to be a bill at the end of each month."

I raise an eyebrow, perplexed by the thought that she assumes I'm going to make her pay for a present. "It's a *gift*," I reiterate. "For safety measures."

"I'm surprised Dr. Smith didn't mention it in session," she mutters with a scoff, looking down at the carpet.

My eyes scan over her frame, taking in her body language. She's not hostile exactly, but she's also thrown off by something. I decide to pry, because *everything* is a need-to-know basis for me.

"What did Christopher say to you?" I ask, straight to the point.

Avery lifts her head to meet my gaze. "He was very chatty today. Told me all about how he framed me with the damn staff card."

It's not very often that I'm surprised, but I can say with ease that I didn't expect Christopher to admit that to her face.

It was on my to-do list to fill her in once she was settled, but as usual, he'll do anything to beat me to the punch.

"He did," I answer, confirming it. "Fucking idiot has quite the chip on his shoulder—*savior complex*."

Her lips twitch at my response, but her eyes turn cool—her gray irises flashing with knowledge. "He also mentioned that Alexander couldn't have given two shits about my return. But you cut a deal with him."

That statement actually makes me laugh out loud. Classic Christopher.

"I did," I nod. "More so because he doesn't consider that actions have consequences—one of those would have been the facility dealing with an out of control Grey had you not returned."

"But he hated me at the time," she points out.

I shrug. "Hate and love often toe the same line. Either way, it was one less issue for me to deal with."

Avery folds her arms, straightening to full height. I know she's trying to be intimidating but given the fact I still have to glance down at her, I can't say I'm fazed.

"Everything is for your benefit," she points out casually.

"We've been over this several times now."

"Is that why you kissed me?"

I'm caught off guard by her accusation, the statement coming out of left field. Something curls and tightly clenches inside me.

"Yes," I answer matter-of-factly. "You were making too much fucking noise."

"I don't believe you," she answers smoothly. "If we had been caught, they probably would have let you go."

A smirk tugs on the corners of my lips. "Not every guard is an acquaintance, Avery. Plus, even if they did let me go—you would still have been in danger."

"So, you did it to protect me," she shoots back, popping a hand on her hip thinking she's got me in some *gotcha* moment.

"Once again, a raging Grey is not on my agenda," I answer, deflecting her silly thoughts. "I'm responsible for keeping everyone in line, you included."

Her face pulls into a frown, clearly not satisfied with my answer—and dare I say it, a little *disappointed.*

And that simple little observation makes me feel... guilty.

I've replayed the kiss a dozen times in my mind, telling myself that I needed to do what had to be done in the moment. Like I said to Grey, I have no desire to kiss her again—even with his looming threats.

Despite how much I've convinced myself that it was a tactic, there's still a part of me that craves doing it again.

I have no idea why—and that's the part I hate the most.

My whole existence is centered around staying in control—whether that's a group of people, my mind, or my body. So, why am I struggling with something as ridiculous as a temptation to kiss a woman I've barely even begun to like.

You sure you only just like her? The doubt is frustrating, and I quickly shove it aside, taking back control of the situation.

"Now, the cell phones—"

I fill her in with the rest of the information, ensuring she knows who is allocated to what number on speed dial and helping her set a passcode.

When we're done, I check the time, expecting Grey to return any minute now with Ashwood not far behind. For the first time ever, Grey had volunteered to willingly do a psych session, on the condition that it was with Elsher. I'm oddly excited for him to report back—hopefully by the time Grey is finished with him, Elsher will need a strait-jacket. Or a casket.

To my knowledge, Ashwood was off enjoying the quiet. He *should* be in his room but I asked Byrone and Jillian to set him up with in-and-out access like the rest of us. I've accepted him as an ally now, so to ensure everyone is available and freely able to move, I've granted him that luxury.

But not Avery.

I don't like the idea of her potentially walking around on her own free-will when she's still a fresh target. For now, keeping her locked up is better than letting Arthur's goons get their grubby hands on her again. At least with the current plan, she's locked away in the evenings, with us watching nearby. And now she has the cell to communicate with us.

We need to call for another meeting to work out the next steps. We don't have long before things shift again. There's too much silence for my liking.

That also means we need to fill the others in on Ashwood's adventure yesterday. But I plan on disclosing that information to Avery once the other two arrive, rather than springing it on Avery during a meeting. She's likely to lose her shit and it's better if we can control that in a more intimate setting.

"Your boyfriends should be here shortly," I say teasingly, sitting down on my usual chair at the end of the table.

Even in the almost empty room, the air still crackles with electricity. Avery senses it too, lingering next to the table, but she just nods, walking slowly toward me.

She surprises me when she sits on the end of the desk next to my hand, legs dangling off the side.

"So..." she starts, quickly getting stuck on her words.

I roll my eyes, her obvious awkwardness making it clear she has something on her mind. "What? Spit it out."

"If this is your own personal hellhole," she mutters quietly. "Then you knew Lily."

I should have known this question would come up eventually. In fact, I'm surprised it's taken this long for the words to fumble from her pink lips.

"I did," I answer monotonously. "She was a nice woman."

Avery's gaze flickers over to me, frown lines appearing on her forehead. "There's roses everywhere," she points out quietly. "It's almost suffocating. But your room... it's the only one with lilies."

Her eyes stay on me, waiting for some kind of confirmation about the connection she's found. But she doesn't say anything further, waiting for me to make the next move.

"Yes," I finally answer. "It's also why my room is number one. I was the first patient admitted to honor Lily's memory."

I can't help that my tone is now snarky, a darkness clutching at my insides.

"Lily Emerson-Dale," Avery murmurs softly. "She was your mother, wasn't she?"

My hands move so quickly that she lets out a gasp as I grab her knees, stilling her legs from swaying back and forth. I rise to my feet, towering over her seated frame. I scan her face for a reaction, expecting fear. But while her legs have now stilled and her eyes are wide, there's no alarm on her face—just regret and sorrow.

"She was the sole person on this forsaken earth who loved me," I say in a low tone. "And he took her away from me."

"He murdered her," Avery answers, mimicking my thoughts and earlier words.

I nod. "Her so-called mental illness was nothing short of a direct response to his actions. But even in death, she made sure I came out on top over him."

It takes a few seconds for the last dots to align, but when her mouth falls open in a softly spoken *'oh'*, I know she's got it.

"It was her money."

I dip my head, closing the distance between our faces until our noses nearly touch. "And greed knows no limit. He's still trying to get his hands on it. Anything to save his crumbling empire."

It's rare that I tell someone this information. Besides Grey and Byrone, no one else here knows about my mother.

Her breath hitches as she becomes aware of our close proximity, but I don't move away. I hold her gaze, watching the emotions dart across her face.

"Dead," she mutters. "Or at least... D-E-D. That's why Grey calls you *Deadman*."

My eyebrow shoots up at her revelation, perplexed that we've made the jump from that information to my adored nickname so suddenly.

"Damon Emerson Alexander Dale," I tell her with a smirk, the memory bringing some joy to the situation. "Despite my father's protests, my mother made sure that I carried her family name too."

Avery's gaze dives down, eyes focusing on my lips. I don't think she realizes she's doing it and I inch forward slightly, so close that I can feel her breath on my own lips. She sucks in sharply, eyes quickly moving back up to mine, and I hold it for a few seconds longer, before slowly stepping back.

"Don't lose the cell," I tease, sitting back down in my chair. "I doubt Christopher will be as assisting a second time."

Almost on instinct, her legs start swaying again. "How about a truth for a truth?"

"I don't play those types of games, but alright—I'll bite."

Avery grins, chewing her lip thoughtfully. "What was the deal you cut? For my return?"

I laugh, once again floored by the newly ascertained fact that perhaps I don't have as good a read on her as I thought.

"What do you think it was?" I ask, leaning forward and cupping my hands together on the desk.

She thinks for a moment before confidently answering. "Money."

I nod. "Something along those lines."

It's close enough to the truth that she has no reason to pry for further information. *Of course* it involves money—but my father is too smart for that. Greedy or not, he still obsesses over something else more... something I gave away that I swore I never would. I still haven't even disclosed the full story to Grey yet. Even though it doesn't concern him, it puts things in jeopardy.

"My turn," she murmurs softly.

"Go on then," I say, entertaining her little game with a wave of my hand.

"What I asked you before..." she pauses. "I liked—"

The rest of her sentence is caught in my throat. Her unspoken words linger in the air between us.

I become painfully aware of my beating heart, eyes narrowing suspiciously as she flushes with embarrassment, looking over at the bookshelves.

Before I can inquire further into her incomplete admission, the library door swings open. Grey struts in, a grin wide on his face and arms outstretched.

"I love a good game," he remarks happily to us both, heading straight to Avery. He grabs the sides of her face in his palms, leaning down to kiss her with an overexaggerated *mwah* as their mouths separate.

It appears we're all playing dangerous games.

But that's the thing about games—for every winner, there has to be a loser.

Chapter 20

Grey

"Elsher is going to be no match for me," I insist proudly. "I think he was close to throwing his coffee mug at my head."

Avery shakes her head in disbelief. "You willingly went to a session with him? You must love torture."

"Only the best kind of torture," I say with a wink.

My eyes glance over to Deadman, his bored expression masking whatever is running through his head. There's a sharp flash in his eyes before he gives a quick nod, confirming that he's provided Avery with the cell.

To be fair, I thought I was going to have to *persuade* Christopher to help. It's disappointing that he was a willing volunteer—I would love to grace my knuckles with his face again.

"Ashwood better get his ass into gear," Damon grumbles. "It will be lunch time soon and we need to get things under-way."

"I'm sure he's not far off," I humor him, jumping up to sit on the table next to Avery. She immediately wiggles closer to me when my arm snakes around her waist, dropping her head to rest it against my shoulder. "What did you think of your present?"

She tilts her head up to look at me. "It's great," she answers. "I feel better knowing I'll have a way to contact you all."

"Make sure you send me plenty of selfies when you're in your room—preferably undressed."

I laugh when she straightens up to smack my arm, cheeks tinging pink. "It's a *work* cell," she argues playfully. "The last thing we need is you draining the battery by sending pictures all night long."

"You know what else is long?" I tease. "It also gets longer if you send some pictures."

"You disgust me," Damon interjects, groaning. "Knowing my luck you'll accidentally send it to me."

Avery snorts with amusement. "Then you'll really be traumatized."

"Hey!" I gape at her, feigning offense. "I didn't hear you complaining yesterday."

The amusement drops from her face as her eyes flash in alarm. "Grey..." she warns.

I swish my hand around coolly. "Deadman doesn't care. I think we're past that."

If anything, his jawline twitched a little when I suggested Avery sending nude photos. Not in a negative way—almost like he's intrigued.

Seeing them together, relaxed for once, eases the built-in baggage I carry around. Maybe I've been looking at this the wrong way. They have both come far, and if I can trust Theo to look after her, then I should, logically, be able to trust my best friend. But we've reached that critical point where I realize how much of a cockblock I have been.

If there is something there between them, neither of them will act upon it now—or ever. Damon will shut down any emotion that he perceives as weakness, entering a state of tunnel vision to focus on the task at hand. While he's not one to listen to threats, I know he respects me enough that he won't touch Avery again because I told him not to. And Avery... she'll be stuck in a carousel of people pleasing tendencies, afraid to lose me.

And that's not a good enough reason anymore.

She's not going to lose me.

But it will always be in the back of her mind that I could abandon her—like I did before.

Regardless of her feelings toward Damon, she won't accept them fully until I do. She needs a push... well, a fucking shove, to take the step. It can't come from Theo—he's already open about our dynamic that it doesn't hold as much personal weight as my opinion.

She'd listen to him, agreeing and feeling relief that her emotions are validated. Knowing she's not a bad person will always comfort that mentality she has for herself. But it still won't be enough.

I'm holding her back.

And for what? So I can prove that I'm not like my fucking father. To inflict my trauma onto the person I love? That's no way to live, and Avery doesn't deserve that burden. She's always so focused on wanting to fix people, as if she's trying to prove that if she can do it, then she's fixable too.

She's not fucking broken.

Avery is perfect the way she is.

Then there's Damon. My unhinged best friend who has the most to lose. Yet, he doesn't focus on that—he puts everyone else first. People may not believe it, but he's a protector in his own ways.

At the end of the day, he deserves better too.

My life improved tenfold when Avery came into it. She's the light in my darkness, healing the ugly parts of me that I learned to accept. The only other person who ever accepted me just the way I am... is Damon.

I'm doing both of them a disservice by standing in the way. I think it was just a shock. No one could have predicted that they would get under each other's skin in this way. It was just assumed that they might kill each other.

The library door swings open and the three of us snap our attention to Theo as he stalks in casually. Hands wedged in his pockets, he looks completely at ease as he approaches.

As if on instinct, I find myself turning my attention to Avery. You know when you go to a wedding and the music starts, and all the guests turn to look at the bride? I was the weird teenager who used to watch the groom. That was one of the truest and most underrated displays of emotion. To be fair, it was only two weddings—both distant cousins on my mother's side who got married seven months apart. But I loved the idea of studying that level of body language—the pure, untainted raw emotion.

On cue, Avery's face lights up—not just her sweet lips, tilting up into a huge smile, but her eyes too. The gray sparkles as she soaks in Theo's presence, body relaxing as that sense of safety wraps around her.

"You're late," Damon growls.

Theo shrugs. "You'll survive. I doubt I missed much."

I cover a laugh with my hand as Damon reaches into his pocket, flinging a cell at him. Theo catches it easily, turning it over in between his fingers.

"A cell?"

"Obviously," Damon scoffs. "We need to be able to communicate at all times. The other numbers are pre-saved into the contact list. I've also saved our three numbers to speed dial. Avery is on one, me on two, and Grey on three."

Theo nods, shoving the cell into his pocket. "Have you told her yet?" he asks, giving Avery a smile.

A wave of confusion crosses her face. "Told me what?"

"No, I haven't," Damon answers. "You can do the honors."

Avery stiffens beside me, attention on Theo. "What is it?"

Without breaking eye contact with her, he smiles, trying to put her at ease before he drops the bombshell. "I went for a walk downstairs—to the lab."

"You what?" Avery yelps. "When?"

"Yesterday," Theo replies casually. "We needed to see if there was any evidence left behind. It looks like they have taken it all."

Avery narrows her eyes at him. "That was a really stupid thing to do. What if anyone had seen you?"

It's hard to miss the smirk that threatens to form on his face. "They did. But I took care of them."

"Of course you did," she grumbles.

"Does the name Dr. West mean anything to you?" Theo asks.

The change in atmosphere is immediate. Avery pauses, her nails digging into the table. The air feels thinner and charged with electricity as she slowly slides off the table toward him.

"Dr. West?" she repeats. "What do you know about him?"

My eyes shift to Damon, a frown appearing on his face as he looks back at me. She hasn't mentioned names to us, but it's obvious by her body language that he was involved in what happened to her.

"He was downstairs, trying to save equipment," Theo answers easily. I resist the urge to snort in amusement because he makes it sound so casual. But I'm willing to bet it's anything more than a fleeting encounter.

"What did you do?" Avery asks confidently. It's not an accusation nor does she seem angry—but it's something else.

"I merely showed him what it feels like to be a patient," he responds. "My finger may have *slipped* on the machine."

Avery frowns, nodding slightly as she takes in this information. "He's dead, isn't he?"

Theo's gaze snaps over to Damon, then me, before resting back on her.

"Yes."

There's no elaboration, just silence as we all watch Avery carefully. When she realizes, she looks around at all of us, shrugging.

"I don't feel anything. He deserved it."

"Was he the one who tortured you?" I ask gently.

Avery nods once. "There was another doctor too—a female. But she wasn't as cruel and heartless as him."

My hands curl into fists. Theo did the right thing—he did exactly what I would have done.

"I saw the machines," Theo says, filling the silence. "And he mentioned some of the experiments."

She peers up at him, face blank. "Thank you," she mutters. "It's nice knowing he won't come after me again..." She trails off, but some of the tension disappears from her body.

"We should anticipate some backlash," Damon informs us. "I suspect they would have found him by now."

"That's why it's a good idea to keep the cells on us," I finish. "Just make sure the guards don't see."

Everyone mutters in agreement as the bell signalling the beginning of lunch echoes outside the library door. The four of us wait a few minutes until we hear the sounds of footsteps from incoming groups of people.

"Call a meeting tonight," Damon mutters to me as we walk into the hall behind a small group. "We need to set things into motion while we have the chance."

I nod. "On it. What are we going to do about Arthur?"

Damon's eyes hover on Avery's back as her and Theo venture ahead, sitting down at our usual table. "I'll pay him a visit. It will help us get an idea on what could be coming next."

Following his line of vision, I reach for his shoulder, halting him in his tracks. He looks at me with curiosity as I pull my attention away from Avery.

"Don't hurt her," I mutter quietly so only he can hear.

"What are you talking about now?" he replies, annoyed.

"I mean it," I grumble. "I'm not going to stop you from going after her if that's what you both want. But if you hurt her, you and I will not only be done, but I'll end you too."

Damon's eyebrows shoot up at my words. I wait for some snarky response about how he doesn't care for her, that there's nothing between them—but he just looks at me for a few seconds longer before turning away and walking over to the table.

I don't make an effort to follow him, instead sneaking back out of the hall to loiter outside the door. When the coast is clear, I whip my cell out of my pocket, writing a quick text.

As soon as I hit send, I shove it back into my pocket, heading back inside the hall. Up ahead, I watch as Avery stiffens with confusion, before she recognizes where the vibration came from. Her chin dips toward her chest, and I know she's glancing under the table at my message.

Suddenly she looks back up, eyes scanning the hall to find me. When our eyes meet, I give her a quick nod, heading to join the queue of people for food.

I replay my own words over and over, tossing up between feeling uncomfortable and feeling accomplished. But this is the right thing to do, I know it.

Little Killer – You are my absolute everything. Everyone deserves the chance to love you too. So, if your heart belongs to three people, then that's okay. I'm not going anywhere, no matter what happens.

Chapter 21

Avery

It's a whole different feeling being able to walk freely through Lilydale, doing things that other patients can't.

Even more overwhelming is the power to tell the staff you need something and them just say okay.

I mean, Damon is beside me, lingering close by, but he instructed me to handle it. They might have been reluctant to do so if I was alone, but I can't help but feel a little giddy at having a drop of authority.

Tony comes stalking back over, his stained chef apron hanging around his waist. He taps a notepad with his pen, glancing at us with mild-irritation.

"What do you want?" he asks, ready to write.

I turn my head to look at Damon. He gives a small nod, gesturing for me to speak up.

A meeting has been called for tonight and while Grey is off informing everyone, he had proudly volunteered for me to handle the food and beverages. It was a little exciting at first, but now that I need to make executive decisions, I'm tongue-tied.

All the past *Cirque des Morts* meetings have been filled with delicious meats, grazing foods, and desserts. I have no idea if

Grey specifically requested them or just suggested a type of dish to be inspired by. As the seconds tick by, I can tell Tony is getting annoyed with my silence.

"Pizza," I finally say, blurting out the first food that springs to mind. "A few actually. Pineapple on one."

Tony starts making notes, giving me more confidence.

"And some type of antipasto platter. In fact, if we could get a variety of cheeses, that would be nice."

He looks up from his notepad, clearly thrown off by the change in menu. "Cured meats, cheeses, olives. Things like that?"

I nod, starting to lose my nerve a little. "And for dessert, peach cobbler. Do we need alcohol?" I ask Damon, hesitantly.

"Grey Goose, whatever IPAs you have left, and my usual whiskey," he answers.

Tony nods, stabbing the notepad with emphasis on his full stop. "Got it. I'll have it ready at the usual time. We'll leave it on the bench for you."

"Actually," I interject before I realize what I'm doing. "I think it would be better if you brought it straight over to the library this time."

It's clear this isn't a method of delivery that has been used before. Tony looks at me in disbelief, at my audacity to give him extra work off the clock. I expect Damon to say something to me, to tell me that's not how this works, but instead he answers calmly. "That's a good idea. We'll say eight sharp—it's earlier than usual but you'll only need to stay back an hour longer."

My head turns to follow his voice, smiling. Having him back me up means everything. I'm not trying to be difficult to the staff or make them feel inferior but ever since I was drugged, I'm terrified of people slipping things into my food or drink.

I wouldn't put it past Whittingham to sneak into the kitchen and drug our food if he got wind of the meeting. It would be the perfect opportunity—taking down the entire society in one go.

Tony sighs, partly rolling his eyes. "Fine. See you then."

He stalks off without another word, clearly pissed at us. I know that's our cue to leave so I turn, walking through the doors to the hall. Damon is quick to follow and I pause to let him catch up.

"Was that okay?" I ask nervously. "I don't know what I'm doing."

"It was good," he says. "Don't worry about him. He despises Arthur as much as we do."

"Not hard to do," I mutter. "Did you know him on the outside?"

Damon smiles. "No. But Arthur doesn't treat the hospitality staff well—or any staff to be honest. There's a few that worship him, but the rest just deal with it for the money. By comparison, we're the better enemies to have in your corner."

"Do the staff know about your connection to the place?" I ask hesitantly.

He shrugs. "Probably. I know Arthur likes to gloat from time to time. Otherwise, the staff just recognize the hold I have and fall into line. When you earn the respect, natural born followers will just obey."

I nod, glancing around at the empty hall. My eyes stop on the tables, a question popping to mind.

"I once asked Grey about the number system," I start. "He said I'd find out if I needed to know."

Damon crosses his arms coolly. "And this is your way of asking if it's time?"

"It can't be as big of a secret as the other things you've told me," I muse. "I'm just curious. It's been bugging me since day one."

He laughs, running a hand through his hair. I don't know why but I like seeing this side of him—it's carefree, almost *normal*. When he's in these moods, he's a whole different person—like he can be himself, not the leader and protector of this hellhole. I've come to realize that much of what you see with him is a shield.

"The number system is our own personal tally. We group people by the risk we think they are to Lilydale. Group one is the most critical—likely on Arthur's hit list. Group five is the people we are least concerned about—patients like Ashwood. We know they won't be targeted."

"Oh," I mutter, lost for words. "That's why I moved up to group one."

Damon nods. "We have people stationed around the exits. Groups leave based on the system and time of day so we can monitor them—make sure they reach their next destination safely."

"I was group three when I arrived," I point out. "The middle."

"We needed time to collect more information. The board picks patients from the court system on who they think would fit in here for their benefit. But that's all on paper. Once a patient is inside, seeing the professionals, and having their behavior monitored, we then get a sense of whether they become of interest for the experiments."

Frowning, I wrap my arms around my frame protectively. "What made me stand out?"

He looks down at me, stepping closer. "It could be that you were just a really interesting individual. When you arrived, you were naturally submissive, almost willing to do what they asked—except you put up a fight too."

"Or?"

"Or maybe you were just collateral damage," he murmurs softly. "Their way of trying to get back at us. Arthur knew how important you were to us, so he turned his attention to you."

I think back to all the punishments. The times I was made to spend in his office sorting out paperwork that never needed to be sorted, or cleaning bathrooms with dangerous chemicals. "He wanted to distract you, make you angry," I point out. "But he was wrong—I wasn't important to you then."

"You were, Avery. It's just unfortunate that they recognized it before I did."

My heart pounds in my chest. Grey's text message has been playing on my mind since yesterday. It caught me off guard at first. I re-read it at least a dozen times to make sure I was understanding it correctly. It felt like he was giving me his blessing, but that couldn't be the case. I overanalyzed the message to search for hidden meanings and alternate interpretations, but I just ended up at the same conclusion.

You can do whatever you like with Damon.

The man himself seems to be acting strange—more approachable, patient... softer. The whole situation is confusing, and now his words are intensifying that skepticism.

"I'm important to you?" I ask quietly.

"Of course you are," he answers, grabbing a strand of my black hair and playing with it between his fingers. "You're also an important member of the society."

I nod, unsure of what else to say. Never in a million years did I expect to end up here.

Shifting on my feet, my head drops as I finally lose my cool. I'm scared to look him in the eye in case he sees everything that I want to hide.

I don't know how I feel about him—about us. We've been through so much, and the only thing I am sure of is that I *don't* hate him like I tried to convince myself. But I don't know where to go from here.

"Come on," Damon says when I don't reply out loud, placing the strand carefully over my collarbone. "Let's go find the others."

"You did good, little killer," Grey murmurs, leaning down to my ear.

"Except there's fucking pineapple on that pizza," Theo grumbles, raising an eyebrow at me.

I laugh at him, shrugging. The three of us are standing in front of the food, waiting for the last stragglers to arrive. "Pineapple belongs on pizza, Theo. Deal with it."

He scrunches up his nose in disgust. "You're lucky I adore you."

"Aw, thanks," I taunt. "It's my trauma that makes me cute."

I nearly burst out laughing as his face falls, his eyes narrowing incredulously at me. Grey reaches across me to grab a cube of cheese, popping it into his mouth.

"Food is food," he says happily. "I'd prefer *you* sprawled out on the buffet, but this is good too."

Shaking my head, I look over my shoulder as I hear the library door. A few people are already sitting at the table, waiting patiently, while others are standing, talking among themselves.

Damon is leaning against the far wall, chatting with Byrone and Jillian, and when he senses me watching, his eyes snap over to me without pausing conversation. I offer a smile before checking to see if the remaining members have arrived.

"I think that's everyone," I say to Grey, nodding my head toward Leighton as he approaches the group. "Leave the cheese alone."

When he thinks I'm not looking, he grabs a few more pieces in the palm of his hand before leading us over to the table. The two men sit on either side of me as others begin to take their seats as well.

Jillian gives me a warm nod as she passes by which I return before the room falls silent. I've been told she was an important part of my rescue and I'm so thankful for her skills—it's obvious why Damon respects her and Byrone so much.

With everyone seated, Damon stands at attention at the end of the table.

"Thank you for attending on short notice," he begins. "As you are aware, things have escalated quickly."

A few people look in my direction, but I'm not bothered by it this time.

"Despite our efforts, it appears the facility was determined to recommence experimentation. I expect some form of retaliation from Arthur, but at present, he's been rather quiet."

Grey nods on Damon's right, throwing a cube of cheese into his mouth. "We're going to continue on with the usual operations, but everyone needs to be on guard."

"Where does that leave Operation Clown?" Byrone asks, his voice loud and clear.

The weird names for their missions trigger flashbacks for me, remembering the earlier days when I was in the dark about all this. Did the whole society know about the secrets below? Or were they just acting on instructions back then?

"Keep trying to decrypt the firewall," Damon directs him. "I suspect their IT people would be on high alert now. Maybe we can use their panic as leverage."

"Possibly," Byrone replies, but doesn't sound confident. "At present we're still only able to see what they are feeding us, along with the minimal control we have at turning the cameras on and off."

"Why don't we just fuck with them?" Grey offers. "Start turning them off at random times—make them think we are on the move."

Damon nods slowly. "That's not a bad idea. If we make it known that we are trying to get in, they will scramble to stop us. Eventually, they might let their guard down enough when they realize nothing is happening and we can use that opportunity to sneak in. In the meantime, work behind the scenes to ascertain what we are dealing with."

"What should we be looking out for?" Jillian asks.

"We need a camera in Arthur's office," he shoots back. "It's our blind spot."

"Can't we sneak one in?" I question.

Heads turn to look at me, but I'm focused on Damon. "Can we get more equipment and plant it?"

I suspect Damon knows what I'm hinting at. If Dr. Smith was willing to bring in cells for us, maybe we can ask him for help again.

"That's not a bad idea," Byrone agrees. "We would be able to set the system up separately from the Lilydale feed. We wouldn't have to worry about them cutting off access, and we would have flexibility to place them where we like."

Grey beams at me—like I've just solved the problem of world peace. "I think we should do it. Especially since we've destroyed their equipment downstairs, we can only assume that they are planning something. It would put us two steps ahead."

"I'll look into it," Damon answers. "The tricky part will be getting them placed without being seen. But perhaps we can turn off their access to the feeds temporarily to give us time. How long does it normally take them to get control back?"

"Four to five minutes if we make them work for it," Jillian replies. "But if we have it planned out and people are stationed nearby, we should have enough time."

"Okay. Let's put that under a new operation. Any name suggestions?" Damon asks, looking around the table.

I run through a list of words in my head, snorting. "How about Operation Magic Trick?" I offer, amused.

A few people laugh around the table, some nodding. Damon's lips twitch as he resists the urge to show *emotion*. "Alright, Magic Trick it is."

"Now they see us... now they don't," Grey laughs. "Hopefully Arthur doesn't bang his assistant in his office. That's one image I don't want to see."

I shrug. "They have sex tapes of other people. Maybe it's time they got a dose of their own medicine."

Chapter 22

Avery

The meeting wraps up and despite the dark storm cloud that looms over our heads, Damon still directs his team to hang around and enjoy the food and party aisles.

I stay back at the table with Damon, Grey, Theo, and Leighton while the others explore the library. Theo continues to give me shit about the pineapple, while Grey chimes in and provides scientific evidence of why pineapple is good for their *bodies*.

I'm not sure I buy into the whole *changing taste* thing, but I have to laugh as they start arguing about it.

My eyes move over to find Damon, his chair tilted back slightly as he half-listens. Leighton is scribbling on a piece of paper, making notes about something and pretending he's not being subjected to the weirdest sperm argument in history.

"If you're so confident, then *you* eat it," Theo snaps.

"I'll happily eat the pineapple, but Avery should be the judge," Grey replies, giving me a wink.

I shake my head, pushing my chair back. "I need alcohol."

They continue to fire shots at each other while I stand at the food and beverage table, reaching to grab a beer. I sense him behind me, well before he appears in my peripheral vision.

"That's not strong enough," Damon mutters, pouring a glass of straight whiskey. "Not by a long shot."

"Yeah, well I'm not the best at holding my alcohol so probably best I know my limits," I laugh. "Knowing my luck, I'd drink too much, and they would try to make a move tonight."

Damon doesn't seem amused by my comment, his jaw tensing. "I'm on guard tonight. No one is going to bother you."

I turn to face him, eyes scanning for his reaction. "Doesn't it bother you having to stay up all night?"

"Not really. I'd rather know that you're safe than have something happen while I'm sleeping."

"It makes me feel bad," I admit quietly, bringing the bottle to my lips. "It can't be healthy being on alert all the time, especially if you are missing out on sleep."

Damon shrugs, unfazed. "I'll catch up on sleep tomorrow night when Theo is on duty."

The word is foreign coming off his tongue, my face freezing as I glance him over.

"What now?" he groans.

"You called him Theo," I point out with surprise. "Not Ashwood."

It's as if he's just registering that fact now too, eyes narrowing slightly as he thinks back. "Well, that's his name, is it not?" he quickly answers. "Besides, he's one of us now."

"I'm still going to call you Demon Boy every now and again," I say playfully. "Besides, those masks you wear seem to fit."

"They do, don't they?" he smiles. "I was pretty happy when I found them. It's a nice reminder to Lilydale that we can unleash hell."

I lean against the table, my hip pressing into it as I nibble on some cured meat. "Maybe so, but this," I pause, nodding to the aisles. "Is a nice present for us. Makes hell feel a little less lonely."

"Just because we're in hell, Avery, doesn't mean we aren't in charge. It's all an illusion. But illusions shatter. Besides, this is my own hell—you shouldn't have to suffer in here."

"I deserve it though," I murmur, meaning every single word. "But to be honest, being in here is the most freedom I have ever felt. It's fucked up, isn't it? I earned my place here but it also saved me."

Damon frowns. "No one deserves to be here. We're the products of a broken system that's controlled by wealth."

"That's what I mean though. Maybe I was always meant to end up here—not as a punishment, but as a way to find my place."

"I disagree."

Reaching over, I grab the glass of whiskey from his hand, taking a sip. "That's foul," I cough, passing it back. "But look how far we've all come. The whole reason we ended up in here is because of shit things that happened to us. In the outside world, that broke us. But in here, we've overcome it. There's no judgment, no need to pretend."

It's clear by the look on his face that he still doesn't agree with me, but he just nods once, staying quiet.

Humming to myself, I turn my attention back to Theo and Grey, noting that their discussions have finally stopped. Both of them are looking over at us, and realizing it's safe to go back to the table since the pineapple discussion has stopped, I grab a piece of pizza and sit back down between them.

"Pineapple?" I offer sweetly to Theo.

He looks at it in disgust. "Don't you start."

"Or what?" I ask with a smile.

The look of resentment for the pizza vanishes, replaced by a challenging stare. "Do you really want to find out?"

I shrug, acting unfazed, even though my heart is starting to pick up pace. "I've eaten a fair bit of pineapple."

Grey cackles loudly, putting his hand on my thigh. "Okay, better alternative. We see if Avery tastes better with pineapple."

"I doubt she can get any sweeter," Theo replies. "But I'm willing to give it a go. How about free time tomorrow?"

My thighs snap together, Grey's fingers getting caught in between them. He squeezes my leg tightly, leaning down to my ear.

"I hope that's all you can think about between now and then."

Raising an eyebrow, I smile at him. "I hope you do as well."

I'm too wired after the meeting to sleep. Even though it's nearly midnight, I'm unable to get my mind to stop spinning.

It's a spider web of thoughts, all coming back to a central point. I don't know how to make it stop.

On one side of the web, my body is spiraling, thinking about Theo and Grey tomorrow. On the other, I get lost in the fear that Whittingham is going to make a move at any second.

My mind flashes with images of Dr. West, still in disbelief that he's dead. It makes me wonder if his sidekick, Dr. Cromwell, is still around. Will they replace him?

And then there's Damon. His whole life is tangled around Lilydale, a constant reminder of his mother. It's a sick and twisted level of torture that far outperforms anything I've been subjected to.

Of course, the moment I let myself fall down that rabbit hole of thoughts, another question arises—what is happening between us?

He's outside at the moment, standing guard. I have no idea where they watch from or whether the guards know. It's dark and cold, and the idea of standing in a deserted corridor for seven hours sounds like torture.

I wonder if he's lonely...

Pulling out my new cell from under my thin pillow, I flick open the message screen. It's been a while since I sent a text, but it's nice knowing I can again. It brings me a sense of security, a connection to life outside of this shoebox.

Avery: Are you still out there?

Damon: Yes. Why?

Sitting up, I swing my legs over the side of the bed, foot tapping on the floor.

Avery: Are you okay?

Damon: You should be asleep.

I scoff quietly at the redirection, fingers quickly punching out a reply.

Avery: I'm not tired. And I asked you a question.

Damon: I'm fine. Go to sleep.

Avery: You go to sleep.

Laughing to myself, I can just imagine the look on his face. It's easier to be stubborn toward him in messages. But as the seconds tick by, no reply comes.

Shit—maybe I pushed it too far.

Just when I consider sending another message, it vibrates with a response.

Damon: Be careful, Avery. You're not as protected as you think.

I frown. What the hell does that mean?

Avery: It's a joke, Damon. Not a dick. Don't take it so hard.

After I hit send, panic surges through me. I've definitely overstepped the delicate line that the two of us hover constantly.

Before I can backtrack or pretend to fall asleep, there's a click, followed by the sound of beeping.

I gasp quietly as the door opens to my room, a tall shadowy figure appearing in the doorway.

"A dick? Really?" Damon asks, annoyed.

"Just let yourself in," I mumble sarcastically.

Damon steps forward, pushing the door closed behind him—not enough to make it latch, but closed enough that no one would be able to see in through the gap if they walked past.

"You're meant to be sleeping," he points out again.

"I know," I groan. "I can't sleep. And I'm paranoid about you standing out there alone."

He laughs, stepping closer. A patch of light from the barred window shines on his face and even though I'm in the dark against the wall, I have no doubt he can see me too.

"I think they are more frightened of me. The guards know to keep away."

"But not all the guards are on our side," I argue. "What if someone tries to take you out?"

"I hope they do," he says happily. "It would make for great entertainment."

Shaking my head, I lift my legs and cross them on the bed. "Do you at least have backup?"

Damon holds up the cell. "Another reason we have these. Grey is on my speed dial too. Stop stressing about shit and go to sleep."

"Can we just sit and talk for a little bit?" I ask quietly. It then hits me. It's not Damon that's lonely...

It's me.

For the past few months, I've grown accustomed to having these guys around. Even though nights were still spent alone, I realize now that after what happened downstairs, the silence is deafening. When I'm alone with my thoughts, monsters creep in, bringing images of electricity and ice water.

I'm afraid to be alone.

Footsteps come closer until the bed dips with Damon's weight. He pushes himself back against the wall, stretching his legs out next to me.

I'm thankful for him—for not laughing at me or telling me that I'm ridiculous.

Why is it that the night makes it harder to hide our vulnerability? During the day, it's easy to pretend we are okay. There's something about shadows and exhaustion that make it that much harder to fight away the demons.

"What's wrong?" Damon asks. It's softly spoken, a genuine question.

"I don't know how to deal with myself," I admit. "I feel fine, but every now and again, I'm... not. I hate being alone."

"It's easier to distract yourself when surrounded by others," he says, summing it up perfectly.

I nod, my head brushing against the wall. "Exactly. It was so quiet down there. It felt like time didn't exist—it was just separated into being a test subject or being alone. But even though being alone was better, I was in constant fear that they would return at any moment. And now that's all I can think about."

"You're not alone. We're always nearby," he answers. "We won't let them near you again."

"I know. I just keep waiting, expecting them to come back. It feels like I'm standing on the edge of a cliff, waiting for the drop."

Something brushes against my hand, and it takes me a few seconds to realize it's his. He doesn't grab it, but our hands rest against each other, touching slightly.

"That's survival mode," Damon points out. "You're running on adrenaline."

"I know he's dead," I whisper. "But the rest aren't. I just can't afford to crack right now."

"Avery," he says firmly. "I promise they won't put their hands on you again."

Taking a deep breath, I lift my hand, placing it on top of his. I half-expect him to move or recoil, but he doesn't, his knuckles warm under my palm. "I know," I reply. "It's just going to take time."

Dr. Smith's words come back to me. I can't help but wonder if the bucket is nearly full. But for whatever reason, the shaking stops for the rest of the night.

I must fall asleep at some stage because when I wake up, the sun is shining through the window, and the only sign of Damon is the faint lingering scent of him on my bed.

Chapter 23

Theo

"Keep still," I growl at Avery. She tilts her head back, peering at me through her lashes.

"It's not that easy," she shoots back, ignoring my scowl.

When we came into the library at the start of free time, her eyes lit up at the sight of the tattoo kit. But even though she begged me to do a new tattoo on her, apparently it's *my* fault for not warning her that it was going to hurt like a bitch.

That's generally the case with rib cages. I don't make the rules.

Grey is perched by her knees, munching on a chocolate bar that he whipped out of nowhere. He gives her knees a playful slap. "It's going to be all wonky if you don't control yourself."

"It fucking hurts," she hisses, covering her eyes with her forearm.

"I know," Grey says. "I have the same placement. Suck it up."

Avery grumbles something to herself and I resist the urge to laugh. That was the exact reason she opted to have a tattoo on the side of her torso—because Grey and I both have one there too.

"Love is pain," I tell her, pressing my hand against her waist to steady her. "The sooner you keep still, the sooner it will be over."

Her body stills and I quickly resume before she starts moving like a drunk octopus again. Grey pats her knee in a soothing gesture, watching the needle closely.

"You're doing well. Hang in there," he says encouragingly.

She mumbles something against her arm that sounds oddly like *fuck my life* but I keep going. As I start to move over a bonier part of her torso, she tenses up. I have to hand it to her—she's fighting the urge to move.

Grey frowns, looking at me for support. I shrug, nodding my head toward her skirt. Maybe if she's distracted from the pain she'll focus on something else.

His eyes light up, a sly grin crossing his face as he pushes off from his chair, moving to the end of the table where her feet are positioned flat against the wood. We had her lay on the table so I could access her side more easily, and in hindsight, it also gives Grey the perfect height to distract her.

As he changes chairs, sitting in Damon's usual spot for meetings, I lift the needle away from her skin, already anticipating what's about to happen. Grey's hands grab her knees and widen them, giving him a literal front-row view of her pussy. Avery shoots up onto her elbows, glancing at him.

"What are you doing?" she squeaks.

Grey blinks at her innocently, a small smile on his lips. "Distracting you. I recommend staying still though."

"Are you insane?" she hammers out. "I'll move even more."

"You followed instructions well the other day when reading the book. I'm sure you're more than capable of controlling yourself now," he teases.

Her cheeks flush as she clenches her jaw. Slowly, she turns her head to me.

"Please don't let me fuck it up."

I laugh at her. She's downright adorable and every day I fall even harder. "It will be fine," I promise her, giving Grey a nod.

Avery lets out a little sound of surprise as Grey grabs her underwear, pulling them down her legs. He bunches them up in his hand, tossing them to me across the table. I catch them easily, wrapping them around my left wrist like a bracelet.

I wait for his head to disappear under her skirt, and as soon as her head falls back and a moan spills from her lips, I carefully put the needle tip back to her skin. She barely acknowledges the pain, but her breathing gets heavier, rib cage expanding and contracting against my hand.

"How does she taste?" I ask Grey with a smirk, eyes laser locked on the half-completed tattoo.

"Fucking incredible," he murmurs from under her skirt. "You can really taste the pineapple."

Avery breaks out of her trance, snorting as she laughs.

My nose wrinkles in disgust at the mention of the fruity abomination. "Funny."

Her laughter quickly turns to breathy moans again and for a split second, she jerks an inch up the table. Looking at me with big eyes, she smiles sheepishly. "Sorry."

"Get back on my tongue," Grey growls, wrapping his arms around the back of her knees and yanking her forward again.

Shaking my head, I move my hand to the top of her body, applying pressure to keep her still. I do my best to finish the tattoo, noticing her legs shaking. Her torso pushes against my hand, and I carefully put the needle down, inspecting my work. Satisfied, I run my hand down her body, cupping her breast through her shirt.

Gray stormy eyes find mine as she looks at me with a silent plea. My thumb strokes her nipple, noticing that it hardens instantly under my touch. I give it a small tug, making her back arch to chase my hand.

"You're all finished," I tell her, standing up to get a better view of her face. "That wasn't so bad."

She nods, cheeks flushed as she wets her lips. I lean down, kissing her and she moans into my mouth, arm shooting up to blindly grab my bicep.

My tongue pushes through her lips, slowly sliding against hers as if I was flicking her clit. I continue to tease her while my hand fondles her breast, giving it a light squeeze before tugging her nipple sharply.

I can tell she's getting close, her body stilling as she chases the high. Pulling back slightly, I flick my tongue over her cupid's bow. "Come on his face, Aves. Let him taste that sweet fucking pussy."

Avery lets out a cry, pushing her mouth into mine as her back arches off the table. Her orgasm hits her hard, body shaking as Grey relentlessly keeps going until she's flat on the table again.

Pulling back, I smile at her, taking in her post-climatic, glowing face. Grey stands up at the end of the table, grinning at her.

"Definitely sweeter," he muses, walking around the side of the table. "I think Theo should see for himself."

There's a strange glint in his eye and when he stops in front of me, I shake my head, amused.

"Taste our girl," he says, throat bobbing as he grabs my jaw.

Resisting the urge to laugh out loud, I open my mouth just as Grey spits into it. Avery lets out a startled, throaty whimper at the scene, and I turn my head to face her.

"He's right," I say calmly. "You do taste fucking incredible."

Her eyes are wide, breathing shallow as she tries to comprehend what just happened. The two of us laugh, stepping away from each other as I grab a new needle and start sterilizing it.

"Grey's turn next?" I say, her head snapping to look at me with disbelief. "For ink."

Avery manages to collect herself together, sitting up as she snatches the needle from my hand. "My turn to draw. It's payback time. And you may as well keep my panties. They suit your skin tone."

I'm lined up, waiting to enter the showers with my usual group when a guard taps me on the shoulder, pulling me out of my thoughts—all of which involve Avery.

Turning around, I give him a bored, pissed-off expression, noticing that I'm at least a head taller than him. It doesn't take much to intimidate him, his eyes flashing with fear.

"What?!"

He recoils slightly as if I've slapped him, but quickly pulls himself together, straightening up.

"Come with me, please. Mr. Whittingham would like a word."

Does he now? Well, this ought to be good.

I stay in place for a few seconds, watching as panic fills the guard's face as he contemplates how he's going to get me to move if I don't comply.

Narrowing my eyes on him, I step out of line, walking down the corridor without him. He quickly catches up, hand placed tightly over his gun as a precaution.

When we reach the end of the corridor, I look at him expectantly while he fumbles to swipe the tag and punch in the code. Somehow, he manages to drop the card twice, and I roll my eyes at their so-called security. If this is the best they can recruit, then it's no wonder they have problems.

"Hurry the fuck up," I hiss at him, making him jump.

"Right, yep," he mutters to himself, swinging the door open.

I don't wait for him yet again, crossing the threshold to Whittingham's office. I've only been in here twice before—once on my arrival, and the first time I broke another patient's nose for getting in my face. Given how little remorse I showed—along with the fact I threw Whittingham's paper weight into his glass window as I was aiming for his head—I was no longer welcome in here. It was straight to solitary confinement, which worked great for me.

So, I can't help but wonder why I'm here now.

If I had to guess—either they know I went downstairs, or they are trying to hunt for information from someone other than Damon and Grey.

The door is open as I approach and I barge straight in, not stopping until I'm at the edge of his desk. It happens so suddenly that Whittingham barely has time to react, his chair rolling backwards as he quickly stands to his feet.

"Mr. Ashwood," he growls, frustrated.

"What the fuck do you want?" I snap at him.

Clearing his throat, he points to the chair beside me. "Take a seat."

"No."

"Fine, suit yourself," he grumbles, sitting back down. His eyes dart to the door where the guard lingers back. I don't turn around, but I know his tiny hand is still resting on the top of the gun. Judging by how close he was to shitting himself, I doubt he'd be much use if I did start a fight. Still, Whittingham motions for him to stay put.

"Can we get this over with?" I say sternly. "I'm allergic to your presence."

Whittingham scowls, flipping open a folder on the desk. There are photos inside—and it's easy to recognize my own figure in the video still.

"We have repeatedly told you not to go out of bounds," he scolds.

"I couldn't give a shit what you have asked," I shoot back. "Are we done?"

He leans forward, glaring angrily at me. "We know you killed that doctor."

I shrug. "Prove it."

Whittingham looks like he's been slapped with a fish, mouth agape. Of course, he has the evidence right in front of him. But that still doesn't mean anything. That's why I'm here and not in police custody. Because the only evidence they currently have is tied to their secret operation. If he wants me to go down for a crime, it would mean revealing their source of income.

While I have no doubt the contract is legitimate, they still have a reputation on the line. If people found out their *wonderful* rehabilitation center was just a ruse to cover up inhumane treatment of victims let down by the system, they would lose everything.

Whittingham's mistake is banking on the fact that I won't see through his bullshit.

Sadly, that's not the case.

"We have video evidence," he throws back, flinging one of the photos toward me.

I casually pick it up, smiling at the still. Dr. West is strapped into the chair, my hand on the machine, *accidentally* increasing the voltage.

Ahh... good times.

"Can I keep this?" I ask warmly. "Souvenir?"

"You're disgusting!" he yells, jolting to his feet. "Have you no decency?"

My eyes darken as my smile vanishes. Instantly, my change in demeanor hits him, his feet taking two steps back. "You want to argue about *decency*?" I ask in a low tone. "Really? How about we start with the fact that you are torturing individuals here for money?"

His eyes flash—but I suspect it's just confirmation. It's obvious I would know since I'm with Avery often. Still, he seems troubled by my knowledge.

"You have no idea what you are talking about," he sneers. "You've left me no choice—either you confess and spend a week in solitary confinement, or I report this to the authorities."

Smiling, I lean forward, placing my hands on his desk. He steps further back, a look of concern appearing on his face.

"You decide, you old washed-up cunt. Because I don't play these games. You and I both know you have nothing in your hands. But if you even think about coming after anyone I love, you better run fast. If I get my hands on you, I'll gut your Achilles tendons so you never run again while ripping out your tongue with my bare hands so that no one has to ever listen again to the bullshit that comes out of your mouth."

A moment of fear crosses his face before he quickly composes himself, straightening his jacket. He clears his throat, motioning for the guard.

"Take him to solitary confinement. And if he tries anything, you have permission to shoot him."

I laugh loudly, startling both of them. A gun presses into my lower back, and I turn my head to send an amused look to the guard. "Do I scare you, little one?"

The guard feigns confidence, jabbing it harder into my back. "Move."

Sending Whittingham a quick wink, I head toward the door, the gun still pressed to my spine. Just as we start to exit, his gravelly voice calls out, making me see red.

"You can't protect her all the time," he taunts. "Let's see you try when you are locked up."

I'm jolted forward by the gun, the guard sensing my growing rage. Against my better judgment, I keep walking, despite the urge to turn around and slaughter him.

Because it's only for the simple fact that I pressed the speed dial on the cell hidden in my pocket, calling Damon before I entered the office, knowing that he just heard everything.

Chapter 24

Avery

When we're led into the hall for breakfast, my eyes immediately search our table for the others. I'm happy to find Damon and Grey already sitting there, whispering hastily at each other.

"Good morning," I say cheerfully, sliding into the chair next to Grey.

The two of them look at me with stoic faces, my heart missing a beat as I take in their expressions.

"What's wrong?" I ask, eyes darting between them. "Something's wrong..."

Grey reaches over, grabbing my hand and clenching it. "Don't panic, babe."

My eyes widen. "That's literally always followed by bad news which I know will absolutely make me panic."

"Theo got dragged into Arthur's office last night," Damon interjects, getting straight to the point. "They know he went downstairs. He's currently in solitary confinement."

A sharp pain shoots across my chest while I stare at the two of them closely, hoping for the *'you should see the look on your face'* punchline. It doesn't come and I sag in my chair, letting out a shaky breath. "Fuck."

"It's just for a week," Grey says soothingly. "We heard the whole conversation. And as far as we are aware, Theo still has his cell on him. They didn't check him for contraband."

"What the fuck happened?" I whisper in a panic. "What do we do?"

Damon shakes his head. "We can't do anything. They are expecting us to react."

"We can't just leave him there," I argue, on the verge of tears.

Grey squeezes my hand. "Little killer, he will be fine. It's you we need to focus on. Arthur made a comment about him not being able to protect you if he's locked up."

A cold rush of trepidation fills me, and in my head, all I can see is the bucket shaking violently.

"They are going to try something..." I echo their thoughts. "They are trying to separate us to make it easier."

"I think he's just bluffing," Damon says firmly. "But I'm coming with you to your session with Christopher. We need to get cameras set up as soon as possible. In the meantime, Grey and I will work out the *ass* schedule again."

I frown, alarmed. "Theo was meant to be watching me last night."

"I stood guard," Grey answers. "Damon already has Byrone and Jillian working on overriding the system again—hopefully more permanently. And Leighton is keeping tabs on Arthur's movements."

The only comforting thought is that Theo likes solitary confinement. It's not a punishment for him. But still, being separated at a time like this is dangerous. I'm not worried for my own safety, but theirs.

"How can we be sure they are bluffing?" I ask Damon. "I don't think they are that predictable."

"Theo destroyed the equipment downstairs," he answers. "They have no way of continuing their research without it. Even if they have no moral compass, the contract is pretty strict. It lists all the exhaustive methods of research they are allowed to conduct—there's very little left that they could do at the moment."

My mind switches back to the ice bath and drugs. There are definitely options that don't require equipment, but I see his point. Doctors and researchers like to be thorough. If they can't draw an inference or check multiple variables, it defeats the purpose of method testing.

"I don't like this," I mutter, frustrated. "They will want revenge for us ruining their project."

"Too fucking bad for them," Damon shoots back. "I have no sympathy for them."

"Me either," Grey murmurs, moving his hand to rub my side. "How does it feel today?"

I give him a tight smile. "It's fine—a little itchy."

Damon pushes his tray of food away—pancakes again—and folds his arms. "I'll pay a visit to Arthur. Maybe I can get some information out of him."

"Be careful, please," I plead. "We don't know what they might do."

He looks over at me, a lop-sided smile on his face. "I think they are more scared of us—as they should be."

"Why am I not surprised to see you here?" Dr. Smith mutters with a deadpan expression.

The two of us are sitting across from him, the cousins having a heated stare-off.

"We need your help," I chime in before Damon can speak. "Whittingham took Theo. Are you able to help us with more tech gear?"

Dr. Smith looks surprised, his face softening slightly as he turns to me. "Such as?"

"Portable cameras," Damon answers sharply. "We need more eyes on Arthur and the other staff."

You can see the switch again instantly as his face darkens with frustration. "I'm not your errand runner, Damon. The cells were one thing, but this is entirely different. It's an invasion of privacy."

"Really? We're going to argue *that* point?" Damon scoffs.

He's right. There's no such thing as privacy in Lilydale. Our files aren't safe, we're locked up like animals—even our showers are monitored. It's not that big of a jump when you're on this side of the fence.

"Please," I ask politely. "We need to make sure they don't pull any more stunts. It's not like we're going to use them to spy on patients. If anything, we're trying to protect them."

An amused look crosses Dr. Smith's face. "The queen protects the king."

I blink slowly, absorbing his words.

Chess.

It dawns on me that perhaps he wasn't spouting random bullshit that day. Maybe he was hinting at something else.

"Checkmate," I murmur back, as Damon stares at me with confusion.

Seconds pass in silence before Dr. Smith starts laughing, relaxing in his chair. "Alright. I'll see what I can do."

As I turn to beam at Damon, I can't help but laugh at the look on his face. For someone who spends his entire life in control, knowing every little bit of information, it's enlightening to see him so perplexed—on the outside of a conversation for once.

He notices me staring and shrugs. "I don't care," he mumbles. "Keep your secrets."

"Oh, don't be upset, Damon," Dr. Smith tsks. "Not everything is about you."

"It technically is," I argue light-heartedly.

Damon smirks in approval, sending his cousin a patronizing glare.

"Don't encourage him, Avery," Dr. Smith mutters. "It will go straight to his head."

It's bizarre seeing new sides to both of these men. It goes to show that everyone has multiple personas, depending on who they are with. I can't help but wonder if this is normal cousin behavior.

Somewhere out there, I have two cousins from my mom's side. I haven't seen them since I was a child, only at the rare family get-together. My memories of extended family are a foggy haze—much like my existence before I came here. But I did always wonder what it would be like to have a sibling or a cousin I was close with.

Paige was the closest family I had after Mom. We all had our demons and battles, so fun adventures and conversation were few and far between. Still, it's nice to imagine what we could have had if life wasn't so shitty.

I picture these two at family events, being competitive as fuck, arguing about rich-boy problems. But let's face it—Damon would have won.

"I'm done with this conversation," Damon announces, standing up. "Avery, I'll be back to get you in forty-five minutes."

"Okay," I answer, watching as he exits the room, closing the door behind him.

When it's just Dr. Smith and I left, we glance at each other, a weird tension between us.

Damon and I have been through several journeys in our relationship—from hating each other, to tolerating, to liking.

And kissing.

The flashback makes me embarrassed, and I'm worried that the psychiatrist in front of me may have mind-reading abilities or be able to see my secrets from my body language. Worse still, he might see what I really think.

I want to kiss him again.

"How are you feeling anyway?" Dr. Smith asks, and I feel relief that I'm not being painfully obvious.

"I'm alright," I mutter. "Just worried about Theo."

He nods, smiling at me. "Good."

"Good?" I question sternly. "It's *good* that I'm worried they took him away?"

That annoys me. Worry and anxiety are horrible emotions to deal with, yet he seems ecstatic about it.

"It's good that you are feeling something," he replies warmly. "And I think it speaks volume that it's about someone you care for."

"Didn't we establish that I have little self-confidence and that I shouldn't rely on other people?" I sigh, feeling argumentative for no reason other than the fact it's Dr. Smith.

"For validation," he chimes in. "But you also came to Lilydale with the struggle to open up to people. You were worried about people leaving, thus being closed off and withdrawn. It's wonderful to see you have developed multiple relationships."

Multiple relationships?

Fuck. Does he know?

We don't hide it by any means, but still... I'm not sure how I feel about it being brought up in session.

I must be silent for too long because he speaks up, clarifying. "Multiple *connections*."

"Right," I mutter, suddenly wishing the floor would open up and swallow me whole. "Good to know I'm succeeding in some way. Not a total failure then."

"Would you prefer to talk about the cameras?" he offers. "Or the cells. I'm sure you have questions."

A dry laugh finds its way out as I slouch back into the chair. "I have many, but if I absorb any more information from you, I might implode. Especially after the last session."

He nods. "That's a fair point. It must be confusing for you."

"That's one way to put it. You make it hard to trust you."

A frown stares back at me. "How so?" he asks.

I tilt my head to the side, gazing at him in exasperation. "What side are you batting for? Because you're a member of staff here, yet you seem to silently beg for me to trust you. I can't trust any of the staff here. I got hurt under your watch, and it's clear you and Damon have a hostile familial relationship, but suddenly you want to help us? It doesn't add up."

He leans back, seemingly letting my words sink in. We have a strange relationship too—always pushing and pulling, tethering on the borderline of professional and non-professional. This session is no different, but after having Damon here, it doesn't leave a sour taste in my mouth like it normally would.

"I'm not sure how much you know about our family," he starts. "But wearing a mask was always a requirement."

"So, who are you then?" I question. "Which mask is your real face?"

"Truthfully, both of them. I *do* care about my position here, and yes, Damon and I have a hostile relationship. But that doesn't mean I'm on Alexander's side."

This voice sounds pained, and it takes me a moment to realize he lost someone too. Lily was his aunt. Maybe he's chained to this place too—just with different colored shackles.

I wouldn't put it past Alexander to blackmail multiple people—*multiple family members*. He seems the type who would step on anyone to rise to the top.

"Why are you here?" I shoot back. "Working in Lilydale? If you have an Ivy League degree, surely you could have gotten a job anywhere."

Dr. Smith smiles—but it's not the warm, friendly one I'm used to. It's riddled with sadness and secrets, a pain I recognize well.

"Let's just say that Alexander has dirt on my immediate family. At the time, it didn't seem like a terrible idea. He wanted me to keep an eye on Damon, help out with certain tasks. But once he realized I wouldn't go as far as he wanted—"

"He hired Elsher," I finish. "He's a piece of shit."

He doesn't say anything, but his agreement reflects back at me in his eyes.

"There are certainly some lines I won't cross," he says. "Not everyone shares that sentiment."

As my eyes drift over to the cabinet, I feel a tightness in my chest. "Were you trying to protect me from Damon at the start?"

"Yes," he answers without hesitation. "But once I realized you didn't need protecting from him, I stopped. It became obvious that he and his friends cared for you—just in their own way."

I snort, amused. "They certainly had a funny way of showing it."

"We all wear our masks well," he replies. "It just takes time to figure out which face is the real one."

Chapter 25

Damon

After I leave Christopher's office, I make a beeline for the door that separates our prison from the hungry leech in designer suits.

He should send me a Christmas card—who knows how much of my money has been spent on his luxury items.

It's obvious my father pays him a pretty penny. From the few times I met Arthur before Lilydale was created, he was a polar opposite shell to his current self. Hideous polo shirts and khakis that belonged in the dumpster instead of the golf course. The type of man who would slosh food and drink all over himself because he was making jeers at people and expressing himself with his hands wildly to seem larger than life.

Now, he's living up a lavish lifestyle thanks to my family.

Sometimes the world is unforgiving. It would be nice to believe that karma is a sure thing, but truthfully, bad guys always win. That made it easier to become one myself—the need to win and succeed drives me further than anything else.

I distinctly remember my parents fighting one day about Arthur. My father spent most of his free time at country clubs and golf courses with his college buddies. Just like now, Arthur was the leech who glued himself to my family's side—money is shiny, after all.

As much as she hated it, Mom heard gossip from the blabbermouths dressed in Louis Vuitton and Chanel. The wives and girlfriends were just as bad as their husbands—obsessed with the money and social ladders they could climb. Any excuse to be higher up than other people. They didn't care who they had to stand on to get there.

Someone let it slip over too many Long Island iced teas that Arthur was cheating on his wife. I had only met her a handful of times with him, but it was clear she was nothing like the snakes in designer clothing. She was the one person my mom got along with, without the need to pretend for the sake of being polite.

They got into a huge argument—Mom was adamant that Mrs. Whittingham should be told about her husband's infidelity. But my father, in his alcohol-fueled toxic masculinity, disagreed.

"He's a man. He can do what he wishes."

"Perhaps she should have spent more time taking care of him as a housewife should do."

"Without him, she'd be worthless. She should feel privileged that she has this lifestyle because of him."

When our maker was handing out cups of morality, my father was last in line. He was of the belief that women were beneath men, there to serve and bear children.

Despite Mom coming from old money, she still loved to work. It gave her a sense of purpose helping others. But my father quickly nipped it in the bud, forcing her to have me and leave the workforce.

To make himself look good, he allowed her to assist him with minor company duties—such as planning and hosting events. You know, jobs designed for *women*.

It was clear from a young age that I only existed to continue his legacy. Even when I was a toddler, he would tell me that it was lucky I was born a man.

I was the product of pain and suffering—but she still loved me. She devoted all her time to my needs, being hands-on unlike the other country club princesses who would pay someone to change their child's diaper.

The only good thing to come out of that mess was the fact that Mrs. Whittingham divorced him. Mom paid for her attorney, and in the end, Mrs. Whittingham walked away with half.

Arthur was furious. My father too.

And it still haunts me that it happened six months before my mother's death.

I don't believe in coincidence. I would wager every single dollar to my name that the grand Whittingham divorce was the beginning of the end for my family. But that's just who my mom was—always the savior, never the saved.

The last time I saw freedom was her funeral. The former Mrs. Whittingham was there—with a male guest—and my father tried to kick her out. I refused, putting him in his place.

Two weeks later I was sedated, placed in a temporary mental health involuntary hold. That part of my life was a blur after her death, and they used that to take advantage of me. At the end of the hold, Lilydale was created—and I was patient number one.

It wasn't just my father's revenge and need to overpower me... it was retaliation for Arthur.

Mom wasn't around to protect me anymore, and why would anyone believe a grieving eighteen-year-old? Especially one that punched his own father repeatedly in the face after a funeral.

He's psychotic. He has Intermittent Explosive Disorder.

He's a danger to society.

They can falsely diagnose me however they want. The jokes on them.

I became the society.

A virus, infecting their pride and joy from the inside-out.

As I enter the foyer, I notice that Arthur's door is wide open. Dorothea jumps in her seat, quickly standing when she spots me.

"You're not supposed to be out here," she scolds, but her words fall flat, coated in fear.

"Shut that dick-gurgling flytrap, Dorothea," I reply casually. "I'm in no mood to deal with you."

I can't see Arthur despite his door being open. He's blocked by a wide-shouldered body—a man standing in front of his desk. I recognize that physique anywhere.

"Well, isn't this just charming?" I sneer, watching as he turns around slowly, anger present on his aging features.

"Damon."

My father stands unfazed, glaring at me as Arthur rises from his chair. The two of them subconsciously straighten up, hoping to intimidate me with their slightly shorter frames.

"I should have known you'd be snooping around," I direct at my father. "Let me guess—there was a bit of a financial setback."

Arthur's fists curl on his desk as he pushes his weight into it. "We're not surprised that you had something to do with it."

I shrug. "I'm not sure what you are referring to. But it must be serious if the great Alexander Dale is making a house call."

"Watch your tone, boy," my father snaps. "I'm in no mood to deal with it."

"That makes two of us," I reply, amused that I just uttered the same words to Dorothea—the apple never falls far from the tree. "But if you're here to discuss business, then I should be involved, no?"

Walking over, I kick one of the guest chairs to the side of the room, sitting down on it. I smile at them, placing my forearms on the armrests as I strum my fingers.

"This doesn't concern you," Arthur spits out. "And I'm fed up with you waltzing around the facility as you please."

"I'm fed up with your existence," I sharply reply. "But alas, we're stuck with each other." Turning to my father, I raise an eyebrow. "Unless, of course, you plan on releasing me?"

My father's cheeks flush red—hopefully a sign of high blood pressure. "You cost the facility hundreds of thousands of dollars with your stunt."

"Oh, no. What a tragedy," I groan sarcastically. "How will you manage?"

Reaching into his briefcase, my father pulls out a stack of paperwork, flinging it into my lap. I calmly pick it up, scanning the front page. "Court proceedings? My, my. Bringing out the big guns."

My eyes hover over the words on the document. My father is seeking a court order to amend my trust, effectively immediately.

At the moment, he is unable to access money from it while I am deemed mentally incapacitated unless it's for specific reasons pertaining to my sole wellbeing and benefit. According to the documents, the facility needs to access the money so that it can stay open—*for my benefit, wellbeing, and the greater good of the community.*

As I read on, finding the section on supporting evidence, I snort. Glancing up at him, I raise an eyebrow mockingly. "You lost the contract."

"Not yet," Arthur interjects angrily. "But unless we pay for new equipment to replace what your lapdog broke, they are terminating the agreement."

I toss the papers onto the ground at my father's feet. "That seems very much like a you problem. You are aware as much as I am that you can't pull the funds from the trust. A judge will never approve this. Guess you'll have to fund it yourself. Maybe sell the Porsche and your vacation house in the Hamptons."

See—I can play nice. Look at me providing financial advice.

"Actually," my father starts, sounding eerily confident. "Our matter was listed on Judge Balknac's docket. You remember him—he's an old friend of mine."

Sadly, I *do* remember Richard Balknac. Mainly because I used to call him Dick Ball Sack. With a name like that, it's hard to forget.

"So, you bribed a judge," I point out in a bored tone. "Not surprised in the least."

"I did no such thing," he refutes. "But he is familiar with our charity work and how *important* it is that we stay in operation."

"Meaning you're terrified of me and had to build a literal prison to lock me up so that your bed feels safe at night."

My father folds his arms, tipping his chin up. "You can keep that copy. It's for you anyhow. By law, we have to notify all shareholders of impending legal action."

I grind my teeth together, realizing where this conversation is heading.

When Lilydale was set up, my father handpicked the board members and key players, including Arthur. But since Lilydale's mission statement was projected to be a mental health institution with my upcoming admission, of which was listed as *indefinite/ongoing*, they had to give me shares. If they wanted to use the trust funds for my admission, it had to be paid for so to speak—an eye for an eye.

Initially, I was the majority shareholder. It didn't matter much at the time—while I am here and deemed mentally unfit to make decisions, I cannot be involved. But I realize now I was set up.

If there's one thing my father loves more than money, it's power. He hated that I held fifty-one percent to his forty-nine thanks to the trust.

But that all changed.

Avery changed that.

The night I bargained with my father to bring her back, to keep her out of federal prison, he only asked for one thing.

Two percent of shares.

He even had Christopher sign off on a legal document stating that I was in a brief lucid state of mind, and capable of temporarily making decisions.

I gave him the position of majority shareholder for Avery's safe return. It's the reason he can bring this request to the court without my permission now. And since it's obvious he's bribed his judicial buddy, the trust fund is finally going to be cracked wide open—just what he's always wanted.

And there's very little I can do to stop him.

"Best of luck with it," I shoot back. "Even if you manage to access the money, I'll make sure those miserable doctors never touch a patient again."

My father smiles at me—his eyes cold and dead. "We'll see. The board has just finished negotiations with them. As your legal guardian, I've given them permission to *attempt to fix your disorder* if they see fit. They seemed eager, given your history."

"Oh, Father," I sigh. "I lived with you for nearly two decades. There's nothing they can do to torture me that you haven't already done."

His jaw ticks with unspoken anger. I look at the clock on the wall, rising to my feet. Turning to look at Arthur, I smile warmly. "As for you—I promise to make *your* life a living hell. The two of you might have money and friends in high places, but what you lack is guts. If your sagging, wrinkly balls weren't dangling around your knees, I'd assume you had none."

"Those are big words coming from someone locked up," Arthur taunts. "Your secret little society can only withstand so much. Eventually, you'll run out of options."

"Try me and see," I dare, smirking at him as I make my way toward the door, stepping on the paperwork without a care. "But you better hope you don't miss with your aim because I'm coming for both of you."

Chapter 26

Avery

Is it possible for someone to change their entire personality in a short amount of time?

Of course, it is. Most of the time it's related to your mood. Even the slightest thing can upheave your state of mind.

But it's still strange to see that somehow in the span of forty-five minutes, Damon's mood entirely flipped.

In Dr. Smith's office he was sarcastic, witty, and warm toward me. But now? It feels like I've gone back in time, and it is day one in Lilydale all over again.

The moment my session ended and I bounced out of the office, Damon's face was cold. He barely spoke two words to me, just gesturing for me to hurry up behind him.

Even when he bothers to look at me, which has been all of three times since then, he's angry.

Grey is nowhere to be seen and with Theo stuck in solitary confinement, I'm left alone with Damon at lunch.

He eats his food silently, only humming in reply any time I try to speak to him.

Is it me? Did I do something?

I know that in reality I couldn't have, but there's still a small—okay, large—part of me that wants to apologize. I want him to look at me warmly again, to display that side that he's shown lately.

After lunch, he walks with me in silence to Charmaine's classroom, turning around and stalking off before I can open my mouth once we reach the door.

It eats me up the entire lesson, especially when I notice that Grey is still missing. I lose track of how many times I stare at his empty chair, panic threatening to take my sanity as I worry that they somehow got their hands on him. But surely if that was the case, Damon would have said something.

By the time the lesson is over and free time has started, I'm on edge. I expect to see Damon or Grey waiting for me when I exit the room, but to my surprise, it's Jillian.

"Hey..." I greet awkwardly.

Jillian kicks off from the wall, her hair swishing behind her in a high ponytail. "Hey, Avery. Damon sent me to keep you company."

"Where is he?" I ask as we follow the rest of the gen-pop toward the hall for commencement of free time.

People ahead of us start to veer off into different directions—some inside the hall, others to the courtyard. Instinctively, I walk into the library. It's the only place that feels like home since I know Theo won't be in one of the empty rooms down the corridor.

"He's in his room," she answers, apparently unbothered by my lead of direction. "And Grey's out dealing with something."

I frown. No one has told me anything, and the fact that there's still secrets between us kind of hurts. Mainly because I'm worried—Whittingham seems determined to separate us. So, why have the men suddenly decided to leave me to my own devices?

"Is Damon okay?" I question quietly.

I have no idea if Jillian knows more than I do. It's clear that she's an important person to Damon and Cirque des Morts, so it's worth a try.

"I think so," she replies, leaning against a bookshelf. "He hasn't said much if that's what you're asking."

Nodding, I do my best to keep the worry off my face, but Jillian notices anyway.

"Don't stress," she murmurs. "I think he's just decompressing."

"Decompressing?" I repeat. "Did something happen?"

Jillian pauses, apparently contemplating how much to give away. "I believe he paid a visit to Whittingham. He's usually pissed off afterward."

That makes sense. He did say that he was going to speak to him. But still, it's Damon we're talking about. He's impenetrable, ruthless. I've never once known him to be cold and detached like this after speaking to Whittingham. Something else must have happened, otherwise he'd be here.

I don't like how much I'm in the dark right now—it's unsettling.

Pulling my cell out of my pocket, Jillian watches me quietly as I quickly send off a text message to Theo and Grey. I consider texting Damon too, but it sounds like I won't get a reply—if he wanted to talk to me, he'd be here.

When I finish, I shove the cell back into my pocket. We stand in silence, the awkward tension growing until I decide to make small talk.

"Where's Byrone?" I ask politely. It's no secret that they are a couple and spend most of their time together when possible.

"He's in his room," she says, and I can tell there's a bit of sadness laced in her tone.

I nod, feeling even more guilty. Everyone keeps putting their lives on hold for me, as if I'm some ancient artifact that needs guarding.

I'm not sure where my train of thought comes from—whether fueled by guilt, anxiety, or the need to be close to one of the guys—but the words fall from my lips before I can stop them.

"Can you get me an access card?"

Jillian listens to my unusual request, not a hint of surprise crossing her face. Instead, she digs into her pocket, pulling out a shiny black plastic card without hesitation.

"Here," she says, holding it out.

Carefully, I reach for it. I'm filled with disbelief that she handed it over so easily, but then again, things have rapidly changed in the past few weeks. I'm no longer the girl being forced to attend meetings while being made an example of. I'm now in Damon's inner circle—something I paid for with my life.

"Thank you," I murmur gratefully, pocketing it next to my cell. "I'll make sure you don't get in trouble for this."

She knows I mean from Damon, not Whittingham, her lips curving into a small smile. "I'm not worried," she says calmly. "Don't forget the pin code."

I listen closely as she rattles off the four digits, repeating them in my head several times so I don't forget.

Together, we walk to the door of the Westwood wing, Jillian letting me do the honors of swiping the card and punching in the code to make sure I've got it correct.

It's oddly empowering having the ability to walk freely without the guys leading the way. It's cathartic in a sense, almost like I'm saying *fuck you* to Lilydale.

The Westwood wing is practically deserted—the only people in here being the ones who can bypass the system. Jillian gives me a little wave as she stops in front of Byrone's door, letting herself in. When it's just me left in the corridor, nerves finally hit as my feet slow down.

I can see the numbers on Damon's door clearly, my heart racing as I pause in front of it.

How will he react?

Better yet... *why am I doing this?*

I shove the questions and doubts aside, letting the part of me that's desperate to check on him win. Swiping the card, I enter the code again, holding my breath as the door clicks open.

Stepping inside the room, my eyes immediately find Damon. He's sitting on his bed, one leg tucked toward his chest as he leans his forearm on his knee. In his other hand is a bottle of whiskey, my nose instantly turning up at the smell.

His gaze is on mine straight away, face almost free of emotion except for a fraction of anger. Even though it's there, it's clear that it's not aimed at me.

"Hey..." I mutter, closing the door behind me.

Damon doesn't answer, bringing the bottle to his lips as he takes another swig.

His guard is up, body tense, but I walk over, standing at the edge of the bed in front of him. "I just wanted to check on you," I add softly.

"You shouldn't be here," he mutters, voice darker than I've heard in some time. "You are supposed to be with—"

"Jillian, yes. But I wanted to see you," I cut him off.

It feels intimidating standing over him, so I slowly drop to my knees, leaning back on my heels. He doesn't move, but his eyes follow my change in position.

In my pocket, I feel my cell buzz—a reply from either Grey or Theo. But I ignore it, keeping my attention on Damon. He must hear the vibration too, his eyes darting to my shorts before finding my face again.

"What happened?" I ask him when he doesn't reply.

Another swig—his eyes finally breaking contact as he turns his head to the left, staring at the wall.

"Nothing."

The response is cold, hostile... and so *obviously* full of shit. It actually makes me hurt a little.

The savage leader, the one always in control, the one who always looks out for everyone else... pained. But I should have known he'd go through something like this alone. It makes me wonder how many times he has retreated to his room to deal with battling emotions.

All the times he scolded me for showing emotion, for not being able to hold it in... it hits me hard. This is what he meant. And for once, I disagree with him.

If I've learned anything from the guys recently, it's that I should process things, not let them hide in the dark corners of my mind. Damon raised that point himself, even going as far as lecturing me on not bottling it up after he rescued me.

"That's fucking bullshit," I murmur. "You're upset about something."

"I don't *do* upset," he snaps back.

I'm still on my knees, gazing up at him, but he refuses to look at me. Reaching forward, I place a hand on his leg, begging him to snap out of his staring contest with the wall.

His muscles tense under my palm but he still doesn't face me.

I drop my head, running through ideas on how to get him to talk. I know I shouldn't push him, but we're supposed to be on the same side now. When one of us goes down, we all do together.

Something red catches my eye poking out from under his bed, and my free hand slips under, pulling it toward me. It scrapes along the concrete, my eyebrows shooting up in surprise at the familiar mask.

It's the same red mask he wore when he pulled me out of that white room, the hard plastic feeling cold under my fingers.

Curiously, I lift it into my lap, letting my hand fall away from his leg. Picking it up, I let the irrational thoughts win, sliding it over my face. I want to see what it looks like from the other side, whether it's comfortable with good visibility. Considering it was late when they found me, I have to wonder if it obstructed their vision in the dark hallways... if the way he fought and defended me against the guards was beyond basic skill.

Surprisingly, the black mesh over the eye sockets doesn't hinder my vision as much as I thought it would. I can see perfectly fine—especially when Damon finally swings his gaze back to me, astonishment on his face.

"What are you doing?" he asks quickly.

I smile at him but quickly realize he can't see that. So, I tilt my head to express my curiosity and innocence. "Nothing," I reply, deliberately using his own frustrating words against him.

Putting my hands on my thighs, I straighten up, staring directly at him. Something flashes in his eyes, his leg dropping from his chest as he scoots to the edge of the bed. He drops his legs on either side of me, leaning forward to glance down at my kneeling frame.

"Avery," he growls.

"What?" I shoot back. "Red not my color?"

We stare at each other for a few seconds longer, until he reaches out, lifting the mask off my face. It rests on the top of my head, my eyes still holding his.

"Fuck it," he snaps.

The air cackles with electricity as he rushes forward, smashing his lips to mine. It's forceful, almost desperate. Our tongues clash as I melt into him, his arms snaking around my back. I'm hoisted up from my kneeling position, clumsily falling into his lap.

There's a small clang as the mask falls off the top of my head, bouncing along the ground, but I'm too caught up in the taste of surprise whiskey to care.

Heat ignites in my stomach, more irrational thoughts winning as I throw my arms around his neck. It feels too good to worry about the *what-ifs* and the *should-I*.

This feels right. I can't explain why.

My chest pushes into his as a hand slides firmly down my spine. When it reaches the waistband of my shorts, he doesn't stop, dipping under the fabric to glide over my ass.

I let out a tiny moan when he grabs my ass firmly. My fingers skate through his hair, tugging on the strands.

I take back what I said about whiskey, because on his lips, it's my new favorite thing.

His hand slips further south, slightly brushing against my pussy and he groans into my mouth. My own moan seems to pull him from his trance, his body suddenly tensing up.

Damon doesn't move his hand away though, his forehead pressed against mine. We're both slightly breathless, our lips barely touching now.

"Avery," he murmurs, my name sounding like a sin on his lips.

I pull back slightly, checking his face for regret.

"Damon..."

Chapter 27

Grey

I smile to myself as I glance down at the screen of the cell, my fingers quickly typing out a reply.

Knowing that Avery is missing me already, as much as I'm missing her, makes this a little easier.

I hate being away from her—even for a second. If I had my way, we'd never leave my bed. Hell, even the library.

Fuck me. Especially the library.

I've replayed our last library visit dozens of times in my head. It's bad enough that I'm constantly turned on and eerily aware in her presence but having visual images to get me through our time apart, is torture.

Well, it's torture for whoever I'm dealing with at the time.

My left hand is firmly pressed against the nape of Rian Thatcher while my foot crushes his calf. I finish sending my reply to Avery, shoving the cell into my right pocket.

"I don't know what the fuck you're talking about," he growls again, whining as I tighten my grip.

"We saw you emerging from the office. Don't lie," I say calmly. "Just tell me what you were there for."

For a scrawny thing, he's quite strong. Despite my hand holding his head down, he manages well to push back and engage his neck muscles. Though, when you have the right motivation...

We're in the male restrooms, Rian dangling over the urinal basin. If his strength gives out at any point, he'll land face first in a puddle of piss—and whatever that *red* stuff is.

Okay—I might be exaggerating a little bit. I know the red stuff is blood. I put it there for dramatic flair.

As usual, I combed through the new kid's file, getting an idea of his wonderful *personality* traits. It turns out that he has a phobia of bodily fluids—a germaphobe.

Which, in the grand scheme of it, seems a bit strange considering when he was arrested, he was apparently covered in *a lot* of blood.

Normally, I'd be more understanding of trauma but considering we know that Arthur had words with him when he first arrived, it's clear our warning didn't hit the intended mark.

Andy spotted him returning from Arthur's office again, and with recent events, it's safe to say I have no fucking limitations or boundaries when it comes to protecting my girl.

I'll happily break this fucker into a thousand pieces without a second thought.

"I was called there," Rian snaps back, eyes narrowing into slits at the mess below him. "I didn't have a choice."

"What did he want?" I ask, his voice grating on my final nerve. "I already *know* you were there. *Why* is the answer I need."

I'm a bit more forceful this time, shoving my weight and pressure against his neck while my foot squishes his calf painfully. The two actions make him jolt, head dipping lower as he lets out a grunt of pain.

"He asked... he just asked if I was doing alright," he grumbles.

I tsk at him, shaking my head. Arthur doesn't have a caring bone in his body—the idea that he was solely conducting a welfare check on the new kid smells of bullshit. "I can feel your pulse jumping under my fingers. Don't lie to me, Rian."

Moving my foot from his leg, I rest it on his glutes, shoving him. The movement forces him down further, his spine unable to bear the weight in this position.

"I'll make you lick this up if you don't come clean to me," I warn, now holding his head up. The piss is right under his nose, his body dry-heaving as the smell assaults his senses. Part of me hopes he does vomit to add to the mess.

"Okay, okay!" he chokes out, making retching noises. "He asked me to befriend someone."

"There we go..." I say in a soothing, praiseful tone, lifting him up slightly. "Give me the name."

Rian takes large gulping breaths through his mouth, eyes squeezed shut. "That blonde haired girl—Victoria or something."

"Vivian?"

"Yeah, her."

I push him down harshly, kicking him simultaneously as I release him. He slips and fumbles, landing in the urinal face first with a squeal as I step back, just out of the way of the splashback.

"If I can offer any advice," I say, watching as he scrambles to the sink to scrub his face, feet slipping on the tiles. "Don't."

He throws water on his face, rubbing his hands vigorously over his skin. "Why do you even care?" he pants. "She's not your girlfriend. You're with that other girl."

That other girl.

I don't take kindly to the fact that he's referring to Avery as if she's just some average female, not even worthy of a name. I storm toward him, my hand grabbing a fistful of his hair as I pull back, slamming his face forward. The glass mirror shatters against his forehead, the loud bang and echo of fallen glass bouncing around the tiled room.

Rian drops to his knees in a daze, groaning in pain as he clutches his bleeding forehead.

"Her name is Avery," I snap. "You better remember that for next time. As for Capello—*Vivian*—keep away from her. She doesn't need any pathetic attempts of fake friendship. Do you understand?"

He nods furiously, eyes tightly closed as a trickle of blood drips down his nose.

Satisfied, I turn and leave the bathroom, nearly colliding with a guard in the process.

The guard pauses when he recognizes me, the two of us entering a stare-off. I raise my eyebrows at him, daring him to try something.

When he doesn't make a move toward me, I give him a smile—warm and friendly like two old associates passing each other at the grocery store.

"There was an *accident*," I tell him, nodding my head toward the doorway. "Best you assist Mr. Thatcher to Markel's office."

Without waiting for a reply, I stalk past him, heading down the hall.

It's free time, so people are wandering around, chatting among themselves. A few stumble out of my way, giving me a wide berth as I pass, while others freeze in fear.

The next item on my list is a little less fun, but still important.

Heading past the classrooms, I give a little wave to Charmaine as she finishes packing up her room. Her face flashes with disappointment when she sees me, but she returns a small wave nonetheless, obviously annoyed that I was absent from her lesson.

The corridor is quiet and emptier the further I go, heading into official out-of-bounds territory. When I reach the familiar steps, I walk down after scanning my card at the first door, coming face to face with the sole room down here.

A large metal door stands in my way, and for good measure, I try to swipe the card. As expected, the access pad flashes red instead of the usual green—confirming what I already know.

It's the one access code in the entire building that differs from the rest. In hindsight, it makes me question why Arthur doesn't just change all of them to stop us moving around freely. I suspect he can't be fucked, because he'd be changing it daily which is too much paperwork for the staff. It would be a logistical nightmare having to brief everyone on the change every single day. People would forget or get locked out—*or in*—and he knows we'd just find a way around it anyway.

Arthur isn't the most intelligent man, but he knows we have some of the guards wrapped around our finger, so we'd easily find out and continue as we were. It's a small sacrifice to make—he lets us walk around, and in return, they monitor us and follow our whereabouts.

But it grinds my gears that the one door we can't access is solitary confinement. Despite Byrone and Jillian's hard work, we are still yet to figure out the code. According to their logs, the system automatically updates this particular door on a daily basis, with only specialized cards programmed to unlock it. To this day, we only know of two cards that work—one that Arthur keeps on him and another that Teddy normally holds onto as a backup. It's probably up her cunt like Arthur is.

My hand knocks on the door twice, my ears straining to listen for sounds.

"What?" A muffled voice shouts, annoyed.

"It's me," I answer in a sing-song tune. "Your favorite boyfriend-in-law."

Even through the door, I hear Theo let out an exasperated groan. "Can't let me have a moment's peace, even in here?"

The pipes clang above me as I laugh. "Just checking you are alive."

"Of course I'm alive," he shoots back sarcastically. "What else would I be doing in here?"

He has a fair point, but still, taunting him is becoming my new favorite thing—after being with Avery, of course. Besides, what else can you do with your girlfriend's other boyfriend if not mock and make his existence a nightmare?

"Byrone is looking into the system to see if we can get the door open," I tell him. "But chances are it's a no-go without getting our hand on Arthur's card."

"I'm enjoying the peace and quiet away from you," he says, but there's no malice in his tone.

"I'm touched that you think of me. How's the cell service down here?"

There's a moment of silence, presumably as he digs it out. "One bar—but comes and goes."

I nod to myself. "Avery is worried about you."

At the mention of her name, I hear movement behind the door, his voice a little clearer and closer when he responds. "Keep her safe, Grey."

"I will," I promise him, meaning every fucking word. "I'll pop down each day to update you on things."

"Alright."

My eyebrows furrow as I reach my hand out, placing it against the cold, metal door. I hate that I can't do anything for him. If I was kept away from Avery, I'd end up breaking every bone in my hands trying to claw this door open. But on the flipside, Theo knows he can trust us. We'll keep her safe—and at the very least, we know he's somewhat safe too.

The thing about solitary confinement is they barely come down to check on you. That's part of the torture—only bringing the occasional food, leaving the patients in literal darkness. And given Theo's aggressive nature toward guards and staff members, no one is keen to try to go inside with him. That would be the equivalent of getting in a cage with a hungry, blood-thirsty lion.

"If you get enough signal, send her a message," I say, stepping back from the door. "I don't know what the charge is like on the cells, but hopefully it lasts a few days."

"It's currently at fifty-eight percent," he replies. "I'll move around and find a spot. The pipes probably don't help with the signal. But when you see her, tell Avery I love her."

I knock on the door twice with my knuckles. "Will do, asshole."

"Thanks, fuckwit."

Chapter 28

Damon

"God-*fucking*-dammit!" I snap, irritable at myself.

My control slipped—again. I've rarely lost it at all the past few years, and now, it's happening more frequently. And there's one common denominator in all of it.

Avery.

Just hearing her say my name like that is more intoxicating than the expensive bottle of whiskey that's now forgotten about on the floor. I don't even remember placing it down. One minute I was fine, then the next it's as if my invisible cord snapped. My mouth was on hers, breathing her in like my life depended on it.

When I look up, I notice her watching me closely, forehead wrinkled with tension. I can see the worry in her eyes—the panic and fear that I regret what just happened.

I don't.

It just happened so suddenly. I'm mad at myself for losing control.

Mad at myself for hating how much I place my own value in her.

Mad for hating the way she makes me believe I'm not as bad of a monster as I think I am.

I hate that she sees good in me when I know there's none. But furious that sometimes I let myself indulge in that thought, believing it briefly.

Everything is so different in her eyes. She's too trusting, too quick to search for good. That's what's landed her in trouble before.

I don't want her to be so complacent. *She needs to hate me. I need her to hate me.*

It would all be much easier.

But at the same time, the thought of her hating me makes it feel like my body is being torn apart from the inside out.

I've grown to like how she looks at me. While everyone watches me with fear, she gazes at me like the sun shines out of my fucking asshole. And I know that's how she feels... because that's how she looks at Grey too.

Despite everything that has happened in Lilydale, she always smiles at me. But she should hate me. The bad things that happen to her are because of me. And now because of my actions, she'll never leave Lilydale. By giving away that two percent, I've signed everyone's death warrants.

Arthur wants people to believe they leave this place once they are *rehabilitated.* But the truth is most people vanish downstairs. The rare exception when people do leave is because Arthur entices them with presents—blackmail in a pretty bow. He gets them on his side, doing a favor for their release—but there's always a catch. Even on the outside, you're never free of this place. You're still under his control, tied to him for life.

The ultimate goal was to get Lilydale shut down. If we overwhelmed the system, the courts would have no choice but to reevaluate everyone's sentences. One person trying to leave—easy for the federal prison system to handle. But trying to find spots for one hundred patients? Impossible.

By losing the contract, we would have forced Lilydale's financial hand. But it didn't dawn on me that signing away that two percent would be a mistake. It saved Avery initially—but at what cost?

I've just sentenced her to a lifetime of pain and suffering here. If that court order succeeds, there's enough funds in the trust to sustain the facility for the foreseeable future. They could easily replace the equipment, securing the continuance of the contract.

We will be overpowered, and eventually, it will just be a matter of time before they resume their activities. We can protect everyone, but not indefinitely. They will corner us somehow, starting with low-risk patients. Our focus will shift, and they will attack.

And it's all my fault.

I never make mistakes like that. I didn't stop and fully consider the consequences—I was determined to bring Avery back. And it sickens me that part of that reason was to continue tormenting her and having her under my control.

It all leads back to those gray eyes that are still staring at me with way too much emotion. I don't deserve it.

I don't deserve her.

"Damon..." she repeats, voice breaking slightly.

I cup her face in my hands, pulling back slightly to look at her. She relaxes in my grip, the guilt eating at me even more.

"It's fine," I mutter. "You're okay."

She frowns, clearly puzzled by my words. I want to reassure her, but the words get stuck on the tip of my tongue. I know I need to tell everyone about what happened, especially Grey, but a part of me is afraid. What if I tell her and she never looks at me like this again? I want to savor the moment for as long as possible before I'm the big, bad monster again.

"What happened?" she asks softly, resting her hands over mine on her face.

"My father happened," I hiss quietly, as if the familial tie is poison. "I fucked up."

Avery tilts her head slightly, her right cheek pushing into my hand. "What do you mean?"

I sigh, closing my eyes. "He's going to get access to the funds. Once he does, there's nothing to stop them from coming at us again."

"We knew this was a possibility," she defends. "We will sort it out."

Shaking my head, I open my eyes, letting her see how serious this is. "He is only able to do this because I gave him the power to do so."

I relax my hands on her face, giving her the opportunity to move away if she wants. She doesn't—her hands squeezing mine, holding them in place.

"Power?"

"The deal I cut with him for your return," I tell her, unable to stop the anger in my tone. "I gave him a percentage of my shares in Lilydale. It wasn't much—but enough to give him the ability to pull stunts like this."

Avery lets go of my hands as I anticipated, and I ignore the pain in my chest. I knew she'd see me for the mess I am eventually.

But her hands are suddenly on *my* cheeks, forcing me to face her.

"You did the best you could in a bad situation. We couldn't have anticipated that they would do this—you saved me. Both times, actually. And that counts for something."

Oh, my little innocent lamb.

If only you realized.

Leaving her hands on my face, I grab her waist, running my palms down the curve of her body. She shivers underneath my touch, sending an electric shock straight to my cock.

She's so soft and warm, and despite wanting to disagree with her, I simply fall victim to my selfish needs again. I kiss her, this time more slowly but with the same heat and intensity as before.

It's the least I can do. I can't turn back time, I can't change what I did. But I can change this. I can stop shoving her away to prove something to myself.

My strength is fading fast, and for once, I just want to forget—to give into the all-consuming thoughts that revolve around her.

I don't know what's going to happen. And I'm fucked beyond reason because I can't control the outcome. But I can control this at least.

We match energy, tongues dancing, and when I slow mine, dragging it teasingly along hers, she moans, hips jerking into me.

And fucking hell she feels good.

My hand skates along her thigh, caressing the inside of her leg until I reach the center of her shorts. Slipping inside the loose material past her thighs, my fingers brush against her underwear. When I feel her arousal starting to seep through the fabric, something snaps.

I grab the side of her underwear, ripping it aside forcefully. Avery lets out a gasp into my mouth as my finger wastes no time in running along her wet slit. I cup her pussy with my palm, pressing my middle finger in until it slides into her warmth. She's already wet, just from kissing me, and I store that knowledge away to reflect on later when she no doubt runs from me.

My finger glides in and out of her, feeling her clench around me. It's not enough for either of us, so I add another one while my thumb finds her clit. I draw circles around it, thrusting my fingers rhythmically into her eager body as she rolls her hips with need.

"Damon..." she moans, and I hear myself growl, dragging my teeth along her bottom lip.

I need to see her, reluctantly pulling my face back. Avery's lips are kiss-bruised, swollen and pink, while her eyes appear hazy. But she's looking right back at me, lips parted as she pants softly.

"Show me," I say, curling my fingers inside of her. "Show me what you look like when you come. I want to make you come so hard that it will ruin your life in the best fucking way possible."

Her breath hitches at my words, eyes widening slightly. There's a glint in them, her lip curving into a smile even as she struggles to breathe properly.

"You've already ruined me," she murmurs.

"Then what's one more bit of destruction?" I press harder into her body, dragging my thumb over her clit.

She squeezes hard around me, almost stopping me from withdrawing, like her body can't bear the idea of my fingers leaving. My head dips to the side, lips locking onto her neck as I suck and lick the soft skin. The combination sends her over the edge, a whimper breaking free as she shudders, hips pushing down as she rides the high, moaning my name.

Our hips grind together, my cock threatening to bust through the dull gray material. I'm frustrated at the clothing between us, wanting to feel her naked body against mine. But it's not the time. I don't deserve it yet. Making her come was the most rewarding prize anyway, and I treat myself to a taste.

Bringing my hand up to my lips, I lock eyes with her, popping my fingers into my mouth. Avery's eyes flash with heat and when she leans forward to grip my wrist, I nearly turn feral as she encloses her mouth around my finger.

My hand shoots forward, grabbing her throat to hold her in place as she sucks my finger. She stills, but the lustful look doesn't disappear. I strum my fingers along the side of her neck, a smirk pulling on my face at the pretty red marks that decorate her throat now. I take pleasure in that alone, as if she's now my proud trophy—a *fuck you* to the system that's tried hard to keep us apart and destroy my life.

"Are you scared?" I ask her, applying more pressure.

She shakes her head slightly. "No," she breathes out in a staggered effort.

"I should tell you to run," I reply. "But I fear I'd just chase you now."

Slowly, I let go of her throat, watching as she takes deep breaths to calm herself back from the post-climatic high.

We stay like this for a few more minutes, until I notice that her legs are starting to cramp. I help lift her off my lap, shifting her over to the bed. She stretches out her legs, leaning against the wall.

Her face glows, eyes unfocused as we sit in silence. I think we both realize that we've now crossed the line and there's no going back. Not that I want to—I can't.

Having her light here is what's keeping me grounded in the dark. I was so close to letting myself fall after speaking to my father, but she pulled me back from the brink.

She's the reason I have to stay strong. I can't let her down—or Grey, or Byrone, any of the society members... hell, even Theo fucking Ashwood.

I promised my father a painful death and I intend to keep that promise. And if he gets that judge to grant his request, it just means we need to find another way to shut down Lilydale.

This place is a mockery of my mother's life and death. I'm going to destroy it, so that her true legacy can live on.

I'm not going to stop until we're all free.

Chapter 29

Avery

Toward the end of free time we meet up with Grey in the library. He fills us in on his day, and to be honest, I didn't even realize the new guy was an issue and on our radar. But Damon and Grey rarely miss things.

While telling us about Rian's unfortunate incident in the bathrooms, I spot Grey's eyes darting down to my neck. He doesn't comment on it, but the frequent glances set alarm bells off in my mind. I haven't checked myself in a mirror since we left Damon's room, but my mind is a whirlwind of flashbacks—his mouth on my neck as he made me explode.

It dawns on me that I might have marks on me, but for once, Grey doesn't appear bothered by it. If anything... he seems *amused?*

Even though I don't want to get my hopes up, I'm starting to believe his text message was exactly as it seemed—a green light. I practically tortured myself searching for answers and hidden meanings, scared to hurt him. But it was loud and clear as day.

I don't know what has changed for him, but judging by the way he looks at me, it's not his feelings. That's a relief because I don't ever want to lose him. Maybe I'm a little fucked up for liking multiple people, but I can't fight how I really feel. If Theo's sister's story has taught me anything, it's that being untrue to yourself can be damaging. I was already lost before I came here, and for the first time in my life, I feel like I belong. I don't want to lose that.

Because dare I say it... I'm actually starting to *like* myself. No longer does my father's voice live in my head, feeding me toxic thoughts about my existence. It's been replaced by my own words, fueled by the attention and affection from these men in my life. As much as I struggled with it, I've come to the realization now that I can't be as horrible as people made me out to be because look at how many people care. And that number far outweighs any measurement my father had.

"So, all we know at this stage is Arthur is keeping tabs on Vivian," Damon says. "That's interesting."

"How so?" I ask, swallowing as I turn my attention away from Grey. I can feel my cheeks heating up under his careful gaze, but I do my best to act somewhat normal and com-posed.

Honestly, I'm falling apart inside.

In a good way.

What happened between us? One minute we were talking, then the next Damon was kissing me. If I thought the kiss downstairs in the morgue was the limit to how mind-blow-ing it could be, I was very much mistaken. That was just a warm-up. The intensity between us in his room is still mak-ing my head spin. It feels like his walls have finally come down and I can see the real Damon.

"Arthur has his attention on Vivian rather than you," Grey answers. "Or, at least, that's what he's wanting us to believe."

"He'd have to know we'd go after Thatcher," Damon adds. "It could be a setup to distract us."

Grey nods in agreement. "I'll instruct Leighton and Andy to continue to watch her."

"We need to protect her," I interject firmly. "She's acting fine, but I know it's probably a disguise."

The two men look at me with sympathetic expressions. If anyone knows and understands what's potentially going on in Vivian's head, it's me.

I hate that we're somewhat bonded by our experience. After all she did to torment me with Sam, leaking my private file to humiliate me, we're now tied together. Seeing her downstairs was the lifeline I needed to fight back. Dr. West had tried to use her as leverage; to convince me I was safe under their care, but I saw it for what it was. And it made me fight back harder. I wanted to protect her, to save her from their torture.

"We'll make sure she's safe," Grey says to me with a soft smile. "And speaking of, I spoke to Theo today."

My heart skips a beat as I look at him with wide eyes. "How?"

"I went down to solitary confinement. We can't get inside the room, but I spoke to him through the door."

"Oh," I mutter, despondent. "Is he okay?"

"He wanted me to tell you that he loves you. And he'll try to message when he can. Apparently, the service is terrible down there."

I nod sadly. "Thank you. It makes me feel a little better that we can check on him."

"Just a few more days," he responds encouragingly, rubbing my arm with his knuckles.

We step forward at the same time, his arms pulling me into his side. Leaning my head against him, I look at Damon, offering a small smile.

"You should tell him," I say gently. "It will help if we're all on the same page."

He looks at me warily, probably trying to decipher what news I'm hinting for him to share. Obviously, I'm referring to his father and Whittingham, because I would bet money that Grey already knows that something happened between us thanks to the state of my neck.

"Alexander," he starts, an angry undertone to his voice as he refers to his father by name. "And Arthur. We've run into a bit of a situation."

Grey frowns but motions for him to continue. "Go on."

Damon takes a moment, letting out a frustrated sigh. "I should have told you when you asked, but the deal I cut for Avery's return was offering up a two percent share. He's now the majority stakeholder. Unfortunately, he's now able to make decisions without my permission. He and the board are filing an urgent court order to access the trust fund. The judge is his friend."

"So, he's going to get access," Grey mimics darkly. "He'll blow through the funds."

"I know," Damon agrees, annoyed. "The federal contract is at risk of being terminated if Lilydale doesn't replace the broken equipment. He'll be able to do it if he has access to the money."

Grey's arm tightens around me, almost as if he's trying to permanently attach me to his side at the mention of the experiments. "It just means we'll need to find another way to stop them."

"We might not be able to."

I scan Damon's face, spotting the guilt. I want to comfort him so badly, but I know right now, he'll be trying to focus on ideas.

"Of course we'll be able to," Grey replies confidently. "We will figure it out. We won't let those bastards win."

Damon opens his mouth to speak but the familiar sound signaling the end of free time cuts him off. He frowns, glancing over at me.

"Keep your cell on you. We'll charge them tomorrow, but for now, we'll regroup by text message. Grey's on watch duty tonight so he'll be close by."

"Ass duty," I correct playfully, unable to hide a grin as Grey reaches down and grabs me to emphasize his agreement.

I'm in line on my way back from the showers when I spot two guards walking toward our group, their faces tight with intent.

When our guard stops, we all pause behind him, watching as they whisper to each other. One of the guards looks down the line, my heart stopping when his eyes fall and stay on me.

"White!" I hear my name being called, our guard turning and pointing to me. "With them." He motions to the other guards, my throat seizing up as I slowly step out of line.

My fight-or-flight reflex is definitely kicking in, running through a hundred ways to potentially get out of another kidnapping. We had every single scenario covered—except for shower time because it seemed unlikely that I would be targeted due to being in a group full of witnesses.

I approach them hesitantly, quickly looking over my shoulder at the rest of the group. Maybe one of them can sound the alarm somehow, but there's no one in line close enough to Cirque des Morts.

What I wouldn't give to have Jillian in my group.

Before I rip my gaze back to the guards, I find Eliana's eyes, her soft features curling into a supportive smile.

Maybe... just maybe.

There's no time to return the gesture, my feet pausing as I stand in front of the guards.

"Mr. Whittingham would like a word," one says, jerking his head to the other end of the corridor.

They don't wait for a response, turning and walking with my arms in their rough grasp. I have no choice but to follow as they drag me along, taking deep breaths to calm myself.

A few minutes later, I find myself at the edge of Whittingham's desk, his cold, dead eyes boring into me.

It's fairly dark in here, only the light from his desk lamp and a lit citrus smelling candle casting any illumination. I nearly gag as I look carefully at the candle, spotting a picture of the receptionist taped on the glass candle holder—a gift from her apparently.

"Ms. White," he greets disinterestedly. "I trust you're doing well since your episode."

Unprecedented anger washes through me at his words. Just like how he announced my arrival back to the other patients, he's making me out to be the problem.

It's insulting. We both know what really happened downstairs, yet he pretends I'm a martyr to my mental health battles.

"You mean since you drugged me and threw me into the hands of doctors to torture?" I snap back. "I'm feeling peachy-fucking-fine."

He looks unfazed, shuffling some paperwork on his desk. "Well, needless to say, it appears their methods weren't very successful."

Okay, I was wrong. Pretending it didn't happen was bad enough, but to insinuate that I'm unfixable despite what I went through is a whole other level.

"I guess that's why those particular methods were largely banned in medical practice," I fire back. "But if you disagree, feel free to volunteer yourself."

His eyes snap up to mine, the hard exterior finally cracking.

I'm playing with fire—I shouldn't piss off the one person who could hurt me the most, but I can't seem to stop it.

Violent thoughts and images flash through my mind quickly, overwhelming me. My hands curl into fists, trembling as I try desperately to calm myself like Grey would be able to.

It's shaking again. The bucket is full, and I take two deep breaths, relaxing my shoulders as I picture Damon in my mind.

Control your emotions. Stay in control. Don't let him win by setting you off.

"I'm not the one who killed their father," Whittingham murmurs. "But I wouldn't expect rationality from someone like *you*."

Don't lose control, Avery.

"Someone like me?" I repeat, gob smacked. "Where the fuck do you get your audacity?"

"Do try to better yourself, Ms. White," he replies, ignoring me. "It's quite childish."

I shake my head, knuckles turning white. When I don't say anything further, he folds his arms, a sly smirk making its way onto his slimy face.

"You've been assigned duty for the next week. You and Ms. Kennedy will be assisting Dr. Elsher with administrative tasks."

All I can see is red, unable to piece together who my companion will be. Instead, I only focus on the fact that I'm being placed with Elsher. Even a second with him is a second too long.

He's the other monster in my nightmares. It wasn't just Whittingham that instigated my kidnapping, but the psychiatrist too.

It's clear this is retaliation for being switched back to Dr. Smith's patient list, and no doubt my last encounter with Elsher where I fought back against his snarky remarks.

They are separating us.

First, they took Theo, sending him to solitary confinement for a week. Then, Alexander dug his claws into Damon. Now, they are coming after me, forcing me to be on duty, away from the guys every day, with one of the people who helped to kidnap me.

Damon and Grey were right—they are going to make a move soon.

Is this that time? Am I going to be taken right now? Tomorrow?

I can't do it again. I can't go through that a second time.

I can't.

I can't.

I can't fucking do it. I won't!

My hand moves on its own, swinging out at the items on his desk before I can realize what is happening. The stationery canister and candle go flying, and for a handful of seconds, both of us stare in shock and disbelief as a piece of paper catches alight.

Whittingham is the first to react, grabbing a jacket from the coat rack in the corner and slapping it over the small flame to fan it out. It quickly extinguishes, but the sight of fire brings new memories to the surface. I stand frozen, no longer seeing him behind the desk, but my empty bedroom as flames lick the doorway, blocking an escape that I don't want.

Somewhere below the roar of the fire, I can hear my father's voice, screaming.

Hands grab me roughly from behind, snapping me out of my trance. I jolt, swinging my head to find the guard holding onto me. I'm back in the present, eyes turning back to Whittingham as he glares angrily at me, face red.

"Consider yourself lucky, Ms. White! Fortunately for you, solitary confinement is currently occupied. Otherwise, I'd be sending you down there right this second."

Chapter 30

Avery

Oh, shit.

Shit, oh shit. Fuck.

I pace my room when I get back, adrenaline spiking.

I lost control in Whittingham's office—exactly what I said I wouldn't do. My body reacted on its own, spiraling because of his words and threats.

It feels like everything is starting to fall apart again—too soon. I had just started to feel almost normal after what happened downstairs, feeling happy because the connection I have with Theo, Grey, and Damon supersedes everything else. They make me feel safe... seen. But like every other villain in my life, Whittingham took that away from me.

Everyone takes and takes—always using me.

Except them.

The ones that are painted as villains by society.

It makes no sense, but the world rarely does. All I know is that I'd give my life to protect them. They already have my mind, body, and soul—they could take my life and I'd ask *'was it good for you too?'*

My feet stop moving as I stand in the middle of my bland room. Inhaling, I reach under my mattress for my cell, flipping it open.

Tears well up in my eyes when I see I have an unread text message from Theo, my fingers quickly hitting the keys to open it.

Theo: It's boring down here without you. Grey better have passed on my message otherwise I'll pin him down and tattoo your name across his forehead.

Laughing, a tear falls down my cheek. I quickly swipe it away, punching out a reply.

Avery: He's safe for now then. I love you too. Are you okay?

After I hit send, I decide I need to text Damon and let him know what happened. There's going to be some fallout from it that we need to prepare for. Or maybe there were warning signs there that I've missed that Damon can pull apart and examine.

I sit on the edge of the bed, leaning on my knees as I gather my thoughts. It's important that I jot it all down, but my mind is still frazzled by the events that I can barely think straight.

The whole thing only happened fifteen minutes ago, but it feels like a fever dream—bits are hazy and disorientated, while other parts are burned into my mind.

Avery: I got dragged to Whittingham's office after showers. Been assigned duty with Elsher for a week. He provoked me and I snapped... accidentally set his desk on fire. He said it's lucky Theo is in solitary confinement otherwise I'd be dragged there.

As I sit and wait for his reply, I listen to my shaky breaths. Hopefully I covered everything. No doubt I'll have to relay all this again tomorrow in person, but at least he knows what happened for now.

It's been dark for quite a while, so I assume Grey should be lurking the hallways soon. The thought brings a little comfort, but also a weight of sadness. He's so close, yet so far away.

I fucking hate this place.

The cell vibrates in my hand with a reply, and I quickly glance at it.

Damon: Fucking asshole is testing my patience. I'm with Grey—I'll fill him in. If that happens again, call me.

I curse myself. The one time I didn't take the cell with me because I was in the shower and this happens. He's right though—I need to keep it on me so I can contact them to listen. That damn cell is coming with me to Elsher's office. I don't trust him one bit.

Avery: I know, I'm sorry. I didn't take it to the showers because I thought I'd be safe.

His reply comes back quickly, and for the first time since my encounter with Whittingham, I forget about it for a second.

Damon: I'm picturing your naked body now.

The small gasp that falls from my mouth startles me. I re-read the simple sentence four more times until I compose myself enough to write back.

Avery: At least you got to feel it today.

Damon: Not enough though.

My mouth curves into a smile at the playful response. If I'm being honest, it wasn't enough for me either. I wasn't lying when I said he'd ruined my life—they all have.

But in the ruins, they are rebuilding me into something stronger. The old Avery is dead—she perished in the fire. And for a while, my ghost haunted these walls, going through the motions of each day, never really understanding how or when things got so bad.

Piece by piece, they put me back together. My flaws are no longer diminishing—they are loved and accepted. The parts of me I hated, I've grown to adapt.

And best of all, I finally forgive myself.

To the rest of the world, I was broken, and I blamed myself for it. I deserved the pain and agony, settled for less than what I needed to truly survive. But I forgive myself for it all. I'm not the person they painted me as. I forgive myself for taking all the abuse and hating myself when I should have pointed my finger at the true culprits.

Avery: It will never be enough. More is always better.

I sit and stare at the cell, waiting for a reply—but nothing comes. Minutes continue to tick by, the light in the room fading as the moon settles overhead casting shadows on the walls and plunging me into darkness. Eventually, I give up and decide to chase sleep, curling up into bed with the cell by my head.

Sleep doesn't come and I keep replaying things in my mind. But I'm somewhat settled and at peace. The shock and adrenaline from earlier have faded. The earlier texts from Theo and Damon have thankfully calmed me, and I know

Grey is outside in full guard dog mode. Everything is okay for tonight... We will sort it out tomorrow. All we can do at the moment is take it one day at a time, and we survived today.

That's enough.

There's a quiet rhythmic echo outside the door, so faint that it could be the pipes or guards doing their rounds. When my cell vibrates next to my head, I hastily grab it to make sure everything is okay. It's probably Grey texting since there's not much else to do while on ass duty.

Opening the inbox, I'm surprised to find it's not Grey, but Damon.

Damon: *Are you awake?*

I laugh to myself, more sarcastically than anything since sleep seems to be missing in action.

Avery: *Not by a long shot.*

His reply comes quickly—just one word.

Damon: *Good.*

My brows furrow in confusion as I sit up in bed. Maybe there's an emergency meeting or more updates that can't wait until morning.

Before I can start writing back, the cell buzzes again.

Damon: *I want you to do something for me.*

Instantly, more messages come through, one after the other.

Damon: *In about twenty seconds, I'm going to unlock your door.*

Damon: *We're going to play a game.*

Damon: *You run.*

Damon: *I catch you.*

My eyes widen as I read the chain of messages, heart beginning to race. The sound outside grows louder before... silence.

Click.

I jolt my head up as my door creaks open an inch. Slowly, I stand, crossing the room to pull it open.

The corridor is dark except for sections of patchy moonlight. As I step outside the room, I look right toward the direction of the library, squinting my eyes. When I'm positive there's nothing there, I look to my left.

At first, I see nothing there, but a faint glint catches my attention, and I do a double take. There, in the dark at the end of the corridor, a figure stands, hidden in the shadows.

My heart starts beating so rapidly in my chest that I'm almost certain I can hear it echo around me.

I tense up, staring at the figure with uncertainty. They take a step forward into a shard of moonlight and I finally see their face.

Hard red and black, twisted features... *Devilish.* I recognize it immediately—the *Cirque des Morts* signature mask and black attire. It's the exact same getup that Damon wore when he rescued me.

The. Exact. Same.

My hand squeezes the cell in my palm, reminding me of his messages as heat rushes through my entire body.

Just one word comes to mind... the one instruction he gave.

Run.

As if reading my mind, he takes a step toward me, forcing my body to spring into action. I turn and take off down the corridor, the sound of footsteps quickly following behind.

I have no idea where to go. In the dark, I can barely see anything. I've grown uncomfortably familiar with the layout of Lilydale, but in the dark, it might as well be a maze.

My first instinct is to run into the library, wondering if I can barricade the door like Grey did. I dismiss it quickly because I wouldn't be fast enough—plus it's too *obvious*.

Instead, I turn right, slamming open the doors to the hall. I keep running to the end, pushing my way into the empty kitchen.

It's eerily quiet, sounds distorted by the stainless appliances and countertops. Faint light reflects off silver, the smell of antibacterial spray still lingering in the air from the end of day cleanup.

Ducking behind a counter, I crouch low, holding my breath as slow approaching footsteps make their way toward the kitchen.

There's a small gap under the counter and through it, I see the door swing open deliberately slow, revealing a pair of black sweatpants.

Even though my heart is racing, there's no fear—I feel safe.

And... I want him to catch me.

As he walks around the kitchen, I quietly move forward, sneaking to the other side. His footsteps pause, body hidden from view by metal countertops.

I can feel the electricity in the air—the two of us trying to seek the other out. I can *almost* sense where he is, but then the air suddenly goes dead still.

There's nothing but silence, not even the faint echo of footsteps or the sound of breathing.

I don't dare move, my hand gripping a support bar underneath the countertop to steady my crouched body.

Has he even moved yet? I can't hear anything at all. It's almost as if he's not even in the room anymore...

Suddenly, there's a flash of movement in my peripheral vision before a hand wraps around my ankle, taking my footing out from underneath me. I let out a small scream, back hitting the cold tiles as I'm dragged across the kitchen floor.

A body moves over mine, hands slamming onto the ground next to my head as he looms over me and boxes me in.

My eyes scan over the mask, staring into the black eyes as my chest rises rapidly with heavy breaths.

His right hand lifts, stroking the side of my face with his knuckles before dipping lower. Fingers dance along my neck, grasping it as I let out a small gasp of surprise.

"Found you," he murmurs, his low voice almost a growl.

Reaching out with shaky hands, I grab the bottom of the mask. He doesn't try to stop me, and I push it all the way up, Damon's heated green eyes staring directly back at me.

I lift my head, pressing into his hand. His fingers tighten around my neck as he brings me forward, our mouths meeting in a frenzied kiss.

Shoving the mask all the way off, it lands with a clatter on the floor as I wrap my arms around his neck. His tongue seeks out mine, the two smashing against each other as I moan quietly into his mouth.

The pressure disappears from my neck, his hands snaking around my back as he shifts back into a kneel, bringing me off the floor with him. Holding onto me tight, I'm hoisted off the floor as he stands, my legs wrapping around his waist.

Damon slides me onto the edge of the counter, pushing my legs apart to stand in between them. His lips move from my mouth, kissing along my jawline, down to my neck.

Every inch of skin he touches feels like fire in my abdomen. It feels like I'm free falling with nothing to catch me but him.

His hands push under my shirt, firmly sliding up my waist. I reach down and grab the bunched-up material, flinging it over my head and dropping it on the floor. Damon pauses his movements, taking a moment to stare at my bare chest.

"Fucking perfect," he murmurs, dragging a finger down my sternum.

I shiver slightly from his touch, nipples hardening as he draws a lazy circle around one.

We're both watching his curious fingers move over my skin, his thumb brushing over the pink peak. He trails further down until he finds the waistband of my shorts, hooking his hands under as he starts pushing them over my hips.

I flatten my hands on the cold metal underneath me, lifting myself so he can slide my shorts and underwear down my legs. My ass barely comes back down onto the countertop when his hands shove my thighs further apart, putting my entire body on display for him.

Damon's eyes fall straight to my pussy, heat flashing through them as he takes in the sight of me. "I've been thinking about *this* all afternoon," he admits, one hand gripping my thigh while the other traces the pathway toward my clit.

Words get caught in my throat as I stare at him in a daze. He drops to his knees in front of me, head level with my pelvis as he uses his thumbs to open me wider.

It feels like I might die when he looks up at me, the two of us locking eyes as his tongue swipes out to glide over my clit. I jolt forward, back hunching over slightly, as my hand rests on the back of his head for stability as he covers me with his mouth, sucking my clit then replacing it with the tip of his tongue.

I can't look away—mesmerized by the sight of him gazing up from his knees while his mouth is glued to me.

Finally, he pulls back, brushing his thumb over the scar on my thigh—the markings left behind from Grey claiming me.

"Mine," he reads, tracing the scarred letters, but it feels more personal, like he's making his own statement.

"I want to see you," I tell him with an edge of desperation, tugging on his hoodie.

Damon stands, a smile visible on his face as he quickly disposes of the hoodie revealing his bare torso underneath. Hard, toned muscles ripple under my touch when my fingers reach out to stroke him.

I slide off the counter, my feet barely hitting the floor before my hands are tugging on the drawstring of his sweatpants. He lets me take the lead, glancing down as my hands grab the top of his sweatpants, pushing them to the floor. There's nothing underneath, my stomach twisting in knots at the realization that this was definitely planned. If it wasn't obvious in his messages, it is now.

He kicks his discarded sweatpants to the side, but my eyes are focused on only one thing. Damon grabs my hand, guiding it to the center of my attention, my fingers wrapping around his hard cock.

"Touch me, Avery," he growls, words sounding more like an order than a plea.

I swallow hard, cheeks a hot shade of pink as I stroke my hand along his length. He's as thick and long as Grey and Theo, my breath catching as I watch him shudder under my touch.

To be able to make him react like that, to watch his face twist in pleasure, it's an intoxicating feeling that I want to drown in.

My confidence grows as I move faster, my hand gripping him firmly—but I can't stop watching his face. His eyes are closed, face full of pleasure but it looks like he's trying to control himself, to let me have this moment and be in charge.

Him. The Circus of the Dead's controlling, emotionless leader.

And now he's mine.

To know that he trusts me enough to do this, to hand over control—it means everything.

Dropping to my knees, I pull my eyes away from his face, gazing in awe at his cock in front of me. I feel his eyes on me, but I don't look up, instead leaning forward to run my tongue along the tip.

"Fuck," he hisses under his breath, hands shooting out to grab my head. There's no pressure though, he waits for me to sink him into my mouth at my own pace, a moan vibrating against his length as I taste him.

I feel his fingers dig into my scalp, hips jerking slightly on their own as my lips drag along his skin. I'm going deliberately slow—for my benefit—to take my time getting to know this part of him. But I can sense his control is nearing breaking point.

When my tongue slides along the bottom of his shaft, he lets out a growl, suddenly stepping back so he falls out of my mouth. Hands tighten around my arms as I'm lifted from the floor, before I'm spun around and bent over the countertop.

I let out a gasp as the cold metal presses against my skin, nipples hardening even more. Behind me, Damon kicks my legs apart as his hand cups my pussy, sliding two fingers in.

There's no time to prepare as he starts fucking me with his fingers fast, cries spilling from my lips as pleasure shoots through my entire body.

Suddenly, his hands are gone from my body, a moan of protest being cut off as they are replaced by the tip of his cock. It's a difference of night and day, taking his time to enter me, inch by inch.

My body stretches around him, his cock sinking into my heat as my fingers attempt to grip the cool metal beneath me. When he bottoms out, he pauses, letting us both relish in the feel of our joined bodies.

Damon leans over me, his chest pressing into my back as he kisses my shoulder blades, brushing my hair aside. "I've waited so long to be inside you," he murmurs against my skin. "You feel even better than I imagined in my dreams."

He pulls back before I can reply, slamming his cock into me. I slide forward with a whimper, reaching an arm back to feel him. My hand rests on his waist as he thrusts into me, keeping my body boxed in against the countertop.

As his hips mold into mine, he grabs a fistful of my hair, ripping my head back. Lips find my neck, attacking my skin as he nips and sucks it into his mouth. He makes his way along my jaw, until he finally gets to my mouth, pressing his lips to mine.

I push my ass back in rhythm with him, his tongue forcefully shoving past my lips. Damon lets go of my hair, hand instead snaking around to grab the side of my face to hold me in place.

My body clenches around him, the sound of our skin slapping against each other echoing around the kitchen. I feel his other hand slide down my waist, curling around the front of my thighs until his index finger touches my clit.

Electricity shoots through my body, my back arching violently into him as he rubs my clit firmly.

My toes curl, feet pushing up as I stand on my tippy toes, shoving my ass back as much as possible to take him deeper. The pleasure continues to build, rolling through me intensely as I feel myself ready to crash.

"Come on me," he growls against my mouth. "I want to feel you again."

Even if I wanted to fight it, there's no way I would win. With three more deep thrusts, I fall over the edge, a scream ricocheting around the room as I shake beneath him. Damon slams into me a few more times, but my body squeezes him so tight that he joins me in the blissful high seconds later.

His face pushes into my neck, his low growl and curse vibrating against my skin as he stills, fingers pressing into me hard enough to leave marks.

I drop my head, the side of my face resting on the cool surface as the two of us breathe heavily, still joined together.

"*Maintenant tu es à moi aussi*," he whispers, placing kisses over my neck and jawline. I don't know what the words mean, but I do know one thing.

Now that I have him, I'm not letting him go.

Chapter 31

Damon

Fuck everything.

I no longer care about the personal consequences or retaliation from Arthur or my father.

Let them come for me.

In fact, I fucking *dare* them. Because right now, the only thing that matters is this feeling—this moment.

The sun is just starting to peak over the horizon, little whispers of light creeping into my room. The usual morning chill is non-existent, the blanket pushed down and resting low on my hips. Avery's warm naked body is curled up against me, her breathing steady as she sleeps soundly.

My arm is wrapped around her, fingers stroking her back as I stare at the ceiling. I'm not sure if I slept at all last night, but I feel more energized than ever before.

After we left the kitchen, I dragged her straight back here to the Westwood Wing before fucking her again—*and again.*

There was no way I was going to send her back to her room alone. Even if I stood outside her room all night, not being able to touch or see her would be torture. Plus, she deserves more than being made to sleep alone after what we did.

I saw red last night when she texted me, filling me in on Arthur's latest bullshit move. Grey was equally as mad, ready to go on the warpath and storm down to Arthur's office if I wanted him to. When I said no, he offered me something else, to my surprise.

"Switch places with me tonight. Go see her."

Neither of us needed to exchange more words after that, the silent conversation and meaning was loud and clear. After having her come on my hand yesterday, I knew we were past the point of no return. I couldn't hold back any longer. And apparently, that was obvious to Grey too.

It's still over an hour or so until the guards wake everyone for breakfast. I'm well aware that I'm about to set in motion a chain of events that may throw gasoline on the already burning fire. But I'm done with their bullshit and antics. Grey's right—we're going to find another solution to stop them. And in a few hours, word will spread about this.

A domino effect will ripple through Lilydale. Avery being in my room is not only a *fuck you* to Arthur's rules—it means more than that.

It means I've claimed her.

She was already untouchable before, tied to Grey and Ashwood, but now with my mark and protection, she's going to be on a pedestal beyond that. The other patients will respect it, but the staff... that's another ballgame.

I'm well aware that this also means putting a target on her back. They already went after her for the connection she had to Cirque des Morts. But knowing that she's now *mine?* My father will lose his shit. Arthur will be furious—they will want to hurt me. But I'll be perfectly fucking clear with everyone...

Touch her and I'll make your nightmares seem like a happy place. I'll burn everything and everyone without blinking.

They will beg for death because it will be the easy way out.

With my free hand, I reach for my cell, sending a text off to Grey. It's early but he'll be awake—best to prepare him so we can come up with a plan. The last thing we need is for him to be hit by surprise, even if he knows what I was doing last night. The guards will raise the alarm once they find her room empty and it's our opportunity to take a stand by escorting her out together.

A warning.

There's a coup coming and we're not afraid to spill blood.

The only stipulation I have is I'll be the one to kill my father. Grey can have Arthur if he pleases—I'll happily watch him tear Arthur limb from limb.

We exchange a few messages back and forth, agreeing to meet in the hallway before the guards arrive. It wouldn't be the first time they have seen us moving freely in the mornings, making a mockery of their security system. But this time, it's a statement.

"What are you doing?" Avery mumbles sleepily, eyes still closed as she rests her head on my shoulder.

I look away from the cell, glancing down at her relaxed frame. She's still wrapped around me, fitting into the edges of my body perfectly.

Smiling, I throw the cell to the end of the bed, discarding it entirely as I grab the blanket and pull it over our heads.

"You," I murmur, rolling over and straddling her.

By late morning, word has already spread like wildfire.

I can hear the heated whispers and feel the stares from the patients. I have no doubt the guards also reported back to Arthur after breakfast, so when Christopher corners me in the hallway while we're standing outside Markel's office waiting for Avery, I assume he's coming to make some snarky comment.

"I'm not interested in whatever you have to say," I tell him lazily before he can speak.

Christopher stops a few feet away, hands in his pockets. "I think you will be."

His eyes shift to Grey, before returning his attention back to me.

"Get on with it," Grey states, clearly already irritated by his presence as well.

My dear cousin half-rolls his eyes at the command, pulling something out of his pocket. He quickly shoves it into my chest and my hand darts up, catching his fingers and crunching them painfully before he can pull back.

But curiosity gets the better of me and I let him go, looking down at the plastic card in my hand.

"What the hell is this?" I ask him.

Grey straightens up with interest, unfolding his arms. His eyebrows are raised, likely thinking the same as me.

"It's the spare card to solitary confinement," Christopher murmurs low, confirming our suspicions. "I swiped it from Dorothea's drawer this morning on the way in. She's called out today."

I pass the card over my shoulder to Grey who quickly snatches it up, putting it in his pocket. "Why?"

"Get Theo out and come meet me in my office as soon as possible. She's written down the latest code with a sharpie on the back."

There's an urgency to his voice that triggers alarm bells. And instantly I know why.

"The order went through, didn't it?"

Christopher nods, face stern. "First thing this morning. I have a copy of it on my laptop."

I close my eyes for a second, taking a breath and practicing my usual *mediation* tactic—imagining my father in a pool of blood. It does the trick, and I open my eyes again, locking them with his.

"Grey," I say with a silent command, not taking my eyes off Christopher.

"On it," he replies, immediately taking off down the hallway.

When my eyes glance over at Markel's closed door, Christopher's face flashes with worry. "Wait here," he says, knocking on the door and cracking it open.

I can hear muffled words exchange before he closes the door, gesturing for me to follow him. Raising an eyebrow, I stay put. He pauses, looking back at me.

"Markel is going to bring her to my office himself. I told him she has a session immediately after he is finished with her."

"And you think I'm going to leave her alone with that old dingbat?" I question with a scoff. "Is he going to protect her against Arthur?"

"Arthur is out for lunch," Christopher snaps back. "*Celebrating* with your father. My office is less than thirty feet away. We'll leave the door open if you like."

I narrow my eyes on him, silently making a promise to kill Markel *and Christopher* if anything happens. I hold up my hand to his face, pulling my cell out with the other to text Byrone.

We could be three feet away with Arthur on the other side of the planet, and it still wouldn't be good enough for me.

Byrone and Leighton appear less than two minutes later, giving me a nod as I pass them on the way to Christopher's office. I give one last check to make sure they are in position in front of Markel's door before I step inside the office.

Christopher walks around to the other side of his desk, leaning over to type his password into his laptop. A few seconds later, the printer whirls to life in the corner, pieces of paper spitting out while we stand in silence.

He starts collating it, and I realize he's printed out multiple copies. Footsteps appear behind me and when I turn to look, I spot Grey with Theo close behind.

I give the latter a sharp nod, impressed that even in solitary confinement for days, he still looks kept together.

A bundle of documents is shoved into my chest grabbing my attention, and I start flicking through them as Christopher passes a copy each to the other two.

"I've had a quick glance over it," he says, stapling his own copy together and flicking through. "The order is on the front, and they have annexed the amended trust to the back."

"Fucking cunt," Grey mumbles, sitting down on one of the seats as he scans the document. "He got on that fast."

"Bribery," I confirm, eyes reading over the familiar trust clauses. It always made me laugh that even in death, my mother made sure to fuck over my father. She did her best to make sure he didn't get a single cent. As much as he wanted to contest it, he knew what that would look like publicly—so, locking me up was the next best thing. He got to play the concerned father, while being my only surviving legal guardian. The trust prohibited him from taking funds for himself, but I guess he finally found a loophole.

Theo holds his bundle up, brows pulling together. "Clearly, I've missed a few things."

"Apparently so," I murmur with playful mocking. He raises an eyebrow at me, Grey snorting with insider knowledge.

I probably shouldn't antagonize Theo—though I do want him to know I've been buried inside Avery multiple times the past fifteen hours. Not because I think he'll care, but because *I do.*

Christopher glances between the three of us, picking up on the undertone. Theo is right there with him, but he just shrugs, unfazed as he turns his attention back to the paper-work. "About time."

"Damon," Christopher warns.

"Don't start with me," I shoot back, voice dark. I know he already knows—everyone does. I'm in no mood to deal with his poor attempt at worry for Avery's sake or fucking witty remarks about *my feelings*.

He looks at the other two, shaking his head as he moves on with a sigh. "I wouldn't be surprised if Alexander has already started moving funds out."

"No doubt I'm buying them lunch right now," I grumble. "But at least we have a small window to figure out a plan. How did you even get this anyway?"

Grey looks up, eyes narrowing on Christopher suspicious-ly. We know that Alexander wouldn't just share this with anyone.

"Arthur accidentally forwarded the email from Alexander to the staff this morning," he says. "He recalled it, but I was up early going for a run before work, so I saved a copy of the PDF straight away."

"That's one hell of a Freudian slip," Grey scoffs, anger splashed across his face.

"Bastard does love to gloat," I confirm, skimming over the trust clauses. Everything is familiar, but it's been a while since I perused it. Suddenly, a section catches my atten-tion—one I remember but never paid any mind to.

My mother was thorough with things, always trying to cover every base possible. I frown, trying to work out if I've just found a potential solution.

"What is it?" Grey asks, noticing my face.

I look up at him. "Turn to page thirty-four, section sixteen."

The sound of paper fills the room as the others all follow, a silence falling over as they read the clause. Christopher looks up first, eyes slightly wide.

"You're kidding me..." he says in disbelief. "You can't possibly be considering that."

"What other choice do we have?" I retort. "We only have a small window of opportunity here."

My eyes dart over to Grey to assess his reaction. His face is scrunched up, clearly not thrilled at the idea, but considering it anyway.

"I don't love it," he admits. "But it might be our only shot."

"Theo," I say, turning my attention to him. "Thoughts?"

He glances up, face blank. I can tell he's surprised that I'm asking for his opinion, but this isn't a decision I can make on my own.

"I think we need to do whatever we need to do," he replies. "It's not infinite and seems like the only solution based on what Grey has told me."

I nod slowly, trying to work out logistics. "Christopher, we need you for this."

Asking him for cells and equipment is one thing, but *this*...

"I don't know," he murmurs. "The repercussions will be extreme."

"Either you fight with us, or you go down with the sinking ship," I shoot back heatedly. "Because you know as well as I do that once they start, it will be like trying to stop a boulder from rolling down a hill."

Christopher throws the paperwork down on his desk, running a hand over his face as he battles internal thoughts. "Alright," he says slowly. "I'll do it. But you realize once they get wind of this, I'll be out the door. I won't be able to protect any of you anymore."

"It's a risk we're going to have to take," I acknowledge, nodding toward a box on the floor. "Is that the surveillance equipment?"

He nods. "You're going to have a hell of a difficult time."

"We need to do it now," Grey says urgently. "While Teddy is out sick and Arthur is away from the building."

I walk over and pick up the box, giving Christopher a nod. "Get started on it. We'll do it tomorrow."

"Tomorrow is your birthday," he points out with uncertainty.

"Even more reason to do it—"

I'm cut off with the sound of approaching voices, the four of us falling silent just in time to see Avery appear in the doorway, flanked by Byrone and Leighton, with a confused Markel behind her.

"Hey..." she says suspiciously, looking around the room, her eyes lighting up when they find Theo.

Grey instantly snaps out of his mood, grinning as he slings an arm around her shoulders, walking her over to Theo. "Hey, little killer. Someone has missed you."

Chapter 32

Avery

I barely had time to catch up with Theo before the guards came looking for me.

It took every bit of willpower I had to not vomit on the floor at the thought of being near Elsher. The guys seemed nervous as well, but I heard them whisper something about keeping him occupied while Byrone sorted something out.

Despite Elsher's scowl and protests, Theo and Grey positioned themselves outside his door in the hallway, standing guard while I did my *duties*.

It turns out my companion for this week is Siobhan, her face confirming she's equally annoyed at being placed here.

Elsher has us sort out paperwork—much like Arthur did when I had my punishments with him. Except this time, it isn't confidential information or unnecessary copies.

Research papers depicting studies of mental health and treatment methods keep us occupied, and I spend the entire hour literally biting my tongue at the silent jab.

Thankfully, Siobhan seems oblivious—just more annoyed at having to be here.

We don't speak at all, just sort through the paperwork as quickly as possible while Elsher leers at us from his desk.

When our time is up, Grey and Theo walk in, glare at Elsher, and promptly escort both of us out. If Siobhan is confused by my entourage, she doesn't show it. If anything, she seems relieved to be getting away, giving me a small careless wave before disappearing into the hall while we wait to get taken to classes.

Grey sticks by my side the entire lesson, much to Charmaine's obvious appreciation that he's present for once. And when free time starts, I fly into Theo's arms in the library.

"Fuck, I was so worried about you," I grumble into his chest.

Theo's arms tighten around me as he laughs softly. "I think of it as a mini vacation. The only downside is being away from you."

The three of us sit at the table, and despite their heated stares on me, I can sense tension in the room. When they make no move to throw themselves at me, I finally snap, throwing up my hands in exasperation.

"What the hell is going on?" I ask.

It's clear something has happened behind the scenes. Damon has gone to deal with something, and I'm still suspicious as fuck that I found all of them in Dr. Smith's office. And as happy as I am to see Theo, there's no way Whittingham freed him early. Something is going down and I want answers.

"Alexander's judge friend passed the order," Grey answers calmly. "We're just trying to figure out what to do next."

I frown, heart sinking. "Oh," I mutter. "Shit—is Damon okay?"

Grey raises an eyebrow at me suggestively. "I don't know, little killer. *Is he okay?*"

My cheeks flush and I look away. I can feel them both staring at me, amused. I guess that answers the question about whether or not Grey would have a problem with my new *situation*.

"He was fine," I mumble, embarrassed. "I only assume you had a helping hand in it."

Grey laughs, grinning at Theo. "I bet you're so proud."

"That you finally listened to my advice?" Theo shoots back. "I was starting to think you were a lost cause."

The playful banter brings a smile to my face, and I look back, giving them both a gaze of appreciation. "Thank you."

"It will be good for him," Grey says quietly, scratching the table with his black nail. "And for you."

"Are you okay?" I ask, genuinely concerned.

He looks up, giving me a soft smile. "I'm more than okay," he says, reassuring me. "As long as I have you, everything is okay."

"I'm not going anywhere," I tell him, my voice full of promise. "I mean it," I add, looking at Theo.

Theo nods, smiling at me. "We know. But if either of these assholes give you grief, I make no apologies for my reaction."

"Hey," Grey interjects. "I could say the same about you."

"Whatever you say," Theo snorts. "Just remember who ripped Hallman's finger off for touching her."

"And *you* remember what happened to him after that," Grey snipes back. "Just disappeared into worm food—such a tragedy."

There's no sympathy in his tone at all, and my brows furrow, my thoughts returning to Vivian.

"Has anyone checked on Vivian the past few days?" I ask.

Grey gives me a grin, calming my nerves. "We're keeping an eye on her."

He doesn't elaborate on it further, his tone suggesting that something—or someone—else may be involved, but I don't push it.

The library door swings open, the three of us looking up as Damon strolls in.

"It's done," he says, and the other two nod.

"What's done?" I ask, confused.

Damon sits down on a spare chair, giving me an amused look. I'm perched in *his* usual chair—the *Cirque des Morts* throne. "Byrone, Jillian, Leighton, and Andy have set up the cameras. We're feeding the live stream back to our laptops. I have them watching the facility now. We also managed to hide one in Arthur's office."

"That's great," I remark, straightening up. "We'll be able to listen to his conversations. Might give us some leverage on how to stop them."

"Yes," Damon confirms. "Though we suspect they will be digging into the funds straight away."

"Will they bleed the fund dry?" I ask.

Damon shakes his head. "Not for a while. But I have no doubt my father will find ways to funnel money out for his own benefit now. We'll probably see Arthur later when he comes to gloat."

"Fuck him," I breathe out, the three of them glancing over at me with amusement. "I mean it. We're going to bring them down."

"We will," Grey agrees.

A vibration cuts us off, Damon digging into his pocket. He looks at his cell, frowning. "Well, fuck. That was not a development I expected."

"What is it?" Theo asks calmly.

He puts the cell on the table, eyes sliding over to mine. "We need to pay a visit to the morgue."

"Oh, my fucking God," I whisper, horrified.

I've come to accept that there are no lines that Whittingham or Alexander-fucking-Dale will cross. But this... this right here, is not one I could have predicted.

Judging by the expressions on their faces, nearly could Damon, Grey, or Theo.

"She really is fucking dead," Grey murmurs, slamming the cabinet door shut. "Huh—Go figure."

I stare at the closed metal door, eyes wide as images of her stricken face remain in my mind. "He had to have done this. But I thought he liked her..."

Dorothea's cold, rigid body is burned into my brain. When the guys said she was apparently out sick, I thought nothing of it. People take sick days all the time from their jobs. But when Damon got a text from Byrone, telling him that he overheard a guard on the live feed talking about the receptionist being found dead this morning, we needed to come check if that was true.

On the way here, the guys filled me in on how she was absent this morning and Dr. Smith had stolen the card for solitary confinement. It was odd, but gave them the perfect opportunity to get Theo out. Little did we know the truth.

She was here the whole time.

"Arthur doesn't like anyone but himself," Damon comments.

"Could he have really done this though?" I question, honestly terrified.

I've come to love all their darkness, accepting the fact that they have done bad things. But in hindsight, the bad things they did... it was all retribution—a fucked-up version of mental health vigilante shit.

But Whittingham... and maybe Damon's father... if they are capable of turning a blind eye to torture and death here, it probably shouldn't be that much of a surprise that they would kill too.

"Absolutely. He's a selfish pig," Grey points out. "She was probably getting too clingy or just collateral damage. He's too busy focusing on his plan with Alexander. She was likely in the way."

My thoughts go back to his office—the candle on his desk. "She gave him a gift with her face on it," I mutter, unsure how to feel. "I think I broke it though when I set his desk on fire."

Theo looks at me in pleasant surprise. I shrug back sheepishly at him. "It was a whole ass thing."

"Either way, we know he'll cross any line. That's why we have to hit back straight away," Damon interjects.

I let out a breath, shaking my head. I'm disgusted with Arthur. Even though I knew he was a conniving bastard, to hurt someone who obviously cared about him, it's *triggering*.

She was a bitch to me, but she was capable of love. And he used her—tossing her aside when she was no longer valuable to him.

They take. And take. And take.

My vision becomes a sea of red, and once again, before I realize I'm doing it, I'm flinging a metal tray full of medical utensils against the wall in anger.

Inside my head I'm screaming. I keep those in though, pacing the room with my hands on my head as the three of them watch me in concern.

"Aves?" Theo calls out, but I can barely hear him.

"All they do is *use* us," I spit out angrily. "They are revolting creatures. Why did she have to die? Why do they have to torture us?"

My voice is getting louder with each sentence, body shaking as I walk. Someone grabs me from behind, pulling me into a bear hug.

"It's okay," Grey's voice soothes. "We're not going to let them hurt you again."

I spin around, letting him see the frustrated tears that have built up in my eyes. "How can you be sure? Because if it's not me, it's you. They will come after you next. Or Theo, or Damon. Or someone else we love."

He grabs my face in his hands, leaning down close. "Breathe," he says softly. "I know this is a lot."

"I don't *want* to breathe!" I yell. "I want this to stop!"

In my mind, I see the water flooding out. And just like Dr. Smith predicted, I can't seem to stop it.

Suddenly, I feel trapped, like I'm suffocating. I gently shove Grey's chest, taking two steps back as I start throwing more things, smashing them into the wall. I can't seem to stop but I'm grabbed again, someone's warm back pressed up against me.

"Aves," Theo says from behind. "Focus on us."

I struggle, trying to get out of his grasp weakly, but he holds tight. Damon steps in front of me, green eyes scanning my face. He looks like he wants to say something, but he doesn't. Instead, his hand shoots out, wrapping around my throat.

The unexpected squeeze takes me by surprise. I freeze, snapping out of my thoughts to look at him properly.

When he realizes I'm back in the present, he nods at me. "There you are," he says, stroking my jaw with his thumb.

My chest heaves with shaky breaths, but I'm distracted by him. He steps closer, using his hand to tilt my neck back. Soft lips find mine, and it's like a switch on a radio. The chatter turns off, my body relaxing in between him and Theo as I kiss him back.

Damon pulls back, checking my face one more time before dropping to his knees. My lips part in shock as my legs threaten to buckle. It's one thing to be on his knees for me in the kitchen, but to do so in front of others—to show his surrender, his vulnerability at revealing his feelings—that means *something*.

He rips my skirt and underwear down my legs in one clean swoop. Dragging a finger along my slit, he looks up at me, voice firm.

"This belongs to us. And with that, it means we will protect you."

I let out a gasp when he slides a finger into my body, my head falling back onto Theo's chest. I feel Theo's arms tighten around me, holding me up as Damon pumps his finger in and out of my pussy.

"We protect what's ours," Damon murmurs, curling his finger. "Don't we, Grey?"

"That's right," Grey answers, stepping to my side. He grabs my face, turning my head to look at him, so that his lips can press into mine.

The three of them touch me at the same time, silently promising to keep me safe. Having all of their hands on me is blinding, my mind going blank as my heart races.

Theo pulls my shirt off, tossing it aside, followed by my bra. The cold air of the morgue sweeps over my body, but I can't feel it as six hands explore my body in unison.

Another finger slides into my warmth while a hand squeezes my breast. A set of lips press to my neck while Grey smashes his mouth to mine harder, swallowing my moans.

I'm not sure where I start and they begin, and my hands fumble as I try to touch them all. Through my hazy vision, I watch as they pull off their clothes, dumping them into a pile onto the floor.

My body flushes with need as I feel their cocks brushing against me, already hard. I grab Grey's first, wrapping my fist around his length as I pump him slowly, moaning into his mouth.

Damon's thumb brushes over my clit, his warm breath making me shiver before his mouth closes over it. My hips jolt toward him, pushing him closer into my body. His tongue swirls around my clit as his fingers slide eagerly into my body.

"We got you," Theo whispers into my ear, my hand reaching behind me to grab his cock that's pressed into my ass. He growls in response, tugging my nipple with his fingers.

"I need you all," I murmur into Grey's mouth. "Fuck—I need you, please."

A wordless conversation appears to pass between them, the three of them slowing their movements. Damon removes his fingers, and someone lifts me, gently lowering me onto him as he lays back on the ground.

My knees hit the cold floor as my hands fall onto his chest. Our eyes lock, Damon smiling at me as he reaches down between us. He grips his cock, positioning it at my entrance. I don't wait for him to move, slowly sinking down his length until I bottom out.

"Fuck," he growls, eyes flashing at me. "Your tight little cunt was made for us."

His hands grip my waist, holding on as I rock my hips back and forth.

"Yeah?" I say breathlessly, using my hands on his chest to steady myself. "Maybe you were made for me."

Something else flashes across his face, before he jerks his hips up, impaling me. He thrusts hard, bouncing me as he goes as deep as he can.

I feel a hand on my back, pushing me forward. I let it—laying flat against Damon as moans and cries spill from my lips.

Finally, he slows his movements, and I gasp when I feel a tongue on my ass. Damon holds me against his chest, restricting me from glancing behind to see who it is. But then Theo appears at my side, dropping to my level.

"Does his cock feel good?" he asks knowingly. "What about Grey's tongue?"

My pussy clenches around Damon's length in response, my head nodding as the man underneath me lets out a groan. Theo strokes my cheek before standing up, walking over to the cupboards and opening the doors. I'm too distracted by Damon and Grey to pay attention, but he finds whatever he is looking for, throwing something to Grey.

When he moves back from my ass, Damon takes control, thrusting into me again. I let out a cry, digging my nails into his pecs.

Something wet drops onto my ass, followed immediately by a finger massaging it in. The thrusting slows, but doesn't stop, as Grey pushes inside.

"Your ass is just as greedy," he muses, gently stretching me. "I can't wait to fuck it."

I gasp softly at his words, hips jerking at the new sensation. A small rush of panic hits me but he quickly reassures me.

"It's okay, little killer. I'll go slow—I'll stop anytime if you need."

His words comfort me, and I rock back into his hand, testing my limits. He groans as I take him deeper, before his hand squeezes my ass cheek.

"Fuck... you drive me crazy."

"Good thing we're in an asylum," I joke, rolling my hips. Damon growls underneath me, hands squeezing roughly.

Theo returns to my side, dropping to his knees. His eyes are watching Grey's movements, and when I feel his finger leave and the head of his cock push against my ass, Theo reaches between my thighs, finding my clit. He circles it with his finger, round and round, as Grey slowly inches into my ass.

I whine as he stretches me, laying my head flat on Damon's chest. Damon stays still, giving me a moment to adjust as Grey slides in—only a thin wall separating their cocks.

It's uncomfortable, but the feeling quickly subsides as Theo plays with my clit, my whole body clenching around Damon and Grey. And when I let out a loud moan, they both start moving.

Words can't describe it—the utmost feeling of being full while pressed between two bodies. They move in unison, like they always do as the perfect team, complimenting each other's pace.

My head feels foggy as I'm overwhelmed with pleasure, barely able to focus as they thrust into my body.

They move faster, changing rhythm so that one enters me while the other pulls back. Moans and cries spill from my lips in a heated mess, and I reach a hand toward Theo.

"You too," I manage to mumble, grabbing his cock.

His eyes darken even more, slowly removing his hand from between my legs to kneel closer. I lift my head as much as possible, pulling him into my mouth as I wrap my hand around the base. I hollow my cheeks as I suck, pumping my hand as I simultaneously bob my head.

"Look at you taking all of us," Theo murmurs with a groan. "You're fucking perfect, Aves."

"Yes, she is," Damon replies, slamming into me to emphasize his point.

My eyes lock onto Theo's hips, my hand letting go of his cock to drag my finger along the tattoo I placed on him.

This reminds me of that—a sensation that feels painful at first but quickly becomes pleasure. Like the tattoos Theo marked me with, or the cut on my thigh from Grey, it's overwhelming in the best way.

It's raw, unrestricted emotion and need. Enough to shatter my world and make me forget about the horrors that live behind closed doors.

My escape. A fulfillment.

My hips are pulled back slightly to make room as Grey pushes his arm between mine and Damon's bodies. His hand lands on my clit, fingers on either side as he rubs in time with his thrusts.

I moan against Theo's cock as my eyes roll into the back of my head and Grey squeezes my ass with his other hand. "Are you going to come for us, pretty girl?"

"She's clenching down on me so fucking tight," Damon growls, placing his hand on the back of my head. He pushes me forward, making me take Theo deeper into my throat.

Theo lets out a loud throaty groan at the sensation, jolting his hips as he slaps his hand over mine, pinning my fingers against my own name on his skin.

It's all too much—the feeling of all of them in me at once. Hands touch me everywhere while their cocks fill and stretch my body.

I can feel the tension building, higher and higher until it finally breaks free, exploding and shattering me into a million tiny pieces.

As the orgasm rips me apart, my scream is muffled by Theo's cock as I shake between them. Grey lets out a groan, slamming into me before he stills, his own climax hitting him just as hard.

Damon is next, his hand fisting my hair as he pushes me hard onto Theo, hips jerking my body up as he growls deep in his throat. I feel him release inside me and my nails dig into Theo, breaking the skin as I choke on his shaft. But I don't pull back, my lips pressing down hard around him, desperate for him to find his release too.

It doesn't take much more, a string of curse words falling from Theo's mouth as he squeezes my hand, leaning over as he spills into my mouth.

Before I can swallow, Damon grabs my throat, tilting my head back as his fingers dance along my skin. "Show us," he orders. "Open up."

I part my lips at his command, his green eyes flashing proudly. Grey pulls out of me and slides round to my side next to Theo, the three of them staring at Theo's release on my tongue.

"Now, swallow," Damon demands, my neck moving under his hand as I do so.

His thumb caresses my bottom lip as I close my mouth. I'm hit with a wave of exhaustion, my body buzzing as I fight the urge to close my eyes.

"Let's get you back upstairs," Grey says gently. "Before the guards find us naked in the morgue and I have to kill them for seeing your perfect, thoroughly-fucked body."

Chapter 33

Damon

"Well, if it isn't the biggest asshole I know. Happy Birthday."

I raise an eyebrow at Christopher, leaning against his door. "Did you get it done?" I ask sternly, ignoring his subpar wishes regarding my existence.

He nods, holding out a piece of paper. "Just need your signature and we're good to go. I got the other signature this morning."

I step inside the office, grabbing a pen off his desk as I snatch the paper from him. I glance over it, satisfied with the details and quickly sign before handing it back to him.

"And no one suspects anything?"

He shakes his head. "I hope you know what you're doing, Damon," he warns. "This could end badly—for all of us."

"I hope it ends in a massacre," I reply coolly, throwing the pen at him. "The best birthday present would be my father in a pool of blood."

Christopher shakes his head again in disapproval, shoving the signed document into an envelope. "Arthur is in early today. Be forewarned—he's in a good mood."

"I can't wait to ruin it," I answer, turning and walking out of his office. "File that straight away."

His reply is cut off by the door slamming shut behind me. The noise grabs the attention of the others, their faces tight as I head over.

Theo and Grey are stationed outside Elsher's office, standing guard while Avery does *duty* with him again.

"All sorted?" Grey asks casually.

Nodding, we glance down the corridor to see Christopher strolling out of his office with the envelope in hand. He gives us a curt nod as he passes, disappearing through the doors that lead to Arthur's office and the outside world.

And now the countdown begins.

I've spent the morning briefing everyone, preparing for the inevitable fallout that will occur once the news breaks. While Avery slept in Grey's room last night, I watched the recorded footage from our new cameras, listening to Arthur's phone calls yesterday. From them, I know my father is going to make an appearance today—anything to gloat in my face on the one day of the year that he knows he can fuck up.

It's also the same day that he murdered my mother. So, it seems poetically fitting that I ruin today for him just like he ruined my birthday for me.

She'd like this.

Sure, she'd scold me for being harsh, but it's a nice tribute. We can do it together, even beyond the grave. I love that she prepared for everything, like she knew this day would come.

She always knew what I needed before I did.

"Is everyone in place?" I ask, leaning against the wall next to them.

"Yep," Grey confirms. "Byrone and Jillian are watching the cameras and will text us. Everyone else is on standby, ready to go."

"Good."

The hour passes uneventfully, and when Avery emerges with a sneer plastered across her face, I resist the urge to go into Elsher's office and stab him in the throat.

Everything has to go according to plan today—even if that means leaving him in one piece... *for now.*

"God, he's a fucking asshole," Avery mumbles, stopping in front of us. She watches as Siobhan disappears around the corner before she relaxes, smiling at us.

"Want me to rip his intestines out of his ass?" Grey offers, only half-joking.

Avery laughs, the sound brightening my mood. She shakes her head. "Not at the moment. Too much mess."

A door closes to our left and we all look simultaneously as Christopher returns. He spots us still loitering in the hallway, pausing when he reaches our group.

"It's done," he says, holding the envelope out. "Happy Birthday."

"Wait," Avery gasps. "It's your birthday?"

I narrow my eyes at Christopher, who just laughs, continuing on his way like he doesn't care that he just dropped that bombshell.

"Fucking bastard," I mumble, turning to look at Avery.

She stares at me expectantly, until I finally cave, nodding once.

"Oh! Happy Birthday," she gushes, crashing into my chest.

We fall back into the wall, my arms wrapping around her as she squeezes me in a hug.

Grey cackles beside me, clearly amused by her enthusiasm. He knows how much I detest my birthday. I hate people making a big deal out of it. Except, if I'm being honest... I don't exactly hate *this*.

When she pulls back, her eyes fall onto the envelope in my hand, brows furrowing with interest. "What's that?"

"Just paperwork," I tell her, handing it off to Grey.

He grabs it, peeking inside for me. I wait until he gives me a nod, confirming that everything is set.

My cell vibrates in my pocket, and I fetch it out, opening the text from Jillian.

"Arthur is on the move," I say, kicking off from the wall. "Let's go."

The bell for lunch is about to sound at any second, and if Arthur is leaving his office, I can only surmise that he's coming to the hall to make some type of announcement—he's too predictable.

We head into the hall just as the bell goes, taking a seat at our table. My eyes stay glued to the door, watching as other patients file in, until I spot Arthur and his group of guards at the rear, carrying his portable podium.

Instantly, he glances over to our table, locking eyes with me. A smug smirk crosses his face, his back turning away as he directs the guards to set up.

"What do you think it is?" Avery asks.

None of us answer, the room falling silent as everyone watches the center of the room.

I know exactly what's coming—some pathetic excuse to gain sympathy and pretend today is a celebration.

Grey throws me a knowing look as Arthur steps up, and I feel my hands curl into fists under the table.

"Good afternoon, students," he starts happily. "Today is a great day for Lilydale."

Avery gives me a confused look, her face puzzled as she listens carefully.

"Today marks the anniversary of dear, sweet Lily Emerson-Dale's passing. Her legacy lives on in all of you. Her life was not wasted, this facility giving you all a second chance..."

He pauses for dramatic effect, though the other patients just stare blankly at him. Avery's head snaps toward me, her eyes wide as she processes the information. I don't look at her though—not trusting myself to stay calm if I see the empathy and pity in her eyes.

Arthur clears his throat, unfazed by the lack of reaction. "To commemorate, we have been working hard with our team of professionals, and I am pleased to announce that we will be trialing new therapy alternatives."

My spine stiffens as my knuckles turn white. Next to me, Avery tenses up as his words sink in.

"That fucking cunt," Grey whispers angrily, reaching for Avery's leg under the table.

"As an initiative and a show of good faith, we will be offering a reduction on your sentences here for anyone who voluntarily opts in to join the trial. All we need is your signed consent and upon completion of the trial, we anticipate you'll be in a position to leave Lilydale."

There's chatter through the hall as his words finally spark interest in the patients. Avery's head whips around, and even without looking, I know she's seeking out Capello.

I can hear her breathing get deeper as she tries to calm herself, Grey leaning over to whisper into her ear.

"Dr. Elsher will be in his office during your free time," Arthur states loudly. "If you are interested, please make your way there. We are canceling classes today and extending free time which starts now in honor of Lily. The guards will be there to assist with queues. Thank you."

He steps down, throwing one final glance back at me before slinking out of the hall.

When he's out of sight, noise erupts as people talk, excited about the prospect of getting out of here.

"He's going to send them out of here in body bags," Avery snaps quietly. "We have to do something."

"I need to go speak to him," I say, standing up.

Avery's hand swings out, grabbing my wrist. "Damon..." she starts, voice laced with pain.

"Don't, Avery," I murmur, not trusting myself. I'll snap if she looks at me with those pitying eyes. "It's fine."

She hesitates, not letting me go. "I'll come with you. Or Grey," she states, turning to him for support.

Grey reaches out, gently prying her hand back from me. "We've got this under control, little killer. Trust us." He squeezes her hand, entwining their fingers as he gives me a nod.

I take off after Arthur, tapping my pocket to check for the envelope. He vanishes through the door at the end of the corridor, my eyes narrowing on the line of people against the wall waiting to enter Elsher's office.

They are going to sign their own death warrants and don't even realize.

He knows I can't protect them all at once, particularly if they go willingly. I didn't see this coming, but that's okay—they won't see me coming either.

The guard at the end of the corridor steps aside as I approach, clearing the path for me.

"Open the door," I demand.

He quickly swipes his card, punching in my mother's birthday before swinging it open. I cross the threshold of the entrance, passing Dorothea's empty desk, and slam open Arthur's door with my palm.

It bounces off the wall, the two men turning casually to look as if they expected my arrival.

"You're too predictable, Damon," my father sighs with disappointment from his place behind the desk. He's sitting in Arthur's chair while the other man leans against the wall, watching on with a smug smile that I can't wait to wipe off his face.

"Then you should know what's coming next," I taunt. "But I bet you don't because your heads are too far up each other's asses."

My father taps his fingers on the edge of the desk, disinterested. "The order passed yesterday. It's over, Damon."

"It's not over until I say it's over," I retort, glancing between the two of them. "You might have the patients fooled but that order isn't worth the paper it is written on now."

His eyes narrow at me. "What are you talking about?"

I reach into my pocket, pulling out my ammunition. I unfold the envelope, digging inside for the paper. "Mom really did cover all the bases because she knew what a slimy, manipulative bastard you are. And thanks to your recent stunt, it worked out perfectly. So, who's the predictable one now, Father?"

Stepping forward, I slam the paper down in front of him, watching his face harden as he reads it.

"What is this?" he hisses angrily, glaring at me.

"Consider yourself dethroned as the majority shareholder," I answer, throwing a smirk at Arthur for good measure. "You might have the patients for your experiments, but we're filing an injunction as we speak to block your order. And I don't need to bribe judges to pass it—the merit is there. I'm the majority shareholder now, and according to this, I'm also currently in a *lucid state of mind* to make decisions. Good luck funding the equipment now."

Arthur steps forward, reading the document over my father's shoulder with an angry face. "It doesn't matter," he says quickly. "Now that we have the patients, the contract will remain in force. They will be willing to fund the equipment repairs themselves since it will be worth their while."

"Maybe so," I agree. "But the patients trust me a hell of a lot more than they do you. Once word spreads about the true nature and intentions of your little experiments, they will run. And you can't lock them into the contract. If you agree they have consent to sign, then they have consent to withdraw."

The two of them fall silent, veins bulging on the side of their heads as they radiate anger.

Checkmate, indeed.

I reach forward, snatching the paper off the desk and securely placing it back into my pocket. "Your castle is crumbling, Father. Brick by brick I'm bringing it down. And eventually, in the near future, I'll be free from your prison. You better believe I'll be coming for you."

Turning, I stroll out of the office with a shit-eating smirk.

It's not quite the birthday present I had hoped for, but it's a pretty damn good second place.

I find everyone in the library, gathered around Jillian's laptop.

They look up when I enter, grins breaking across their faces. Avery dashes over first, engulfing me in a hug.

I wrap my arms back around her, resting my chin on the top of her head, glaring at the stunned reactions of the rest of the group. They turn away awkwardly, pretending not to notice.

"We heard you on the live feed," Avery says, pulling back with a bright smile. "You were amazing."

Unable to stop myself, I tip her chin up with my finger, pressing my lips to hers. She kisses me back, and when I feel eyes on me again, I open mine and glare at everyone behind her while pushing my tongue into her mouth.

Grey gives me the thumbs up, shaking with silent laughter as Leighton stares at me gob smacked, quickly trying to distract himself with the wall when my eyes fall to him.

Pulling back from Avery, I grab her hand, leading us to the table. My usual seat is free, and I sit, dragging her onto my lap.

"So, what now?" Byrone asks. "How should we warn the others?"

"We need to start spreading the word," I say. "Find out who has signed a consent form, and we'll visit them one by one."

Avery turns her head to look at me. "I can help," she offers. "And maybe Vivian too. If they don't believe you, we can tell them what happened to us."

"Are you sure?" Theo asks with a hint of concern. "You don't have to relive that."

She nods confidently. "If it will protect other people, they should know. There's no way that they are being upfront about these so-called *therapy alternatives*."

"She's right," Grey answers. "The more information we can provide, the better. We can't risk people taking the gamble. They need to know the full details of what they are trying to do to them."

My hand strokes the top of her leg. "Alright. But stay on guard. Arthur knows we're going to try to intervene. We need to be prepared."

It's nearing the end of free time when Jillian suddenly shoots up straight in her chair, a look of panic on her face.

"Damon, they are taking Smith."

She flips her laptop around so that the screen is facing me at the other end of the table. My eyes narrow as I spot two guards escorting Christopher from his office, his arms held down.

"We knew this was a possibility," Grey says lowly, looking at me. "What do you want to do?"

I stand from my chair. "Jillian, keep watching the feed. Make sure it's being recorded. Leighton and Andy, go gather the others. Grey, with me."

Avery jumps to her feet. "I'm coming with you," she declares firmly. "Theo, too."

I turn to argue, but her eyes flash with stubbornness, Theo already on his feet. Begrudgingly, I nod.

"Fine, let's go."

The four of us quickly make our way out of the library, heading toward the staff rooms. Immediately, we spot Christopher, still squished between two guards while my father towers over him, berating the younger man.

Arthur spots us first, whispering to a guard as we approach. Immediately, I throw my arm out, making Avery stumble for a second as I usher her behind me. Grey and Theo cage her in, stopping next to me.

"It appears we've hit a crossroad," my father states, spotting us. "Dr. Smith has just been fired from Lilydale for insubordination."

Chapter 34

Damon

Christopher glances over at me, face stern and defiant. I hear Avery suck in a breath, anger rushing through me. With Christopher gone, she knows she'll be forced back with Elsher.

"It would be a shame if someone was to sue for unlawful termination," I say slowly, locking eyes with Christopher. "And to report inhumane conditions."

My father scoffs. "Christopher wouldn't do that. He'd be risking his place in my family. I'd hate to see him *disowned*."

Typical of my father to hold money over someone's head as a form of blackmail, but judging by Christopher's expression, he's not bothered by the threats.

"No one wants to willingly be in *your* family," I shoot back. "Luckily, family is not just about being blood related. And you're not the head of the Dale empire. You're just a seat warmer."

I hold his gaze when he narrows his eyes on me. Slowly, they slide to my left, landing on Avery.

"And this is *her*, correct? I vaguely remember her insignificance."

Arthur nods. "Yes, that's her."

The monster in me screams to be unleashed, my expression darkening as I step forward. "You touch one hair on her head, and I'll put you six feet under right now."

"She's just another obstacle," my father points out casually. "*Accidents happen.* And it will all revert back to me once again."

"You'll have to go through me first," Grey snaps.

My father raises an eyebrow lazily, taking notice of Grey and Theo. "Wasn't that one meant to be in solitary confinement?" he asks Arthur provocatively, nodding toward Theo.

This time, it's Avery that snaps back, my blood running cold as she addresses my father.

"Don't pretend you don't remember me. And don't you dare fucking touch any of them."

There's a sense of pride in me at her protective outburst, followed by an even stronger desire to gut them both for even looking at her.

Christopher looks at her fondly too, seemingly impressed. It's not often we witness anyone standing up to him.

"Shame they didn't manage to correct that attitude," Arthur sneers. "Perhaps they will get another chance now that operations are recommencing."

Instantly, the hallway erupts into chaos at his words. Grey lunges forward, barreling into Arthur. The two fall to the ground, Grey's fist slamming into Arthur's face with a crunch.

One of the guards hastily lets Christopher go to intervene but Theo tackles him quickly, his head making a cracking sound as it connects with the wall painfully.

Avery shoots forward in alarm when more guards come sprinting down the hallway toward Grey and Theo, but I grab her, wrapping my arms around her protectively.

"They will be okay," I try to tell her, dragging her back from the commotion.

To my surprise, Christopher throws a punch at the other guard still holding him, knocking him to the floor.

Arthur presses himself flat against the wall, managing to get out of the way just in time as Theo throws a guard through the air. He hits the wall next to Arthur, dropping like a stone.

"Guards!" Arthur yells, the sound of more rushing footsteps approaching us from behind.

My father turns to look at me, his cold, hard expression full of blind hatred. Even with the havoc behind him, he manages to stand out, his voice loud.

"Enough," he roars, grabbing a gun from one of the unconscious guards. He lifts it, pointing toward us.

Instinctively, I shove Avery behind me, my hand still gripping her wrist as guards surround us.

"Damon!" she yells, pulling my arm. I jerk her into my side, fighting to keep her back as she tries to step in front of me again, her eyes wide with panic.

"This is between us," I snap at my father. "Leave them out of this."

The hallway falls eerily silent, everyone watching us with trepidation. My eyes dart behind him as I fight to keep the worry off my face, noticing that the guards have managed to get the upper hand against Grey and Theo. We're dangerously outnumbered and I have no doubt that my father would be happy to spill blood.

"Technically," he responds. "It's between us and *her*." He points to Avery with the gun.

My stomach clenches as I shove her back again, feeling guilty for the little pained whine that quietly escapes her mouth from my forcefulness.

The air is thick with tension, no one daring to move. I keep my eyes locked with his, hating him even more than I thought humanly possible.

"I suppose I should congratulate you," he jeers. "Welcome to the family, daughter-in-law."

Avery breathes in sharply. "What?"

Grey looks at me, a flash of panic in his eyes. A guard has him in a headlock, crushing his throat, but that's not what he's afraid of.

"You're married now," my father says sternly. "And apparently, a shareholder in Lilydale. You'll have to excuse me for not being more *delighted*."

She squeezes my arm, falling quiet. I can sense the dots connecting, her eyes darting over to Christopher—probably realizing that the piece of paper he had her sign this morning was a marriage license.

I should have told her, but I didn't want to ruin our little bubble of happiness. I didn't want to put that weight on her shoulders just yet.

My mother really thought of everything—including a clause in the trust that stipulated any shares in a company or organization tied to her inheritance must be partially distributed to my spouse... *from the majority shareholder.*

It was a safeguarding measure. If I was still the majority holder, a small percentage would go to my wife as marital compensation. But in our case, where I no longer held the majority, the clause was designed to protect *my* interests in the inheritance—meaning my father lost a fraction to ensure an equitable split since I'm the sole beneficiary. It's like my mother knew this was a possibility. If he hadn't forced my hand by making me sign over two percent, Avery's small marital percentage would have come from me, making him the majority shareholder even if our combined shares equaled more. But now, our marriage has tipped the scales—*all because of his greedy actions.*

Her five percent share has reduced his to forty-six... allowing me to take back the power with my forty-nine.

Sure, he can have Elsher try to sign off to say I'm not mentally capable, but thanks to Christopher's psychiatric assessment, I've been deemed mentally sound to enter into marriage—at least for today. Plus, he officiated our license, with his freshly ordained credentials off the internet—meaning my father can't strong-arm or bribe an outsider official to say it wasn't legal. We might end up in a stalemate, but we'll be able to stop them dipping their greedy fingers into the fund. The injunction request has already been filed with the marriage license, so for now, we've managed to stop them.

It also means that if he kills me, Avery gets everything.

And he is fucking livid.

"Put the gun down," I say, my voice low.

I never should have let Avery come with me. Grey and Theo struggle against the guards, eyes dark with anger as they fight to get to her, sensing the rising danger. We have to play it sensibly here—one wrong move...

"Arthur," he turns, looking at the other man. "What would you like to do here?"

I'm horribly aware that we are outnumbered. None of the guards seem confident enough to side with me, not while my father and Arthur have the upper hand—and certainly not while he's pointing a gun in our direction.

"Send the birthday boy down to solitary confinement," Arthur replies. "And the other two as well. They can go in together—we'll bend the rules just this once since it's a *special* occasion."

He motions for the guards to step forward, and as soon as one of them lays a hand on me, I snap. There's no way I'm leaving Avery alone with these assholes. I turn around and swing at the guard, punching him square in the face. Another makes a grab for Avery, pulling her away from me and I see *fucking red*.

They aren't taking her away from me—away from *us*.

I lunge forward, breaking his wrist with a loud snap, forcing him to let go of her. More swarm toward me, trying to take me down in pairs, and I slam my body into them, sending them backwards onto the ground.

Behind me, I hear the commotion as Grey and Theo lash out at the guards again, trying to break free from their holds.

Someone manages to get my arm behind my back, but Avery throws her bodyweight into him, tipping him off balance.

In my peripheral vision, I see her throw a punch, managing to get a guard in the nose.

That's my fucking wife.

Smiling, I move onto the next guard closest to me, splattering him against the wall with a loud sickening crack before he drops, motionless.

A roar of voices startles everyone, our heads whipping in unison to the end of the corridor to find the members of *Cirque des Morts* charging down, led by Byrone at the front of the pack. The distraction gives Christopher a moment of leverage, throwing his guard across the hallway. He falls into Arthur, the older man losing his footing as he lands heavily on the ground.

"Get up!" I hear my father yell, urgently.

Immediately, I look for Avery, reaching under a guard's arm to grab her wrist. I kick the guard hard in the kneecap, feeling it break under my foot. When he goes down, I yank her to me, Avery smashing into my chest. Her gray eyes peer up at me in panic, and I'd give anything to take that fear away—to get her out of here safely.

A few guards stumble backwards, trying to move out of the way as my people slam into them. They go flying past me, falling like dominos. I grip Avery in my tight hold, spinning her around just as the sound of a gunshot rings out.

Someone yells, followed by eerie silence as I twist my head to find my father on the ground, knocked over by a guard. The gun is still in his hand, and I quickly scan my eyes over everyone—Avery, Grey, Theo, Christopher, Byrone... trying to figure out where the shot landed.

I breathe a sigh of relief when they all look fine, surveying the carcasses on the ground.

"Damon..." Avery whispers, and I turn quickly to look at her.

Her hands are outstretched, palms up, and my heart stops at the sight of them covered in blood. My gaze darts to her face, finding tears in her eyes as she stares at me wide-eyed and panicked.

"Fuck!" I hear Grey yell, but it's muffled by a ringing in my ears.

A chill runs through me and I glance down, spotting droplets of blood dripping around me onto the floor. That's when it hits me...

I'm the one that's been shot.

"Damon!" Avery screams, pain shooting through me as my legs give out and I hit the ground.

My vision starts to go hazy, darkness creeping around the edges. The last thing I see before it all goes black is Avery and Grey leaning over me, frantically mouthing my name.

Book Four – Exile

Coming soon...

https://books2read.com/u/3GOovP

Stalk the Author

FB Readers Group - Steph Macca's Asylum for Pectoral Perves
https://www.facebook.com/groups/authorstephmacca

Instagram
https://www.instagram.com/authorstephmacca/

TikTok
https://www.tiktok.com/@authorstephmacca

Facebook
www.facebook.com/authorstephmacca/

Online Store
www.stephmacca.com

Other Books by Steph Macca

DANCE WITH MY DEMONS SERIES

(Unhinged, Echoes, Ravage, Exile)

BOYS OF WILLOWBROOK

(The Devils They Are, The Monster I Am)

ALL TOO WELL

THE LIES WE KEEP SERIES

(Vicious Games, Pretty Savages, Recklessly Damaged, Sweet Anarchy)

THE BLACK SPADES SERIES

(King of Spades, Queen of Fire, Aces and Ashes, The Hunter)

THE CHRONICLES OF MAXWELL DUET

(A Day of Ruin, A Day of Chaos)

MIDNIGHT PSYCHOS TRILOGY

(Ruthless Savages, Ruthless Redemption, Ruthless Reign)

WICKEDLY SWEET

SLEIGH

BEAUTIFUL DECEPTIONS & SWEET MISERIES

ANATOMY OF A KILLER

RAYNE